Claus's Revelations
by
Alexandria May Ausman

Book cover illustration by Alexandria May Ausman
Editor: Jon M. Ausman

Library of Congress Control Number: 2025927716

ISBN: 978-1-963335-34-7 (ebook)
ISBN: 978-1-963335-33-0 (paperback)

Published By:
Ausman & Cousins LLC
1700 North Monroe Street
Suite 11, Box 284
Tallahassee, Florida 32303-0501

For author interviews: ausman@embarqmail.com

Das Kaiser Haus Series

The Collar King Series

The Most Brutal Man in Europe Series

Claus's Revelations (Chapters 1 to 8)
Xavier Saves the Haus (Chapter 9 to 16, coming soon)

The Psycho Series

Cemetery Kid (Chapters 1 to 20)
Stop Calling Me Psycho (Chapters 21 to 33)
Motor-Psycho (Chapters 34 to 44)
Delusion of the Collar and the Key (Chapters 45 to 53)
Brutality's Prisoner (Chapters 54 to 64)
Aesthetic Akathisia (Chapters 65 to 74)
Metallic Burden (Chapters 75 to 83)

27 Masters Series

Anita the Benevolent (Chapters 1 to 7)
The Beast and the Witch (Chapters 8 to 16)
High Priestess of Schizophrenia (Chapters 17 to 24)
The Professional Dominatrix (Coming soon)

Stand Alone Books

The Grannybat's Weird Tales & Gothic Stories Volume 1

Book 1 Characters: Claus's Revelations

Agnette Krauss: the mother of Christian Axel

Amos Altergott: a Fur King, succeeded Felicity

Annika: spouse of Gregor

Attilia, Doctor: the Haus physician

Barhard: a Haus Dungeon Master

Barnham Reinhardt: half-brother of Bladrick

Bartram: a Haus Dominant no longer

Bernt Schmidt: brother of Xavier

Bladrick Reinhardt: cousin of Keifer

Borya: a Russian Guard

Byron Schmidt: a Haus Dominant, a Voting Council member, son of Xavier

Cary: the Shadow King

Catarina: spouse of Ivan

Christian: the anger and lust shard

Christina Schmidt: daughter of Ingrid and Xavier

Christian Axel: a Haus Dominant, the Priceless, son of Xavier

Claus Albrecht: an Elder of the Haus

Dämonen: the Demon sharing the shard Maximillian

Deiter: Claus's black collar

Der Goldene Hund: the Voice or the Boss shard; the Conscious shard

Derbeck Schmidt: brother of Xavier

Die Brutale: three shards melded together; Mad Max, Max, and Christian

Drexel Reinhardt: half-brother to Bladrick
Ebba A. Albrecht: spouse of Gerard Albrecht
Evelyn: a Haus black collar kitchen worker
Felicity: the Mother Lamb, a shard
Felicity Albrecht: mother of Claus, the Fur Queen
Florian Schmidt: the first Priceless, deceased
Freidrick Schmidt: a Haus Voter, son of Bernt
Fiona Krauss: a Haus FemDom
Friz Altergott: an orderly at Irsee Abbey
Gerard Albrecht: a deceased sadistic step-father of Christian Axel
Gregor Kraauss: grandfather of Meine Liebe, Fur King of the Danish House
Gretta Albrecht: a Haus FemDom, the Silk Queen
Grisha: a Russian Guard
Grisham Krauss: a Haus Dominant
Gustov Krauss: a Haus Dominant
Heidi Schmidt: sister of Xavier
Heindrick Krauss: a Danish Haus Dominant
Helga Schmidt: sister of Xavier
Hemmel Krauss: a Danish Haus Dominant
Henri: a deceased black collar trainee
Henson Schmidt: son of Ingrid and Xavier
Ingrid Reinhardt: spouse of Xavier, ally of Claus, sister of Keifer
Iosif: a Russian Guard
Ivan: retired captain of the Russian Guard
Jonas Weiss: an Elder of the Haus
Jorge Reinhardt: uncle of Keifer

Joseph Schmidt: an original Founder of the Haus

Julius Krauss: a Haus Dominant

Justus Schmidt: son of Bernt and Ingrid, half-brother to Christian Axel

Keifer Reinhardt: a boyhood friend of Claus, then much more

Kilian Altergott: a Haus Fur King

Kristian Reinhardt: cousin of Keifer

Lars Schmidt: son of Ingrid and Xavier

Leo Albrecht: an Elder of the Haus, cousin of Claus

Lucus: a Haus Dominant, a royal

Mad Max: the sadistic shard of Maximillian, aka the Heart and Judgment

Mad Maxx: husband of Meine Liebe; a Haus Dominant

Mad Maxx: the masochistic shard, also the Brain and Guilt

Mad Maxximillian die Brutal: the most brutal man in Europe

Maksim: a Russian Guard

Malfred Krauss: a Haus Elder

Matilda: a Great Hall black collar

Max: the Soul shard

Max Reinhardt: cousin to Keifer

Maximillian Keifer Schmidt: the twin brother of Christian Axel

Maximillian: the seductive shard, aka the Libido

Meine Liebe: submissive and spouse of Mad Maxx

Muarl Reinhardt: aunt of Keifer

Nestor: a deceased Russian Guard

Noah: a Dungeon Master

Olaf: a deceased black collar door guard
Oliver Schmidt: brother of Rolf, son of Derbeck
Peter Schmidt: a Dominant of Der Kaiser Haus; uncle of Christian Axel, son of Bernt
Rolf Schmidt: a Haus voter, son of Derbeck
Roselina: a Haus black collar, spouse of Cary
Ruslan: Captain of the Russian Guard
Samuel Wagner: a Haus Silk King
Sasha: a Russian Guard
Sergie: assigned son of Ivan
Sofie Albrecht: cousin of Claus
Stephan Krauss: a Haus Dominant
Taube: a Ram, Taube in German is "Dove"
Timor: a Russian Guard
Vern: a silver Haus trainee
Wilhelm: a Haus Dungeon Master
Xavier Schmidt: deceased Fur King, father of Justus, Byron and Christian, brother of Derbeck and Bernt
Xavier Schmidt II: son of Ingrid and Xavier

Preface

The new Haus order has been imposed by Maxximillian who is also known by those who love him as Christian Axel. The Russian Guard leadership is adjusting to the rise of the Mortar King. The replacements for exiled black collars are learning their new positions.

The Fur King, who financed the Mortar King's revolution within the Haus, is on his deathbed. He sends multiple messages to Christian Axel Schmidt to attend him.

Claus Albrecht, the Fur King, tells Christian Axel the story of the Haus. The Haus in 1974 had been formed more than two hundred years earlier as an exclusive Haus for the entertainment of the powerful and the rich. Claus introduces the story upon his arrival as a social refugee in the early 1900s.

The description and history of the Haus, along with the leadership that rises and dies there by Claus, is of little interest to Christian Axel. When Claus finally arrives to tell the story of the beginning of Christian Axel, the Mortar King rebels and believes the verbal history given by Claus is a lie.

Is it a lie? The reader will have to decide whether Claus is telling it as it really happened or whether Christian's denials are more likely to be true.

Language in italics is a conversation between the adult male Master Mad Maxx and his female submissive Meine Liebe. The editor is related to both.

Chapter 1: The Finale
Master Mad Maxx and submissive my Liebe

Noah crept up closer to the lip of the stage and looked below. "For the oppressed of this Haus, these submissives appear to have a touch of sadism within their stomachs. Look at them. Many are smiling as they trample on their own brethren and sisters. Holy hell. Who knew their subdued veneers could so easily be peeled away to reveal the beasts they truthfully are." His expression was that of both disgust and shock.

I chuckled bitterly. "Their violence toward their own is of no surprise to me, Headmaster. You fellows don't know the truth of the people that serve you because you're too busy fighting with each other to climb to the top. Trouble is, that lofty peak you all are trying to reach is nothing more than the tip of a huge turd that floats in the GDR's sewer system."

Jonas clicked his tongue sounding exasperated by my truthful comment, "Is that what you really think, Maxximillian? If you have such a low opinion of Das Kaiser Haus's thrones then I must wonder why be hell bent to bow everyone to their knees before you."

I glared with open animosity toward the Vampire as I gruffly replied, "Because it makes my dick hard to watch you motherfuckers groveling like little bitches, honorable Elder. I must be satisfied by raping the souls that are trapped in the walls with me, since you dirty cocksuckers keep denying me any other avenue to obtain sexual gratification of worth. Anyone else have stupid commentary they wish to assault my last nerve with? Or are you boys finished working hard to convince me to grant the place on that empty stake to you? Hmmm?" I quickly fanned my attention across the anxious faces of Byron, Cary, Noah and Jonas.

The men, including Jonas, rapidly dropped their sights to their boots. I scoffed over the obvious cowardice each demonstrated when it came down to it. Don't get me wrong. I already was aware most of the Dominants and FemDoms of the Haus were nothing but lily-livered bullies. They only are tough when their victims are bound in ropes, or too weak to defend themselves.

Well, Mad Maxximillian wasn't that frail little boy called Christian Axel. I was happy to prove to each of them that they couldn't pick on this big man like they did that poor kid. I understood that there was lots of work to do and plenty of heads to crack before the members of Das Kaiser Haus realized the tables had turned. That wasn't a hardship for your Master Maxx Die Brutale. when it comes to causing another pain, you could say it's my sincerest pleasure. Hahaha.

I trembled slightly as Maxximillian laughed for several moments over his statements of enjoying tormenting others. I didn't utter a peep, terrified to near paralysis over his noises of cruel delight. I was personally aware this wasn't the boasts of a madman but the honest reports of a man-made monster. He ruffled my hair playfully then without his typical move to thud me with his cane continued with his story. Thankfully he did so, yikes!

3

Without a shred of sympathy I watched the hundreds of submissives stomp the thirteen bastards. The atmosphere in the Great Hall became electrified with the sounds of unrestrained brutality. Hundreds of voices, male and female, jeered at the wailing criminals suffering their collective battering. The noise was sweet music to my burning ears. I could've happily listened to that bloody melody for hours.

However, it took less time than one would expect for the entire crowd to get their licks in. Just as I was getting completely immersed in the thrill of the show, the black and silver volunteers come forward from the railing masses.

I didn't bother to disguise my eager interest in witnessing the selected torturers begin their dark work. The first criminal was relieved of her tongue by a lovely silver. She practically ripped the spongy appendage from her restrained victim before the knife she held could complete the job. To my glee, she held up the freed tissue. She led out a wild sounding yip. The crowd broke out in riotous cheers.

That beautiful display of wanton callousness caused me to let out a howl of elation. The agitated audience returned my calls of blood lusting. This stirred the groups deep resentment towards the harshness of their existence. All at once this hidden anger among them erupted to the surface like the cataclysmic volcanic eruption.

The room exploded into a deafening chant, in unison. from the submissives, "Burn, burn, burn the child killers. Burn, burn, burn this motherfucking Haus to the ground."

I lifted my chin and replied to my subjects, "Awroooow! Burn, burn, burn until their bones squirm. Awrooooow! Hahaha." The audience returned my wolf howl and began to bust the furniture and each other into pieces.

Jonas wailed out in terror from behind me, "Holly hell. Noah, Byron and Cary, get ready to shoot. The fucking submissives have gone made as their King Give me a Gott damned weapon if you boys are too pussy to use the ones you are holding. Fuck, Maxximillian, order these people to calm their fit. This is out of hand. Shit, this is bad."

I turned around and glared at him with demons rising in my eyes. "I need only gesture the fire brides to see this Haus and everyone inside of it destroyed Jonas. Are you paying attention, pops? I am the Master of this Haus of disgust. I intend to send it and those that call it home to hell. That's where we fucking belong." A chair, well what was left of one, went sailing past me nearly hitting the Vampire before sliding uselessly across the stage floor.

Noah shouted in the trembling voice, "Please, your majesty, mercy. Call the submissives off. If you don't end this riot soon, they are going to run out of shit to break. Then, no doubt, they will come up here to do to us what they have been doing to the Great Hall furniture." His hue was so pale I think he would have glowed in the dark.

I roared out, "Take your pleas up with the devil, Noah, because your King shall grant no mercy to any of cocksuckers."

Cary's panicked face appeared in front of my with suddenness. "Christian baby, I beg you to order these people to cease their hostilities. I know you are tired of the bullshit and full of grief over your heavy losses. Listen to me lover. This isn't the way to gain what you desire the most in life. I think you've sufficiently frightened the Guard, the Elder and all the Dungeon Masters by this extreme demonstration of your honest powers. Give the command to calm the crowd, if not for yourself, do it for me. Roselina was in labor when you called me to attend you for this party, beloved. I left her side to be at your own. Doesn't my loyalty to you over that of my own son deserve the reward of allowing me to survive to know him?"

I startled when the Shadow King said that. "What? Roselina was giving birth and you didn't tell me? Why would you keep such a secret Cary? Christ, you should be by her side instead of knee deep in this shit. Damn you." I put up my hand and emitted an ear splitting whistle.

The submissives immediately halted their wild rampages and all eyes fell upon me. "On your knees, worms. You will allow the assigned collars to complete the tasks I commanded without interference. No further actions against the Haus, her people or property contained within is to be damaged. Anyone that refuses to obey me shall be joining these low dogs on the stake. Guardsmen, I demand you arrest any person you witness trying to rise from their kneeling until I grant release. Now, finish attending to these bitches sentences in silence." The entire room fell to the floor dropping whatever they had in their hands as they went down.

I returned my attentions to the relieved appearing Cary. "I've done as you wanted lover. Now you will return that service to me. Leave this Hall and go to welcome your baby boy into the world. It's bad luck to mix birth with death, you know that. Get the hell out of here. I will see you later and you better be holding a tiny version of yourself the next time we meet."

The Shadow King chuckled and looked to his boots. "I thank you for the attention you give to your grateful lover. Christian, I wish to do as you tell me but I worry leaving you at this dangerous time isn't wise. The stress of fearing you'll need aid from one that honestly loves you surely will cause me a heart attack. My honest value is here at your side, not sitting like the useless bump next to a woman screaming in the birthing pains. I can swear to you I be as worthless to my wife with the task she doing as I was when she bore our daughter."

I shook my head and cooled my temper. "Beloved, your demonstration that you care is more important to your Frau then you give it credit. If it will calm your anxiety, I can swear to end my plans to set the Haus on fire. There are other ways to punish anyone that gets out of line. Does hearing that change your mind about attending to your task as the father over the duties in your role as Shadow King?"

Cary quickly stole a glance at Jonas, Byron and Noah who were obviously holding their breath praying the Wolf would agree to my offer. "Uhm, if you promise to call off the fire brides and let Noah, not Byron and not Jonas, substitute in my place, then I will go without quarrel or fear."

I narrowed my eyes at Noah then scoffed as I replied, "Deal. I suppose one is as bad as any of them. I accept your conditions Cary. Go before that boy of yours is taking his first steps and trying to court the Fraus." The Shadow King smiled with unabashed pride at the idea of becoming the father of a healthy son.

He started to come toward me for the goodbye kiss but I halted his actions with my cane. "Hold up their stud. I cannot have my subjects privy to my private affairs, Cary. If you must show affection, a handshake will have to do. Otherwise, I make it up to you later. See you soon lover. Tell Roselina hello for me. I wish you and her congratulations on the arrival of the greatest treasure any man can boast to possess. I confess, I call you the jealous bastard all night, but it's this idiot that honestly is turning green over those you can claim love you." He nodded appearing a bit disappointed but without further hesitation rushed for the Great Hall exit.

I watched Cary leaving with a twinge of sadness. It wasn't that I honestly desired him the way he truly does me. That strange tug of despairing was directly related to the knowledge that while he hurried to sooth the cries of his young son. This worthless man was left to bury one whose calls for aid went unheeded.

I confess. The terrified final screams of the violated Heidi and crushed Henri still haunt my nightmares to this very day.

With a long sigh brought on by the growing fatigue I began to limp back to the thrones. My gimp right knee suddenly buckled. The thin frame I called my carcass shifted wildly. I used the cane in the futile attempt to prevent an epic spill in front of the subdued audience of submissives.

All that I managed to do was prolong the inevitable display of my honest weakness. It felt like everything was in slow motion as I wobbled, trembled and then collided with the floor face first. Noah, Byron and Jonas come running but all them failed to catch my fall.

The air was forced from my lungs causing a temporary stun. Jonas pushed the other two men out of his way. My momentary incapacitated state allowed him time to get his nasty paws on my flesh. I groaned in dismay as the Bat rolled me to my back and leaned down close looking right into my eyes.

His expression was that of intense fear as he growled out, "Christian Axel? Are you conscious? Speak to me, baby. Christ, I should have forced you to end this farce and carried you to the clinic hours ago. You aren't fit to do anything but weigh down a coffin at this point. Noah, release these idiots and send for Doctor Attila."

I pitched my flesh with a strength that apparently surprised Jonas. "I told you to keep your filthy clays off of me. Release me or you are going to be the one in need of Attila's services, motherfucker." He let me go but didn't remove himself from his place above my prone frame.

Noah's face joined that of the Elder. "Your Majesty, can I get you anything to provide some comfort for your unfortunate condition? Tell me what you require and I will retrieve it with speed." His face appeared more frightened than that of Jonas's.

I shot a menacing glance at the Vampire as I said, "Ja, Noah, I need a pair of underwear made of garlic and the bodyguard with the surname of Van Helsing. You go get those things for me and I will regain stellar health in no time."

Jonas chuckled, which shocked me I admit. "Ah, there is the rude bitch Maxximillian that I know and love. Here, take my hand and I help you back to your feet, husband." He put his hand out towards me.

I swatted it away with vigor. "Noah, give me a lift here please. Seems someone tripped your King while he was distracted. If I discover the identity of that fool, I swear I'll feed him to the bear." The Dungeon Master moved with silent speed to do as I requested.

The Vampire backed away appearing irritated but unwilling to argue. Noah gently pulled me to my boots by the upper arms. I never stopped glaring hatefully at the Vampire as the Headmaster performed his assigned task.

The Bat returned my stare, but his expression confused me. The notoriously cruel Jonas seemed to be gazing at me like the smitten young boy that was swooning over a gorgeous Frau. I thought maybe it was a hallucination but I couldn't deny he'd been behaving oddly that entire night.

I tore my attentions from the adoring Elder and snuck a longing look at the throne. I wanted badly to sit down but to be honest, that was more than a little uncomfortable thanks to, uhm, personal issues. Fucking Stasi shitheads.

My private thoughts were mildly interrupted by a knock on the doors. Barhard cracked them open and peered out. He nodded then pulled his side ajar slightly to allow the returning Ruslan to enter.

The arrival of the Captain signaled that Ivan had been adequately eliminated as a strong threat to the plan of my assuming sole authority over the Haus factions. I watched my strongest ally quietly rejoining his men. I decided there was no reason to chance another fall or worse wailing out in agony when I tried to sit down. I instead chose to end the festivities earlier than expected.

With a grunt of irritation I shrugged off the Headmaster's attempts to maintain his stabilizing grip on me. Noah took the hint and backed away quickly, mumbling an apology for overstepping his bounds.

Byron cleared his throat appearing more anxious than even the Headmaster seemed. "Uhm, your Majesty? Did by any chance the Fur King grant enough funds to pay for all this damage the submissives have done to the Haus property? I mean, if not, who will claim responsibility for it?" He glanced at what was left of that chair laying next the Vampire.

I growled in response, "Fuck the Fur King, the Great Hall furniture, and everyone that lives in this hell hole. As far as I'm concerned a few broken baubles is a far better outcome than my honest intentions this night. If you fellows were smart you'd fall to your knees and thank the Shadow King in the repeat for the rest of your useless lives. That's because he is the man you can claim the hero of Das Kaiser Haus. If not for his quick thinking the sun would be greeting this spot to find nothing but smoking timbers and shriveled bones. Now, if you are done bothering me with stupid questions, I believe the time has come to move this party to a more appropriate venue." I waved my hand in a command for all to rise.

The entire room of submissives moved in perfect unison to mind my order. I allowed the cane to bear the majority of my weight while I carefully limped to the edge of the stage. Jonas and Noah followed my journey cautiously flanking each side. They were overtly wary of getting too close, but neither man was willing to keep their distance. They were likely afraid I'd stumble or worse, fall off the stage into the crowd below.

With a baleful eye kept on the stalking Dominants I addressed my subjects, "The dawn is beginning to break. We must hurry before the Sun climbs too high in the sky to witness the gifts of flesh and blood we offer to him. Dungeon Masters, you and all the submissives but the thirteen condemned are to redress with speed. You have five minutes and not a minute more to protect your flesh from the rough German winter outside the Haus walls. Ruslan, you, Borya, Shasha, Maksim, Iosof will gather together and follow behind these skilled drummers. Timor. You will come to claim the Schweinehund. Take it to join his brothers in the hound cottages. Do remember if it's discovered that anyone tampers with him other than necessary feeding and medical care, they will take a place next to him in the hound stalls. No one is to speak with him or offer mercy of any kind. In December four years from tonight, he will be offered up as the entertainment sacrifice for the Stasi Party. Grisha, you will select one of the sturdy Dungeon Masters to aid you in hauling Das Haus Mistruck to his new home in the bowels of this hell hole. Noah and Byron, you will gently collect the Mortar Prince and Queen. I desire they be carried in your arms the way a sleeping child is lovingly carted by his mother to his bed. The volunteers that rendered these low children killing criminals useless to fight shall each choose one to guide in the procession. Beware, failure to produce the man or woman entrusted into your care will result in you taking their place upon the stake. The rest of you submissives follow the fire brides. The remaining Dungeon Masters and Guardsmen not already utilized in assigned tasks shall take up the behind the collars. I charge you worthy men to keep these worthless worms in step. If any attempt to flee from the procession or get out of line in anyway, shoot them in a non-lethal place, restrain them, and I will happily add them to the number traveling with my Royal family to Valhalla this day. Barhard and Vilhelm, you fellows will open up when the drummers approach and stand aside to allow every single soul in the room pass. When the final person is clear of the Hall, close the doors and take up the rear of the procession. Are there any fucking questions?" The hundreds of people, Dungeon Masters and Guardsmen quickly bowed their heads without a single sound escaping into the air.

Jonas cleared his throat behind me. "Uhm, what about me Maxximillian? You didn't indicate where I should be in this, uhm, funeral parade."

I turned around with vigor and glared at him full of fury. "You know Gott damned well as the first Prince of the Fur, and substitute for the King of that throne, your place is next to the Collar/Mortar King and his honorable family. Why do you waste my time acting like the novice of high protocol, Jonas? Seriously? Tell me something Vampire. Does it bring you perverted thrill to force me to admit publicly that you and I, at least in this case, are of equal status? If so, then consider your cock stroked to perfection. I mean it husband. Stop fuckin bothering me or I won't be desirous of a divorce, because I will be a widow."

The Vampire chuckled with humor breaking out in his expression. "Damn, I never realized how sexy you are when angered. As it is, I'm honestly honored to be traveling at your side for the sobering journey ahead." He bowed low in a dramatic but graceful fashion toward me then turned and did the same to the silent Queen and her Prince.

I rolled my eyes and then motioned the six drummers. Without hesitation they took up their sticks and pounded out the booming rhythm in announcement that the Royal funeral had begun. I watched quietly, as did all the eyes in the Hall, as these young men slowly marched back the way they entered.

The pallbearers spun around and waited till the drummers passed by. Then in silence grace, they carefully

14

took up the glass casket onto their shoulders. Each man marched in place keeping perfect tempo with the beat. The fire brides and the two shepherd boys navigated though the throngs of submissives that were busy putting on their clothing.

It is almost as if expertly choreographed these professional mourners emerged from the crowd. The brides held their glowing lanterns at breast level moving their feet in the cadence of the pall bearers. The two shepherd boys quickly bypassed their sisters and took up on the heels of their larger brothers. Like all the rest hired for this sober job they also began the act of walking without going anywhere.

Byron and Noah had outfitted themselves in their leather breeches and boots with speed. I turned to observe their handling of their honored duties. Byron approached the Queen and Prince first. With uncommon, for him, gentleness he reached under the broken little boy. The shadow Felicity given Henri by Sergie fell from the Prince's tiny frozen hand.

Byron looked at Noah and said in the pity filled tone. "There, there little one, don't fret. We won't take you to your bed without the comfort you have earned. Noah, please retrieve the Prince's lamb for him. Place it on his chest so that he feels less frightened of the journey he must take." I confess it touched me to hear my brute brother's words of solace to Henri.

Noah picked the shadow Felicity up and patiently waited for Byron to position the boy in his arms. He nodded to the Headmaster that he was ready. The burly Noah carefully arranged the lamb on Henri just as Byron requested with her eyes facing ahead. You know that way she could watch out for trouble, ja?

Byron and Henri approached and took up a spot to the left of me. I gazed into the damaged face of the deceased Prince with intense grief tearing at my soul. I managed to swallow the tears that threatened to cloud my vision just as Noah bent down to collect the Mortar Queen.

He gently cradled Heidi's limp head in his arms. with respectful thoughtfulness he took up her weight from the throne by lifting her from behind the knees instead of her waist. He traveled to takin up the spot on the right side of his King.

I nodded at the reverent men bearing this most precious cargo. "I thank you both in advance for your kind devotion during the Queen and Prince's final journey. I beg of you to take care not to stumble. If you find yourselves fatigued, I grant you permission to request a brief respite. I happily will pause this procession rather than chance the dropping the treasure you carry." The huge men nodded that they understood my concerns and swore to alert me if they were in need of a rest.

Jonas silently joined at my right side when I started limping for the steps. Byron and Noah followed closely behind. I didn't have to turn around to know the Dungeon Masters were keeping pace with the beat of the drummer's call.

The awaiting submissives dropped to their knees and bowed their heads as me, Jonas, Byron/Henri and Noah/Heidi marched by them. It only took a few minutes for the Vampire and I to take our place behind Ruslan and his four men. The Drummers held the line still, all of us marching in place, as Barhard and Wilhelm pulled the Great Hall doors open wide.

The second the exit was unbarred the men drumming allowed their stepping to move them forward. Behind me the fire brides began to vail out in high pitched despair.

The pall bearers and shepherd boys' voices joined their sisters' sounds with a traditional funeral chant, "Requiem æternam dona eis, Domine. Et lux perpetua luceat eis: Requiescat in pace. Amen." Translation: Eternal rest, grant unto them, O Lord, And let perpetual light shine upon them. May they rest in peace. Amen.

The huge procession spewed into the main hall of the Haus from the mouth of the Great Hall. The head of the line, the drummers, assumed a leisure pace keeping perfect step to the thumping of their instruments. The females in the assembling crowd of submissives joined in with the fire brides. Immediately the air-filled with the ear shattering cries of extreme lamentation.

The males of the crowd, *including your Master, and the Vampire*, added our voices to the chanting men folk. This thunderous sound added to the spectacular display of sorrow at the royal level.

Many of the Dominants and FemDoms had been gathering in the main entry outside the Great Hall throughout the night. All had been without the services of their submissives for the last twelve hours. It likely didn't take them long to come snooping around trying hard to gain information about the happenings going on behind the closed doors.

Some had been present to see the terrified Justus rushing to the Haus clinic carrying a naked, badly beaten Silk Queen in his arms. Most had witnessed the awesome sight of the professional mourners and animals they hauled, not to mention the glass casket, when it first arrived.

However, none of that prepared them for what they were about to see. As the royal funeral procession erupted from the confines of the hallowed Hall, a collective gasp escaped all present. The Haus members backed away, each wearing a dumbfounded expression on their face.

This opulent display of power and tradition was obviously not something that been viewed in their lifetimes. Though funerals like this were quite common prior to the modern era even with past generations of the Haus.

To my surprise many of the uninvited Dominants and FemDoms took places behind the trailing Barhard and Wilhelm. Even more stunning was that the unexpected followers reverently joined into the wailing and chanting in perfect unison. Before the mass of mourners reached the front doors, I believe most of the souls that call the Haus home were among our numbers.

It must have been something to see that early dawn as Ruslan and Borya flung the wooden barriers aside. A massive quantity of Das Kaiser Haus spilled into the yard, greeted by the dimly lit cloudy skies of the very early dawn.

A stiff breeze blew in from the north and caressed our cheeks with her wet kisses of promised precipitation. Our sounds of grief rose from the Earth calling in unified strength to the agitated Heavens. The barren ground cracked and popped under our boots. It was frozen deep in her winter slumbering boasting a thin layer of powdery snow.

The cold darkness offered each marching a powerful reminder of their shared fate with the lost Mortar Queen and her Prince. Despite the plunging temperature, the hundreds of voices (including my own) continued their pleas to the Gotts without faltering.

That entire trip to the hill that morning seemed almost surreal. The clouds barely illuminated by the weak light of the rising sun were moving at seemingly unnatural speeds. I sung out the words of the funeral song but inside my chest, my heart seemed as frigid as the German December.

I suppose I expected to be plagued by tears, or at least some minor sign of sadness. Yet as we finally had our destination within sight, I still felt completely numb. It was as if I were as dead as my bride and son.

We slowly approached the shallow grave that had been dug in the place I'd selected. Without being told the entire group of mourners ended their noise, including the drummers. It's tradition to demonstrate quiet reverence when encountering the resting place of the dead.

Not a sound, other than those that cannot be stifled due to the human condition, was uttered as the heads of the group fanned out to give the pall bearers space to attend their duties. I watched the men lower the casket from their shoulders and quickly pull golden colored ropes from inside their jackets.

Each man expertly guided their pieces under the delicate glass. They used a series of artful knots to connect them into a makeshift pully system. It seemed silly to do this since the hole they needed to lower the coffin into was only about three feet deep. I can only assume they wished to be extra careful due to the fragility of the casket and the royal occupants it would soon contain.

Byron, Noah and Jonas reverently gathered around me. Their faces wore expressions of pity as they stood silently watching the men finish their task. I stole a quick glance at the huge crowd that littered the hill behind us. The hundreds of people had their head bowed in a mass display of profound respect for their lost royal family.

With a sigh I leaned in close to Noah and whispered, "When the casket is ready, you will grant me the privilege of taking possession of my wife. I wish to be the one to put my beloved Lady into the wedding bed that fate cruelly selected for us." Noah nodded and to my surprise a tear rolled down his cheek.

It bothered me that this usually stoic Dungeon Master found the emotions that seemed to elude me. I closed my eyes and reached far inside myself as possible. I was hoping that somewhere in the mess I called Maxximillian, a shred of basic compassion could be found.

The sounds of the pall bearers kneeling in unison broke me from my inner searching. I startled as I opened my lids. My ears had reported the happenings correctly. All six men were on their knees next to the open glass container.

At last, the time had come to say my final goodbye. I brace to let go of the only woman that'd found honor in accepting my proposal of marriage and the only soul willing to sacrifice his life to give me a tiny bid of comfort in an existence of nightmares.

Noah gracefully released Heidi into my awaiting arms. I held her close to my naked chest, praying that somehow I could lend her my heartbeat. While I stood there wishing for the impossible, Byron come forward with his own burden ready to follow my lead.

I glanced at him and saw that like Noah, his eyes were leaking water of grief. I nodded to the quietly sobbing brute that I was ready to go. In perfect tempo and without a single misstep we silently carried the lost child the last few steps between us and the glass casket.

I ignored the agony of my hands and aching in my flesh for those moments. You'd never have known that I was nearly in need of a grave myself as I carefully knelt next to the open box.

Gently I deposited my broken Queen laying face up on her pearl adorned pillow. The moment I'd let her go, Byron gracefully fell to his knees beside me. I turned and held out my damaged arms towards him. He didn't hesitate to transfer the tiny boy into my hold. He took possession of Felicity before letting go. With my near useless hands I did my best to arrange Henri to rest upon Heidi, face down upon her breast.

The lovely lost Frau and the brave little boy appeared to all that saw them as the mother that fell asleep while comforting her slumbering son. I motioned Byron to return Henri's property to him.

In an unexpected display of consideration, the brute ex-Voter gently positioned the boy's right arm to clutch the waist of his mother. He sniffed back his erupting tears as he tenderly placed the lamb in the crux of his cuddling upper limb.

I gave him a grateful nod of approval for his sympathetic assistance in this difficult matter. Then, overlooking the horrific pain, I pulled the white rabbit fur blanket up and tucked my lost family in for eternity.

Immediately the fourteen fire brides came rushing from their place in the crowd. They surrounded the grave single file and stood there in silence for a moment. The gold and white sparkled in tragic beauty from the light of dare lanterns.

Then, suddenly one of them lifted her head to the sky and began to sing. The words I knew well, because I had given them to Claus. It was a poem that I'd written for Heidi while I waited in agony for release from Bartram's hold the night before.

The fire bride's beautiful voice rang out in the darkness, "She sang like the bird. Her flaxen hair smelled of Spring wind. The light in her eyes gently waning. In the tragedy of the hellish night, she fell in love with the sounds of my silence. I hold on in vain to the wilting feathers of the songbird who can sing for me no more." When she said the last word her sisters brides joined her as she repeated the poem in the same pretty melody.

When day finished, each girl laid her lantern on the ground forming a circle of light around the grave. Somberly they lined up single file and began walking in the direction of the poles erected for the sacrificial executions. Without being directed, the drummers took off in slow procession tailing the brides. I lifted my arm and motioned Ruslan to lead the watching crowd to the hill.

Quietly my Captain and his men guided the mass away. In only minutes, only Jonas, Byron, Noah, the six pall bearers and me were left. This part of the funeral was private by tradition. I kept my place knelt next to the casket, while the pallbearers took to their boots. It was clear the fellows were anxious to get to their task of completing the burial ritual.

Byron politely backed away to allow the men room to maneuver the coffin into the grave. everyone left stood there casting confused glances at each other when I didn't follow my brothers respectful behaviors.

Jonas approached me and leaned down to whisper in my ear, "Christian, baby, you have to move out of the way or these men cannot do what they are supposed to."

I looked up at him angrily then growled in reply, "I wish to have a final moment alone with my wife. All you back off and give me a little privacy. Now, Gott dammit." The pallbearers, Byron and Noah hauled ass to a safe distance, but the Vampire ignored my demand.

He watched the others scrambling off as he said, "Look at the chickens run. This would be funny to watch if under better circumstances. However, I must ask you Christian, why do you appear to be as stricken with grief as you are? You managed to fool the entire Haus into believing this girl was truthfully your blood bonded Frau. Everyone is headed to the hill to await your command to light up the stakes. You can drop the act and get back to reality."

Without even bothering to look at that heartless bastard I responded, "Shut up, Jonas. You think you know everything about me but you are totally ignorant in that area. Hell, even Byron has demonstrated he understands me better than you likely ever could. Never mind. I honestly don't care that you're an odious bastard. Not right now, anyway. I'm asking you nicely to leave me alone for a few fucking minutes. I believe after all the cruel shit you've done to me for years, you owe me this one small favor."

The Vampire gasped. "I resent what you say to me Christian. I've known you since you were the mere boy not much older than the one laying there locked in eternal youth. I won't lie. It's true that sometimes your behaviors are mysterious to me. That said, believe me when I tell you if you were seeking to put the residents on notice that you've become a man at last. You can consider the job completed. Everyone is righteously frightened. Come away and let the men bury the dead. If for no other reason than it's below freezing and you are ailing and not adequately dressed for the harsh elements. The longer we linger, the more likely you be joining those two in short order."

I continued to gaze upon my broken song bird and replied with a shrug, "Oh, if only it could be that easy to get the Reaper to grant me mercy at last. It's good that you finally are able to admit that it's a man you hold hostage in your creepy grips, Jonas. I suppose hearing you say it is a small consolation during this time of tribulation, but it brings me no comfort. As for your refusal to give me a second of peace, that's not a surprise. You've never cut me any slack, even when I beg. I'm a fool for bothering to ask you for it. Stand dare drinking in my heartbreak if you wish. Just do it in silence. I'm warning you Bat. I won't allow you to sully this time I have with my wife by engaging me in the never ending quarreling."

The Vampire bowed his head with his face taking on an expression of confusion, "So be it, Christian Axel." He held his place, despite that move.

I leaned down into the casket and whispered into Heidi's deaf ear, "Beloved, I beg of you to forgive me. However, I must interrupt your making the birds of the Green Fields jealous as they listen to your glorious singing. Please look upon your worthless Mann to grant him your pity. I've done all that's possible from my place on this side of the universe to undo the harm done unto you."

"I restored your honor as the precious Lady and made you a Queen. Your beautiful flesh adorned the temporal Mortar Throne in a wedding dress fit for a Goddess. I made our entire world bow before you and call you her Majesty."

"I used the power of my grief to find the strength to end the practice that halted our plans of a future together. I even saved your sister and brother silvers from the fate we suffered. I gave them and your family what was denied us. Can you see their expressions of joy and feel their happiness? I hope this makes you smile."

"I punished the man that betrayed your love and dignity. He was forced to worship at your tiny feet. I will torture him more than a thousand days before sending him to taste the pain that took you from me. I send him to you soon my love, for your final judgement."

"I heard you say that your truest dream was to become the Frau and mother. See here, in your arms? I give you a son that belongs to you for all time. His name is Henri, and he's brave and strong my love. Take his hand. He follows the lamb. Henri will keep you from being lonely in the grave.

I pray you love him the way you loved me. I cannot lie. I envy his place in your arms."

"Oh. and see here the lanterns? This fine blanket? They will chase away the inky night and keep you both warm."

"Remember you told me you were scared to be alone in the cold dark grave. I purchase this casket made of glass, then placed your grave on top of the highest hill. I know the sunrise greets this spot with her brilliant smile first and says good night to it last of all the areas in this land."

"Don't worry beloved. This hole is shallow. I won't allow them to bury you deep under the ground. I've commissioned a mausoleum with many windows and a skylight built over your delicate bed. I asked them to be quiet as possible while building it, so your sleep isn't disturbed."

"Then, each night, when the sunsets. The Russian Guard, who blocked the doors while the monsters stole you away from me, will come to do penance for their crimes against you. They've been charged with watching over your home and keeping your royal lanterns lit for eternity."

"I pray that the paltry offerings I've secured for you is enough to give your tormented soul a bit peace. You can see into my heart and know nothing I've done assuages my honest guilt. I failed to protect you and our son Henri. Your useless husband is also breaking his promise to join you with speed. I offer no excuse for my dishonorable survival while your blood freezes in your veins."

"Please know that while fate has been unkind to you, beloved, she's a far crueler Mistress to me. I must live on suffering all the things I've managed to curb for you. Can you see me, beloved? I'm the fool that finds himself lonely in the cold darkness of a grave."

"I must go now, but I promise to return and visit as often as the bastards that caused this terror permit. Do you recall I asking you to grant me a sign that you're pleased with the feeble attempts I make to see the debt owed you paid? Would it be too much to request you let me know you still love me despite my unworthiness of it?" The ground shook under my knees from the rumbling of distant thunder.

I heard the Vampire expel a sudden fearful gasp just as the cloudy sky caught fire from a bolt of lightning. Once again the Earth trembled from the thunderclap. I looked up into the swirling tempest to see a dozen blazing stars falling from the Heavens in a cluster formation. They hurled towards us at unimaginable speed, leaving trails of white light in their wake.

My eyes were unable to tear free of Heidi's signal that our bond remained solid despite our unfortunate separation. The freed stars glow became near blinding in their brilliance. Then moments before reaching the horizon, in a sudden flash, they exploded leaving not a single trace that they ever existed at all.

I gazed at the spot in the sky hoping to catch another glimpse of the beauty waiting for me on the other side of life. Only the sound of the wind howling through the trees and

28

the evidence that Thor was vigorously banging his hammer greeted my searching senses.

The feeling that Heidi was merely sleeping over took me. I returned my attention to my silent bride. I remembered a fairy tale my mother told me when I was little. Quickly I attempted to use the cure the man used in that silly story to reanimate his lost lover. I leaned down and brushed my lips on hers.

The cold taste of her kiss reminded me of the reality of my predicament. Heidi was dead, not sleeping and I was an abused schizophrenic the perverts called their King. I was that fella Prince Charming.

I started to rise when, to my shock, the girl opened her lids. She looked at me through the milky white gaze of a corpse. Fear and elation held me frozen to the spot. I couldn't believe Heidi had found a way to regain consciousness. Yet, the evidence of her amazing powers was staring right at me.

Then my stun was compounded when her colorless lips parted and she said, "My love, I hear your honest pleas for mercy. I wish to grant you such luxury but as you can see, no such thing was gifted me no matter how much I begged for it. I demand you return that service in equality. No mercy, Christian Axel. Listen to me beloved. Hunt down the killers of the innocent. Stamp them out. You hear me? Grant them no mercy. You do this, and I forgive you for letting them defile, then murder, me while you did nothing to stop it." Her eyes fluttered, then closed as her final words to me rose into the air and rode away on the stormy winds.

I sucked in my breath then wailed out into her lifeless face, "I will do as you ask, my love. No mercy. I hear your command. I'm forever your helpless servant. Forgive me, please don't leave me here. Come back, Heidi, I'm afraid. I cannot do this anymore. Take me with you to the Green Fields." I broke down sobbing uncontrollably, burying my face deep in the folds of Heidi's neck as I begged the reaper to take me away.

Jonas come towards my shameful display of grieving. He dropped to his knees next to me. without a word he pulled me out of the coffin and took me into a tight embrace. I struggled, wailed and threatened him, but he refused to let me go.

In the gentle rhythm he rocked back and forth pulling me along in this motion as he whispered, "Easy there, Christian. Let the pain out. Don't hold any of it inside you or it will slowly rot you from within. I didn't realize you honestly loved her. I'm so sorry for your loss. beloved. Losing one so dear is the worst agony a man can ever suffer. I swear in time, this pain you are feeling right now will become less overwhelming. You say to her you are lonely and trapped in the darkness. This is only true if you wish it to be. I'm here with you and I'm never letting you go. If only you could see that I love you, then you can finally find peace in my embrace, without having to search for it in the grave."

The Vampire's words dug into my ears like sharp icicles. With a sudden burst of inhuman strength I pushed Jonas. The surprise force of it sent him and me to our backsides opposite to the other. He was too bewildered to recover quickly. I was able to take to my boots before he fully understood what had happened.

I stood over him with demonic fury raging in my expression. "I stupidly fell for your tricks when I was the easily misled little boy. I've done many foolish things in my worthless life, but one that I never be guilty against is being seduced by your empty promises of false love. I don't need your affection, Bat. In fact, I don't need anyone. Maxximillian is alone and that's fine by him. No mercy, you dirty cocksucker. Are you listening? I grant no fucking mercy because that is what all of you gave to me." I spit at him and took off in the hurried limp to join the crowd waiting at the stakes for the orders of their Mortar King..

Bryon and Noah that been watching this odd show rushed to follow me on the journey to the 'Hill.' Neither man said a single word as they silently joined in my overtly angered marching. Jonas apparently realized he wasn't getting whatever he thought he could from that exchange between us.

To my dismay, he managed to catch up to our small group before we'd traveled very far. Lucky for him, he wisely kept that big mouth of his shut while he took the spot next to me as dictated by protocol rules.

The thunder and lightning of the strong storm grew in intensity as we reached the traditional execution grounds. That northern gale howled wildly, just as the clouds opened and released their frozen tears. A blizzard of unusual vigor broke lose her fury on the fifteen condemned souls, bound to wooden poles surrounded by a fire scorched landscape.

Me, Jonas, Noah and Byron arrived to find none of the original crowd had abandoned their resolve to stick to the end. It seemed the Haus residents, the powerful and the weak, were smitten with the demons of blood lust. Hundreds of eyes followed us as we took a place next to Ruslan and his Russian Guard. He and his men stood at attention, with fifteen of them, one of them being the Captain himself, holding lit torches.

Ruslan nodded his head at me when I took up a spot by him. "The prisoners have been doused with petrol, your Majesty. The weather is too harsh to be assured the usual procedures will yield the desired results, ja?"

I stole a glance at the pathetic people, their naked flesh glistening from their recent accelerant baths. Dmitry and Boris were loudly praying to the Gott that doesn't listen. The other thirteen, blinded and silenced by my orders, merely trembled and wailed out in fear. Satisfied that my Captain had made a wise judgement call, I returned my attentions to the watching mob.

I had to yell at the top of my lungs to be heard over the sounds of mother nature's blustery uproar, "These villains have been found guilty of crimes against the Mortar King and his Prince. By proxy their cruel actions have robbed each of the residents of Das Kaiser Haus of her precious treasures. Since the things they have stolen from us cannot be replace nor restored by fine, or other type of useful penance, their sentence is death as is dictated by law. It is tradition to offer everyone a vote to decide if the accused of such serious infractions have the right to a merciful end before facing an agonizing death by flame. It is your King that is most deeply injured by the actions of these psychopaths. Therefore, I refuse to grant any of you a voice in this matter. For their cruelty towards me and my beloved son, I grant them no mercy. Furthermore, I demand fourteen of those wearing black and silver metal to come forward. You are commanded to takin the fire from the hands of these honorable Guardsmen and do what all of you should have done in the first fucking place. Kill the scum that dare to raise a hand to your Lord and Master or find your own future burnt to ash, damn you." I snatched the torch from Ruslan's surprised grip with speed.

I limped over to sobbing Dmitry and without any expression on my face, dropped the fire at his feet. The flame jumped from that lit stick, gobbling up the petrol like a starving wolf. The Russian brute's skin immediately blistered to black. He writhed and wailed out inhuman sounds as the flames boiled his blood and cooked his flesh. I stood there breathing in the putrid scents of his agony without a shred of sympathy for the murderous bastard.

Behind me, fourteen people wearing a mix of black and silver stepped out of the crowd. Each chose a staked criminal. They were given the execution torch by the Russian standing guard over that particular condemned soul. I watched almost as if in a trace while all fourteen mimicked my callous actions.

The numerous fires likely could have been viewed for miles in any direction. The heat put out by the dying men and women warded off the cold of the winter storm for those in close proximity. The crowd pushed forward in unison, all were eager to utilize the useful side effect of this horrific act of inhumanity.

With all fifteen stakes fully aflame, the powerful thundersnow storm must have felt insulted. It looked upon the hundreds gathered around the flesh bon fires, and decided it was not going to allow the people to ignore its fury. Almost the moment the final criminal was lit up, the turbulent skies let loose every weapon at her disposal.

The crowd exclaimed and shrieked as rain, snow, sleet, ice, wind, thunder, lightning and hail rained down upon their heads. I was sure the entire group would scatter away, with their tails tucked firmly behind their legs like frightened dogs. To my shock, quite the opposite happened.

The fourteen Brides and two Shepard boys broke from the mob. Each of them began to twirl, run, jump and sing as they circled the fiery corpses. Their white dresses flowed in the flickering light, making the girls seem like fleeting ghosts. The mob of onlookers gasped; then began to cheer the ladies and young men on in their pagan celebration. Several even came forward and joined in the wild dancing.

Noah slowly approached while I was distracted by the hypnotic movements of the skilled performers. Byron saw the Headmaster making his move. He took to stalking me from the opposite side. The Vampire, hell bent not to be undone, made his move to cut off the attempts of my men to gain audience with me but he was too late to stop dem.

I didn't realize that the brutes were coming to corner me until all my exits of escape been blocked. Noah made his move before Byron and Jonas could get their own hooks into my flesh. He snatched me by the right upper arm and pulled me toward his burly frame with speed.

With a jell of fury I called out for Ruslan to arrest the Headmaster. He didn't hear my calls of distress. The noise of the storm, crackling of the blazes, and voices of the hundreds attending the execution drowned out my pleas for his aid.

Realizing that help wasn't coming, I turned on Noah battling against his hold with all the strength I had left. Byron arrived to find me engaged in a vicious struggle to break free of the Headmaster's sweaty grip. My brute brother pounced on my back, knocking us both to the snow-covered ground.

I shouted out franticly, "Let me go, you creeps. You dare to rape me, I swear I will make sure you share that empty stake. Get off me Byron, you bastard. And you Noah, let me go. I command you to unhand me, dammit. I gave you Bartram. Isn't that enough to satisfy your base urges without risking your life to illegally taste my favors." I pitched and pulled but even if I'd been in robust health I was no match for the combined strength of both the brutes.

Jonas arrived to find the three of us rolling around in the fast rising snow. He stood there a moment watching the fray.

Then appearing to be convinced the men had obtained the upper hand he let out a shrill whistle to gain our attention.

Me, Byron and Noah ceased our hostilities for that moment and looked at the Vampire. "Christian Axel, stop behaving like the frightened little Frau. These men are not trying to violate you. They are doing their duty to their King by offering him protection against himself. Now you end your struggling this minute before you cause more injury than you already suffered."

I head butted Noah while he was busy listening to what Jonas had to say. "Fuck off. I'm the Master of this Haus. I don't obey you cocksuckers. It's the other way around. I'm Gott. Are you boys enjoying this weather? Well, that's because even the heavens do my bidding. I'm warning you. Keep angering me and I will release the full extent of my fury on your pin heads. Ah, let me go. Ruslan, call the Guard. Arrest these insolent bastards at once. They are kidnapping your sovereign, fool." I began to laugh maniacally as rivers of tears became ice flows upon my cheeks.

The Headmaster swooned for a moment but managed to maintain his hold. "Byron, secure him from your side dammit. Watch out for his forehead and mouth. He's thin and weakened but he sure packs a wallup. Shit, I think he gave me a fuckin concussion." My brother quickly minded Noah's request.

I couldn't stop the men from hauling me to my feet, held hostage between them. I again attempted to assault my Dungeon Master subduers with a series of well-placed smacks of my noggin. This time, the fellows weren't falling for that sneaky move. They grunted and dodged every attempt I made to regain freedom while they slowly dragged me back toward the Haus.

Jonas took up the lead. The blizzard had made seeing but only a few inches ahead difficult to impossible. I must assume that since he knew the Haus grounds better than the rest of us, it made him the natural selection to guide us home. Most likely that Bat managed to find his way back by use of his nightcrawler instincts rather than honest familiarity with that vast terrain.

My fit of rage had calmed substantially be the time the men pulled me through the front door. The uncontrollable urge to hurl threats, struggle, and even that infernal giggling, had ceased. I no longer offered resistance of any kind but also refused to carry my own weight. Though to be honest, it's entirely possible I had lost the ability to walk due to incredible fatigue and untreated injuries.

Neither Byron nor Noah voiced compliant over their burdensome cargo. I hate to confess it but as I was carted up the stairs to Mad Lucus's fourth floor apartment. I was behaving in the most shameful manner. All the way up I wept while mumbling useless apologies to Heidi and Henri in the repeat.

To their credit none of the Dominants present made sport of my pathetic demonstration of repentance. I honestly wouldn't have blamed them if they had. I was truly the picture of a worthless wretch.

When we arrived at Mad Lucus's apartment door, Jonas knocked on it with vigor. He didn't have to pound on the wood long before it come open. The royal Dominant stood there still in his night clothes with an expression of stun on his unshaven face.

The Vampire grumbled out, "You going to stand there like an idiot or are we invited in? I believe we've come across something you keep trying to say belongs to you." He shot a glance full of irritation at me as he said that.

I wailed out suddenly, "Don't give him permission to enter, Lucus. Don't you know vampires cannot enter a Haus until the owners say they are invited in. Hurry, call Superman. Tell him to bring the kryptonite rock that Nestor tried to kill me with. I know they say it takes the stake in the heart, but I bet if we smash his head in with that stone, he won't recover from it."

Mad Lucus stared at me as if he never seen me before that moment. "What the holy hell? What is he babbling about, Jonas? For that matter, Noah, why is Christian Victor wearing the sacred Gold buckles? Where the fuck has he been for the last twelve hours? He and I have the agreement. I don't interfere with his daily business and he always returns home by nine o'clock. Christian Victor, dammit, you accuse me of offering shady deals but you are the one that never keeps his word as the gentlemen."

Jonas rolled his eyes. "Lucus, it turns my stomach to bring Maxximillian here to turn over to your, uhm, care if you could even call it that. Look at him. Before any of us bother to answer your questions, perhaps you'd like to explain to us why you let him out of your sight in the first place. He belongs in the clinic or at the very least in his bed. Did you know the boy had a fucking heart attack early this morning thanks to your neglectful supervision?"

Mad Lucus startled when Jonas said that. "A heart attack, seriously? Doctor Attila said that? When did this happen?"

Noah shook his head. "At around four AM this morning, Nein, Doctor Attila didn't diagnosed him. In fact, his Majesty still has not been attended by that skilled man. That Russian named Shasha staved off disaster by giving the King CPR. Look, I don't mean to appear rude honorable Lucus, but his royal person is heavy as hell. Could we come inside? I don't think I'm out of line to assume Byron agrees we happily will help you put him in bed if you'd grant us mercy in this matter."

I blubbered out through my tears, "No mercy. I don't granny you mercy, motherfucker. Nor you, or you, or you. Hey, you, get over here. Ha, no mercy for you either, hahaha." That crazy giggling erupted before I could put a halt to it.

Mad Lucus's eyes went wide. "Ja, ja. Bring him inside fellows. Follow me. Jonas, honorable Elder would it be too much for me to request you call down to the clinic? Tell Doctor Attila that Christian Victor appears both fevered and quite likely demonstrating trauma driven psychosis. Tell him to bring a strong sedative and I pay for the blood draw to discover any lurking pathogens."

Byron and Noah dragged me along behind the anxiously chattering Dominant. I snickered as I realized how fucking short Lucus truthfully is. *I swear Meine Liebe he was so small that day, I thought he might be a secret lilliput, that's a leprechaun or the elf you know.*

I called out in the jeer at him, "Fie Fi Foe Fum. I smell the blood of the English man. Be he live or be he dead. I grind his bones to make my bread. Hahaha. You hearing that Lucus? I'm the Jolly Giant from the Green Fields. I'm will stomp on you with my humongous boots. Then you won't be accusing me of breaking the contracts with you, only your skull. Oh, Florian. Byron, go get that bonehead. My Lambs, Noah, you stole them from me and gave me this stupid horses harness to wear." The fellows hauling me along stopped at the bedroom door their eyes wide and mouths ajar in utter shock at the sight of, ja, you guessed it, Mad Lucus's gross cock bed.

Noah sucked in his wind then said, "Now there's something you don't see every day."

Byron barely nodded his head as he added, "If you ever seen anything like it on any day before this one, Noah, I swear I'm going to have to start partying with you. Holy Hell, what a piece of amazing art."

I whimpered upon seeing that gross atrocity with these two nasty fellows in the same room with it. "Nein, don't. Someone help me. They are going to rape your King. Hurry up. Where is Superman? Can you hear me in the walls? I will give you anything if you stop them from hurting me Mister DJ. I will even eat that nasty pocket soup you make for me." I began to jerk and twist wildly.

Noah was pulled from his place of astonishment. "Byron, hold him, dammit. Shit, Lucus, get out of the way. We are coming through." The huge men rushed inside the room and practically tossed me onto the spongy mattress of the cock bed. The sheets barely touched my naked back before I was scrambling with vigor trying to evacuate what I was sure was the spot they intended to use for their sexual assault.

Noah blocked me on the right while Byron rushed to prevent my escape on the left. I crawled rapidly down the middle headed for the foot of the mattress with speed. Jonas practically flew through the door and bravely obstructed that getaway route. I wailed and spit nearly ready to collapse from fatigue while I retreated back to the headboard of that monstrosity.

Mad Lucus shouted to the Byron and Noah, "There, in the center are the restraining chains. Capture his wrists and pull them into those cuffs he's wearing. Here." He threw the tiny padlocks at Noah and that brute caught them mid-flight. "That will end his mad attempts to sneak off and prevent further fight out of him."

I saw the Dungeon Masters moving in on me with expressions of determination on their faces. I need not tell you, I wasn't the victor of that battle. I doubt either man was so much as scratched thanks to their unfair advantage over me. All I could do was swear, buck and scream in retaliation while they successfully bonded my by the arms to that cock bed.

Jonas watched me winding down. I always give up against chains and locks. They are stronger than me, ja? Jonas said, "So uhm, honorable Lucus, where do you shop for your furniture?" His dark eyes soaked in the obscene carvings with an unreadable expression on his face.

Mad Lucus flashed a weak smile at the Vampire. "Ah, it's a masterpiece, ja? If you like, I can share the name of the artist with you at a more appropriate time."

Jonas darted his gaze at the royal pervert and responded, "Ja, ja, you do that. However, for this moment if you don't mind, I would like to discuss your plans to gain appropriate medical treatment for my husband and ward."

Mad Lucus narrowed his eyes, "I intend to follow the doctor's orders to the letter honorable Elder. Like I always do for my Lord and Master. Did Doctor Atilla say how long till he arrives?"

Jonas shook his head with a sigh. "He didn't answer. Byron, you are Dungeon Master to the Mortar King and I dare say better fit to move quicker than me or Lucus. Would you please search the Haus until you locate the good doctor. Once you find him, no matter what he's doing, bring his ass here."

Byron nodded and smiled with sadistic joy. "It is my pleasure to serve his Majesty, honorable Elder. I thank you for the mercy of it." He tore out of the room without hesitation.

Mad Lucus glared at Noah for a moment then said, "Wouldn't it make more sense to send two healthy fellows to find the physician? Byron is clever and strong, but there is only the one of him. Double the men, double the chances, ja?"

Jonas's mouth drew up into the taunt smile as he replied, "Byron will manage to complete the task assigned him without Noah's help. Besides, I have more need for his muscle than that conscientious doctor does." Noah shot an anxious glance at the Vampire.

Mad Lucus startled and moved slowly toward the door as he said, "Oh? Are you expecting trouble sometime soon?" I watched helpless to do a thing as the Vampire continued his open threatening of my Regent to be, or at least I hoped it was all chest pounding. I mean Jonas had been acting completely weird since the Wedding Party. If that wasn't bad enough, what the fuck was I gonna tell Claus when he come calling demanding to know why he just spent a fortune to kill a Queen and the bitch still claimed an address in the apartment next door to him.

Chapter 2: Little Boy Blue
Master Mad Maxx and submissive Meine Liebe

So we finally got all three horrific parties in the Great Hall out of the way. Maxximillian has risen to full power as the New Year of 1976 rolls in. The lost boy Christian Axel has been left behind in the ashes of an abusive past and a brutal Monster has replaced him. If Maxximillian wants to completely shed his old life, he must first discover which is the real boy and which of them is only a figment of someone else's imagination.

Mad Lucus stopped in front of the bedroom door appearing ready to run. I could tell he was nervous for some reason. "Honorable Jonas, I must beg your forgiveness for being forward but your statement of needing Noah's strength? Christian Victor cannot escaping the restraints, that's a promise. Is there another issue I'm unaware of causing you to be concerned?"

Da Vampire's taunt lips spread into a sinister smile as he replied, "Ja, there is. Well, actually you are very knowledgeable of the situation that has perked my interest. I'm not going mince words but get right to the crux of the matter. That Gold collar contract you tricked my Mann into. I want you to transfer it to me. You've proven in the repeat the boy is too much for you to manage with any effectiveness. The fact is you never should been involved with him in the first place. If anyone was to takin responsibility for his behaviors, much less look after his best interests, it would be me, his fucking guardian and husband."

Mad Lucus's mouth nearly dropped to the floor as he stammered out, "You must excuse my rudeness, Honorable Elder, but where do you get off making such preposterous demands and in my own haus. Much less my private boudoir. You're demonstrating the poorest of manners for a man of your status. Not to mention you make accusations against my handling of Christian Axel's illness without a bit of validity to them."

Jonas scoffed loudly and shot a glance at Noah as he turned his attentions back to the stunned Dominant. "You dare to deny that Maxximillian's troubles since his return to the Haus from Heslach are not directly related to your mismanagement of his psychotic disorder? Seriously Lucus? Shall I count the stupid shit he's gotten himself mixed up in thanks to your neglectful supervision? I do believe he's wearing a crown that shouldn't be and that's only one of the bloody messes I've watched him struggle through. That bitch Gretta nearly murdered him with that Stasi switch and tonight you don't have a clue what this insane motherfucker been up to, do you? The Great Hall is in shambles, thirteen sturdy collars are burnt to ashes, and look at him. The boy is a fuckin wreak in both flesh and psyche. Where were you Lucus? Up here reading a dusty old book about Haus lore or perhaps commissioning your obscene furniture carver to create a sofa with a hairy asshole theme?"

Noah snickered over that gross comment. Both the arguing Dominant's glared at him with suddenness. He covered his mouth with a hand and mumbled a quick apology for his moment of rash rudeness.

I laid there in the chains trying hard to calm my inner turmoil. I didn't care for the subject the Vampire was bringing up. Mad Lucus may be the pervert extraordinaire but we'd finally worked out our differences. Well, after I threatened to kill the bastard. The one thing I didn't want, okay there were many things I wished to avoid, was to be returned to Jonas's complete dominion. Yikes!

With as much force as I could muster I yelled, "Nein, don't you listen to that Bat, Lucus. He's trying to put the vampy trance on you. Quick, look away. Go find Justus and ask him for the crucifix. I told you not to grant him permissions to enter the apartment. See, he's barely in here a moment and already he is making himself a lair of the place. Do you have any garlic in the kitchenette? That will make him uncomfortable. Go get it and watch that blood sucker fly off."

Jonas bellowed out with force, "You be still, Maxximillian. This conversation is between me and your partner of the Gold. If I desire any input from you, I will beat it out of you." He smacked one of the cock bed posts loudly.

I whimpered from that sudden racket. "Please Lucus, make the Bat go away or let me out of the cuffs and I will do it for you. If you don't, he is going to suck my blood, then fuck me. I'm not feeling well. Is the doctor coming? I think I need medication for the pain. Especially if you are going to let that Vampire and this sonofabitch Headmaster rape me."

Mad Lucus groaned. "Christian Victor, honey at least on this point I must agree with Jonas. You need not be involved in this conversation. Doctor Atilla is on his way to make you feel better. Close your eyes and rest a minute darling. I promise I won't allow Noah or Jonas to touch a hair on your head."

Noah sucked in his breath appearing offended. "You need not make that promise to Mad Maxx on my behalf, honorable Lucus. I have no intention of sexually assaulting his Majesty. I also would like to add, if you're seeking quarrel with this man about his Gold metal the King wears, Jonas, you are on your own. I'm not about to strong arm him nor my sovereign over a legal agreement these fellows have between them. If you had issue with it, you honestly should've taken this shit up with the Council long before tonight. Not like you haven't had plenty of time to do that. Mad Maxx has been under the protection of the honorable Lucus for more than seven months I seem to recall."

Jonas glared at the Headmaster with fires of fury lighting up in his dark eyes. "You dare to refuse to aid me if I require it, Noah? Do you believe that wise knowing that someday soon I will be the King of the Fur? You better be considering your future comfort, boy. The Gold throne rules over the bowels of the Haus and all that reside down there. If you anger me, I promise I will make your life a living hell the second my ass hits that furry seat cushion."

The wily Headmaster grinned at the fuming Vampire. "Maybe his Majesty isn't as crazy as everyone wishes to believe. He said you're getting a little demented at least twice tonight at the party. I must say your words just now are evidence that you possible do suffer dementia, honorable

Elder. Look at Mad Maxx, Jonas. I do believe the Golden Buckles adore his pitiful frame. The Fur Throne used to rule over the Dungeon Masters but not anymore. We answer to our chosen Supreme since yesterday evening. You were there watching his initiation from the front row. Do you remember that hallowed event or should we have Doctor Atilla give you a few tests to check your mentality when he arrives to attend his Majesty?"

Jonas's veins popped out on his forehead, he was pissed. As Mad Lucus gasped and said, "Then that harness he wears is real? He's become the Dungeon Master Supreme? That's where he's been? Holy hell. He never said a word about it to me." The royal Dominant eyed my chest and yellow belt with an expression of awe and a touch of what appeared to be pride. Lucus is weird, you know.

Noah nodded his smile growing even wider likely because he was thinking of that agreement he made with me, the sneaky bastard. "His Majesty only learned of the honor a few minutes before it was bestowed upon him. I can attest he wasn't purposely keeping this wonderful news from you. He was as surprised as you are, as was his Mann Jonas. Perhaps that is the reason he suddenly seeking to have the King's golden collar re-assigned to himself." He shot a look of triumph at the furious Vampire.

Mad Lucus appeared surprised by his response. "I cannot disagree or agree with your assumption about the Elder's interest's in Christian's gold metal, but I must wonder about your motives in putting the sacred Harness on him. He's mentally unstable, overwhelmed by his tasks as the Mortar King, and stressed beyond human imagination. Yet somehow you believe him capable of management of the Dungeon Masters. While I cannot deny the boy is gifted, I'm thinking you've either made an honest mistake or perhaps used underhanded persuasion to gain the upper hand through hijacking of the Priceless game piece." He narrowed his eyes suspiciously at the Headmaster.

Jonas startled and shot a look of concern at Mad Lucus "Speak plainly, damn you. What is this shit you spewing about Noah's designs on Maxximillian?"

Mad Lucus flashed a weak smile at the Vampire and crossed his arms as he replied, "You are so busy trying to snatch Christian Victor from my loving hands that you have been blindsided, Jonas. The Supreme Dungeon Master not only takes control of the boys in leather away from the Golden throne, but he also has the power to raise a Fur King as well as remove one."

The Vampire's wind left his lungs like he'd been sucker punched when Lucus said that. "Holy hell. Noah, you motherfucking snake. I cannot believe I'm about to agree with Lucus, but he's right isn't he? You plan to force Maxximillian to put the Silver crown on your conniving head. With him trapped below in your domain, you'd have plenty of time and the privacy to beat him down till he does as you command. Gott damn you. Well, we will see about that. You better watch your back asshole. This Haus is a dangerous place, from top to bottom. Accidents happen all the time. Don't they?" Jonas glared at the Headmaster menacingly.

Noah smiled widely at him appearing unflustered by his open threat. "They sure do, honorable Elder. People fall off the banister, slip down the stairs, and their heads fall off constantly around here. Especially since this lovely young man took up residence within the hallow halls of Das Kaiser Haus. I suppose it would be wise for all of us to be more cautious going about our daily lives. At least those of us that have been careless about the enemies they have made of fellows worth their weight in gold, ja?" He snuck a glance at me.

I wailed out in distress, "You stole my lambs, Noah. I asked you to watch out for them for a minute. I never said you could have them. Felicity, tell this man to release you. You are going to be in so much trouble when the Mother Lamb gets angry. All she has to do is call Superman. Then that DJ will jump out of the walls and beat your ass. Help me! Fuck, someone kill me please. I cannot take this shit anymore. Heidi, my love, listen to me I beg of you. Send the stars from the sky and crush this Gott damned Haus. No mercy, not even for your Mann." I writhed and pulled on the chains wildly while whimpering from the maddening agony that was short circuiting my good judgement.

Jonas approached the bed and in the overtly calm tone, "It's okay baby, the doctor will come and make the pain go away. Before he gets here, listen to your Mann. This fella Noah is holding your lambs hostage to force your compliance with his cruel plans. That won't stand. You tell Lucus that you want him to remove his collar and give it to me. If you do that, I swear I will make this rat fucker return

Felicity to you and make him pay for stealing them in the first place."

Noah let out a roar, "He's lying to you, your Majesty. I didn't thieve your lambs. I will retrieve them and return them to you immediately, Sire. Jonas is attempting to twist your mind to work in his favor. Don't listen to him."

Mad Lucus put up his hands as he yelled out in frustration, "Enough, both of you. You are upsetting Christian Victor, Gott dammit. Jonas, he's not going to transfer his gold contract to you. Noah, if you honestly didn't take his toys then I suggest you do as you say and bring them to him with haste. Everyone needs to settle down or I'm going to call Ivan and have you both removed by force."

I lost it at that point. "Shut up! I fed Ivan to the Ukrainian bear. I don't give the Vampire anything but my spit. I want Felicity. Let me out of these fucking chains. Help, they are trying to rape me. I want my mother. Taube, where are you? Call Superman."

Jonas moved with the speed of the cat and backhanded me. The shock of that ended my cries of distress. He reared back to strike me a second time, but Mad Lucus came at him. The royal Dominant restrained his arm mid-air cursing the Vampire to hell. Noah didn't waste a moment to place his huge frame between the two feuding men.

Jonas and Lucus ended their fight immediately. The Headmaster was much larger than the both of them and I dare say physically far stronger too. Neither was desirous of getting into a scrap with the notoriously battle experienced Headmaster.

There was a pounding at the door about this time. Mad Lucus shot a hateful glare at Noah and Jonas. Then he quickly rushed off to attend his visitor. I started to pitch and quietly moan while Jonas and Noah stood there watching my torment in silence. Within seconds Mad Lucus reappeared with Byron and Doctor Attila trailing behind him.

As the two men entered the room Doctor Attila stopped dead in his tracks. He stood there pale as the ghost staring in a dumbfounded stun. His shocked eyes rapidly flitted from that horrid cock bed to me laying there a mangled mess, bound to its pornographically themed headboard. There was no doubt this was not the scene he was expecting when my brother demanded he come attend the injured Mortar King.

He shook his head and let out his breath slowly, but loud, as he exclaimed, "I don't know if I'm asleep and having the nightmare or if I should put in my two weeks' notice because this is really happening. What the holy hell! I have no words for this, whatever the fuck this is." He motioned his hands towards me rolling around in absolute agony.

All the men shot each other nervous glances while Mad Lucus cleared his throat and spoke up, "Christian Victor has suffered torture at the hands of the Stasi. He's thankfully survived their cruelty but as you can see, the damage done is extensive. His mind is as traumatized as his flesh. We had to restrain him or he was in danger of harming himself further.

Can you stabilize him here? Moving him without administering a strong sedative is out of the question."

The Doctor glared at Mad Lucus with what appeared to be hatred dripping from his gaze. "This is all your doing, Lucus. I had this young man on the mend only three days ago, until you showed up with your thugs. I complained to the Fur King but was told he wasn't in any real danger. Look at him. I've seen corpses in better health and that is based solely on what I can see with my naked eyes. I'm terrified to examine him more closely. I've the sinking feeling this mess that used to be Mad Maxx will reveal things I'd happily go the rest of my life being unaware can happen to the human being and yet they still cling to life."

Jonas growled out irritably, "Be that as it may, Herr Doctor, you were made aware of the difficulties of the position before you agreed to accept the job. Your comfortable ignorance of harsh realities are not a luxury you are going to be permitted to enjoy today. Get your ass over here and attend my beloved Maxximillian or you will be terminated and I don't mean fired."

Doctor Attila turned his furious sights on the Vampire when he said that. "Honorable Elder Jonas, there is no need to threaten me. I've every intention of doing all that's possible to making Mad Maxx's existence tolerable as possible given the deplorable treatment he receives from the reprobates that surround him. He can always be assured I'll give him my professional best and absolute pity. However, before I walk over there and stitch this poor kid up yet another fucking time, I'm going to voice my disgust about the abuse and neglect he's suffering in the repeat. How many times have I told you Jonas, and you Lucus, that this patient has a severe mental illness? Repeatedly I warned you both that he requires constant supervision, intensive medical and psychiatric care. You continue to ignore his doctor's advice. That's bad enough. But you also never listen when I tell you he needs a stress free environment if any of you desire Mad Maxx to thrive or survive to adulthood. As I look at him this minute, I'm finally realizing all I'm doing each time I pull him from the Reaper's embrace is pissing in the wind, ja? None of you give a Gott damned that his life is the living hell. Nein, just as long as he is compliant with your sick and twisted interests in him, that's good enough. Dare I fucking said it. If you feel the need to have me murdered over it, then I suggest you get on with it. Because my medical and personal opinion won't ever change in this matter."

Mad Lucus stared in bewildered silence at the doctor. Jonas, on the other hand, was visibly angered over his statement. The Vampire shot a demon filled glance at the loitering Noah and Byron. Both of whom wisely kept their mouths shut through the whole situation. He seemed to be doubly outraged when neither brute appeared to be offended over what Attila was accusing Jonas and Lucus of that day.

The Elder sneered at the doctor and said in a scornful tone, "If it makes you sleep better at night that you got that drivel off your chest, who am I to argue. Now, if you are quite finished with insulting the men that pay your lofty salary. Then I suggest you stop with the lip service and start patching up Maxximillian. You know, so he can return to his

54

hellish compliance with our 'sick and twisted interests in him.'"

Doctor Attila rolled his eyes and his sleeves up as he approached the bed side. He did pause for a second to blow out his breath in frustration while looking over the obscene carvings. "I'm gonna need one of you to remain handy while I do a quick assessment of the patient. I brought a few things that may be useful in my travel bag, but if I determine he is stable enough to move to the clinic. I will require assistance to get him down the stairs. I don't think it's a stretch to say the current, uhm, accommodations aren't the appropriate surroundings for his fragile health. As for the rest of you. Undo these chains and then leave this room. I require quiet to work and I'm sure Mad Maxx would appreciate a little privacy to boot." I winced as he reached out and gently grabbed my chin in the effort to look into my eyes. Probably to check the dilation of my pupils for signs of brain damage, yikes.

Another mild argument over the identity of the man permitted to aid Attila broke out. That was solved when Byron correctly pointed out he was the man officially assigned to protect the Mortar King's person.

As for the doctor's demands that I be uncuffed, they all agreed that wasn't going to happen. They told him that I was aggressively psychotic. None of the men believed I could be trusted to comply willingly to his treatment of my wounds and injuries. Attila attempted to reason with the idiots that my state of bondage would hinder his examination, but his protests fell on deaf ears.

Though they all agreed my brother should be the one to stay, the three men continued to linger by the bedroom door. They only left begrudgingly after the doctor threatened to refuse treatment if they persisted in disobeying his orders that they give him space to work.

I won't get into too many details regarding that rough exam. I will say the doctor was horrified to discover besides both my hands being broken to bits, that I'd likely had a stress induced mild heart attack that morning. Byron told him about it, the narc.

On top of all that, he determined I had several busted ribs, a fractured collar bone, a likely concussion, hundreds of contusions (that's severe bruises), deep lacerations and minor cuts, burns of various degrees, a probable hairline fracture of the right knee and the worst of all, severe anal tearing.

That kind Doctor looked like he was about to cry when he gave me the bad news of his findings. He additionally told me that it would take from six to twelve weeks before the bones, cuds, and tearing healed and that's with stitching and tight bindings.

I confess, I assumed the medical report would include worse damage, but to be honest the sheer number of injuries was bad enough to make death seem preferrable.

After his initial assessment, he quickly shot me up with a wonderful pain killer, mixed with a powerful sedative. I barely recall the bite of his needle before everything went dark, and I floated far away from the pain and that hideous cock bed, into the peaceful nothing.

By this time in my shitty life, I'd been under the influence of sedatives hundreds of times. Chronic injuries, cruel experiments at Heslach, and attempts to calm my schizophrenia so the perverts could have their way with me had made me the experienced traveler to the realm of semiconsciousness.

Thanks to the non-stop special service calls, constant scenes of extreme torture, and collection of skulls for Florian's court, another thing I'd become overly familiar with was horrific nightmares.

To be fair, that issue had been going on long before my arrival at Das Kaiser Haus. I cannot recall a time when my sleep wasn't disturbed by some terrible vision of doom or despair. Gerard's brutality began before I turned six years old. Waking up in the cold sweats, screaming like the banshee had followed soon after he dragged me to his barn and chained me to the wall.

The reason I bring this subject up Meine Liebe is because the morning that Attila drugged me to the gills, both issues came together. I had an extremely rough nightmare, but since I was partially conscious, I suspected it wasn't the usual fragments of memory mixing with a traumatized imagination.

More than that, I was able to recall every detail of it later when I was fully alert. As you know, most of the time, a person only remembers bids and pieces of the stories they watch while slumbering. This further convinced me that this was a reclaimed memory rather than a fictional dream.

That frightening assumption would lead me on a hunt to discover the origins of the events that I saw while Doctor Attila worked feverishly to repair my ailing flesh. This is why I'm going to tell you about this but haven't bothered giving details on the thousands of nightmares I've had before or after it.

Anyway, I woke up on the dungeon floor in a small isolation cell. I looked about the hovel and saw it was devoid of furnishings except a small wooden privy, straw on the floor and a rough cut plank to sit on.

I whimpered thinking Jonas, or Lucus had Attila send me to the Palace, but then noticed neither the Mortar throne nor Florian was anywhere to be seen. With a startle I realized I was attached to the wall by a heavy chain, affixed to a silver slave manacle around my neck.

That sent me running in terror. I hit the end of that chain with all my strength and found myself weaker than I recalled being for quite some time. I stopped struggling as I noticed besides being the limp noodle, I also seemed to have shrunk in size.

I held up my arms to look at them. To my absolute shock I discovered the pain that was radiating throughout my flesh wasn't from the Stasi tortures. It was coming from the hundreds of stitches that were holding me together. My numerous scars from Gerard's straight razor had reverted to a state of being unhealed and only weeks old.

It was then that I noticed, besides the scary fresh razor gashings, my arms were that of a tiny little boy. I let out a yelp of terror as I glanced down and saw the legs and feet under me matched the arms.

All at once, the answer to this bizarre scene came to me. The wounds from Gerard appeared new because day were. Somehow I'd time traveled backwards from 1975 to 1966. I was once again only eight years old and I'd just been put into isolation for running away during the collar color selection.

I opened my mouth to call for help and instead of yelling in German I said the words, "Hjælp. Jeg vil have min mor." Translation: Help. I want my mother. I spoke in my native Danish tongue.

That really upset me. I attempted again to speak the German language of the Haus, "Vær så venlig. Du begik en fejl. Jeg er grim og lille. Denne sølvkrave er ikke noget for mig. Jeg tror, du havde til hensigt at give det til drengen ved siden af mig. Ring til min mor. Hun vil fortælle dig, at det var en fejl. Jeg vil hjem nu... Vær så venlig. Jeg lover, at jeg ikke vil stjæle slik mere. Mor. Hjælp mig." (Translation: Please. You made a mistake. I'm ugly and small. This silver collar isn't for me. I think you meant to give it to the boy next to me. Call my mother. She will tell you it was a mistake. I want to go home now please. I promise I won't steal the sweets anymore. Mother. Help me."

I nearly fainted at the discovery that the words coming out of me were not within my power to control. Not only *could I not speak German but I didn't mean to say what I did. It was as if I couldn't resist calling out for Agnette nor could I deny the urge to dispute there placing the silver collar around my throat.*

I backed away from the stone door in fear. Something told me in a moment a bad thing was coming through that entry. My heart was pounding in my chest while I retreated to the furthest stone wall. I crouched down and did all I could to make myself as small as possible. That wasn't hard because I was indeed the itty biddy boy. I covered my face with my chubby baby hands and trembled with terror.

Almost as if on cue I heard the sounds of stone griding on concrete. That door was opening and someone was coming into the cell. I let out a tiny whimper and pressed into the wall with all my might.

A voice that I recognized called out but I only understood a few of the words he said. It was all in German and for some reason I couldn't understand the language. "Christian Axel. Boy blah...blah...blah...trouble...blah...come here. Now. Do...blah...I...blah...blah...beat you. Come here boy." I wailed out uncontrollably and felt my bladder let loose its contents. Ja, I wet myself. Can you believe that shit? Ugh.

The man yelled in fury, "Christian Axel, blah blah blah blah come here." I removed my hands to look at him and immediately felt all the air leave my lungs. It was Noah. He also was a nine years younger Headmaster, but I recognized him without trouble.

I opened my mouth to tell the brute that if he didn't fuck off Florian would have a new head but instead I said, "Jeg vil have min mor. Venligst far. Må jeg se min mor?" Translation: I want my mommy. Please sir. Can I see my mommy?

Noah glared at the little boy me and shook his head. "You blah blah blah. Blah blah blah Beating." With that he rushed me and snatched me by the hair.

I wailed in terror as the huge Dungeon Master dragged me to that wooden privy. "Blah blah blah now, bastard. Blah blah blah little shit." He pointed at my wet crotch and then pulled me to my feet by that handful of mane.

I screamed out in Danish, "No. No. Please don't beat me. I didn't mean to make the water in my breeches. It was an accident. Mommy please help me. I want to go home. I swear I'll be a good boy this time." Noah slammed me onto the hole on the wooden stool then ripped my soiled pants off with force.

That move really sent me into the crying jag. My high pitched childish voice emitted an ear shattering shriek at being half naked. I assumed the man was going to lash my bottom with the cruel looking whip attached to the white belt on his leather outfit.

Noah winced appearing most disturbed by the racket I was making. He reared back his arm and laid a strong backhand across my face. That effectively ended my panicked calls for aid. Hey, he was a fucking giant compared to me.. With my noises squelched, the Dungeon Master reached around my waist and pulled off the dirt encrusted shirt from my ravaged flesh.

All I could do is whimper and sob while Noah effectively stripped me. I was left shivering, trying in vain to cover the exposed skin. A feeling of terrible despair came over me as I helplessly watched the big man headed for the door. Before leaving he reached into the straw strewn floor to snatch up my protections against the chilly temps of that stone prison cell.

Then the Dungeon Master exited. I was left sitting on that privy, nude, confused with salty water burning my eyes and a cheek smarting from his harsh blow. It took many minutes to regain my composure and for my tearful leaking to end. Well, mostly. I had forgotten how much snot a little kid's nose holds. Yikes.

With much apprehension I hopped off that wooden throne and scurried to the corner furthest from the door. I put the wall to my back and sat down. My teeth chattered uncontrollably from the cold. I pulled my knobby little knees close to my chest, desperate to conserve as much heat as possible.

It seemed like hours passed but I couldn't be sure. Time is a difficult thing to determine for the isolated person but this was further complicated by my inexperienced baby brain. I thought I should be comprehending the meaning of this brutal treatment by this man Noah, but try as I might, I couldn't understand.

All I honestly knew is that my mother told me I was going to jail for a little while but she would come get me soon. This terrible crime that landed me in the clink, according to Agnette, was her belief that I'd been eating the candy she had hidden in her pantry.

The trouble with her explanation for the Russian men hauling me away to this terrible prison, was that I was innocent. I didn't steal her sweets. Hell, I didn't even know they existed or believe me I probably would've. Hahaha.

No matter how much I swore it, she didn't believe me. I begged her not to call the police, but she said I was becoming the brute. I'd gotten into a little argument at that school she sent me to because a boy there was teasing me about the razor cuttings. This situation didn't appear that serious at the time, but Agnette swore with this latest infraction of thieving I'd become unmanageable. The teacher called my mother and reported the incident but no punishment in either direction was dealt out.

I believed everything Agnette told me. It's to be expected I would. I was only the confused little boy with a long history of chronic isolation and severe physical abuse. Gerard was a bastard as you may recall. She was the one person on earth that I thought I could trust. I mean, after all, she was my mother.

Mothers are supposed to love their children so much they'd be willing to sacrifice their own lives to protect them, ja? Well, if I ever find the fucker that spreads that lie, I'm will feed his fibbing carcass to the yard dogs and give his noggin to Florian.

Anyway, so this shivering in the chill while sobbing for my worthless mother went on for Gott knows how long before the sounds of the door opening reached my troubled ears once more...

I peeked between my leggy barrier. A gasp of fear escaped me immediately. My red, swollen eyes were set upon a tall figure dressed in a hooded cloak. This person's cowl covered the entire face. To me, being the frightened youngster, this fella appeared to be the Reaper coming to take me to the land beyond living.

I need not tell you that the trembling I'd been suffering doubled the second this death creature closed the door. It was only me and this thing, alone, and I was without a route to escape what I was sure was my doom. With rising terror I watched it, standing there in silence, looking at me.

Then to my shock it spoken to me in my mother tongue, "Christian Axel? Are you afraid? Ah, there is no reason to be. I've come to bring you a gift." He held out his hand, which was human appearing to my surprise, where I could see the contents in his grasp.

I didn't move from that spot despite the things voice sounding friendly. By this time in my short life, I'd learned the painful lessons that people were not to be trusted. My heart was racing in my chest while I cowered there keeping both eyes on that Reaper man.

The fellow stood there for several moments still as calm water. When he realized I wasn't willingly going to take his bait, he took a couple small steps toward me. I whimpered and clung to my legs more tightly, certain that this was curtains for Christian Axel.

Instead of pouncing on me with a straight razor, which is what I expected, the man cleared his throat and said, "I can see you don't believe that I'm your friend, little Christian. That's okay. All the great buddies have the slow start. We have all the time in the world to get to know each other better. To prove to you I mean you no harm, I'm will leave a piece of candy here on the floor and I will go away. It's all yours, my bunny. Maybe tomorrow when I come, you'll think fondly of me, ja?" The fellow knelt and dropped one of the colorful tubes from his hand onto the straw. Then without another word he exited the cell.

I sat there for many minutes shifting my attention in the repeat from the door to that thing he left. It goes without saying I was expecting that he would spring out of the wall the second I attempted to exam this gift he said was my to keep.

As the adult, I could go for the rest of my life resisting the urge to gain a closer look at that curiosity. The eight year old Christian Axel, however, let novelty get the best of him. It goes without saying, soon enough I found myself crawling across the dungeon floor eager to see the present the Reaper man gave to me.

The item wasn't something I'd ever seen before that day. Whatever this thing was, it was cylindrical and wrapped in the blue and white paper. There were a lot of words that I couldn't read written all over it.

At first I was too scared to touch it. I sat there enjoying looking at the pretty thing imagining all kinds of magical stuff that it could do. In my world of empty hours full of greys, browns, and washed out whites, just the sight of its vibrant colors was pleasure enough to keep me entertained for hours.

Finally, I couldn't stand the torment of guessing the contents within. I nervously kept an eye on the door while seizing that wonderful thing. Quick as the roach, I scurried across the floor back to my spot in that corner. I held my breath, sure that the Reaper man would bust in screaming for that Noah fellow to beat me for taking his whatever it was.

When that silly thing didn't happen, I got brave enough to inspect this amazing object more closely. I turned my back on the door, to hide my actions in case anyone was to visiting and rolled the thing in my tiny palms with glee. The paper made a marvelous crinkling noise. That made me giggle.

The sound of my voice frightened me. I was sure that Noah guy heard my sounds of joy. I held still, waiting for trouble but again nothing but the noise of my own breathing greeted my ears.

Eventually I went back to my preoccupation with the Reaper's gift. I accidently ripped the edge of it while *spinning it around like the top. The damage caused by my carelessness caused my heart to sink. With a groan of dismay I examined the tear closely. My nose was suddenly assaulted by the most glorious smell I'd ever encountered.*

I held it closer to sniff in the scent deeply, thrilled at this newest discovery. This aroma called out to me in the most delicious way. Drool began to pour from my mouth, and my tummy rumbled angrily. To be fair, it had been a few days since anyone brought me a piece of bread or sausage scraps. Likely, even shoe polish would have smelled like food by that point.

Before I could think better of it, I tore open the paper and gasped when I saw the brown thing contained within. I admit, it looked like the petrified turd though it sure didn't have the same stink of on). I seriously thought that this was some kind of cruel yoke that Reaper man was playing on me.

However, that scrumptious scent it put out made me wonder if it tasted as good as it smelt. I tightly closed my lids and quickly put it to my tongue. I pulled it away rapidly and waited for the disgust to purge the flavor of cack from my mouth. Of course, that didn't happen.

Instead, I opened my eyes and stared at this incredible gift in awe. Then, before I could stop myself, I crammed that candy bar into my maw munching with urgency. No doubt anyone watching that show would've gotten a chuckle. Putting the starving boy in the same room with the sweets was like putting a horse into the sugar cane field. Hahaha.

All my troubles were temporary forgotten while I let that scrumptious treat tickle my neglected pleasure centers. Without a bid of decency I licked my fingers, that fancy wrapper and went back to the spot the Reaper man left it. I tore through the straw feverishly hoping in vein that I could find another one like it.

I'd just had my first taste of the chocolate. Until that day I'd never had candy. Which proves I didn't steal Agnette's sweets. I need not tell you, I was hooked like the drug junkie immediately.

Much to my dismay, no other candy bar was hidden in the folds of my meager floor covering. I sighed and begrudgingly returned to the spent wrapper. A series of yawns overtook me while I played with the pretty paper. I pretended to be an important man that was addressing a large group of adoring people, reading the fancy words to them. Of course I made that speech up since I still couldn't tell you what the hell was written on that wrapper.

Some time passed and the urge to nap overtook me with vigor. I rolled up around my prize to take a little snooze. This impromptu nap was disturbed before it began by the sounds of the door opening again. I tried to take the stance of defense, but I discovered my arms and legs weighed a ton. All I could do is watch in muted fear as that Reaper man come back into the cell with me.

He approached my floundering flesh and knelt only inches from my face. I whimpered in pure terror as his boney hand come at me. He gently rolled my wobbling head till I was forced to look directly at him. I still couldn't see his identity thanks to that hood but to my surprise a white scraggly beard was poking out within view.

The old man spoke to me in Danish. "Christian...an...an...an? Can you hear me...e...e...e?" A weird echo was trailing all his words.

I grunted and then let out a wail, "Mommy, I want my mother."

The Reaper chuckled and replied, "You be the good boy..e..e..e. You do everything you are told, and soon you will be with your mommy, Christian Axel...el...el...el. Do you understand...and...and...and?" I nodded feebly realizing there was nothing I could do but hope this man was telling the truth of it.

The memory gets hazy here. I recalled this man telling me to track a gold watch he held up in front of my eyes. It swayed in the most appealing fashion and I felt incapable of taking my attention from the movement of it.

Then I woke up to find myself in a valley surrounded by snow covered mountains. The grass is green and full of the wild flowers. The sky is blue. Birds are singing and in the distance I hear the bleating of the lamb flocks. This sound makes me happy. I want to pet the soft baby lambs. With eagerness I begin to run towards the calling of the sheep.

I find them with ease. Hundreds of white fluffy lambs running and hopping about. They see me and come to play with their best friend Christian Axel. It was great fun to be the buddies of all the animals in the Green Fields.

I never wanted to leave this place of peace and smiles, but the lambs tell me there are people wanting to destroy it. That information bothers me. I ask them if there is something I can do to help prevent that from happening. They tell me that I need to speak with their mother. She is the wisest of all the lambs.

The mother of all the lambs approaches me and whispers into my ear, "Christian Axel, I will tell you a secret, my name is Felicity."

I'm honored that Felicity gave me her secret in confidence. "The lambs told me that they are in danger. I want to help. This place is too beautiful to be ruined by the bad heart seeking to damage it."

Felicity nodded. "We need someone to protect the flock of the Green Fields. To do this a list of monstrous men and woman must be sent to the yard. Maybe you can do this for us?"

I nod that I can even though I have no idea what a yard is. "Tell me the names Felicity, and I will make sure they never get the chance to hurt you or the lambs. Then I will come live here with you in the Green Fields, ja?"

The mother lamb frowned. "You won't miss being in the world of men? There are only us lambs here. Won't you be lonely?"

I shook my head. "I'm already lonely, Felicity. Here the lambs speak and play with me. They don't mind that I'm the ugly boy with many scars. None of them hit me, and there are no chains, or stone cells. Everyone is free and I can dance in the sun. I will protect you, if you swear I can return to the Green Fields the minute I'm finished putting all your enemies to the yard."

Felicity smiled at me. "I give you my word, Christian Axel. You do as you are told and your reward shall be to live here in the Green Fields forever."

With a nervous smile I asked, "But how will I find my way back here, Felicity? I don't remember the way."

Felicity gave me a knowing smile as she replied, "You can always find the Green Fields, Christian Axel. Follow the lambs. They know the way, ja?"

I woke up to find the Green Fields replaced by the brown straw. The bleating of the gentle lambs became the sounds of sobbing children in neighboring cells. With a startle I looked around the stone room unsure if everything was only the stressful dreaming.

Then my eyes came upon the crumpled blue and white wrapper in the corner. The chocolate was real but I was unsure about the talking lambs. I'd been chained up in Gerard's barn for over two years with his horses, sheep and pigs. In all that time, none of the animals ever spoke to me. I decided Felicity and the Green Fields were a beautiful fantasy, but my reality was the ugly brutality.

71

Noah arrived soon after that weird dreaming. He threw a wad of clean clothing at me. The shirt and breeches were not mine. I sat there staring at them unsure what to do with them. Noah approached, yelling angrily the entire way. It was obvious he wanted me to do something but I couldn't understand a word that he said. Worst, he didn't appear to speaking my language either.

There was nothing I could do as the brute slapped me around till I was near stupid from his harsh blows. When this aggressive behavior didn't gain him the outcome he was seeking, he picked up the breeches. I wailed and cowered while the Dungeon Master forced them onto my battered flesh. It was at this point I realized he was demanding I put on the materials he brought with him.

I grabbed the discarded shirt and pulled it on with speed before Noah had the chance to hit me again. He stood there gawking at me in the oversized outfit for several minutes appearing stunned I minded him for a change. Then to my surprise, he patted me on the head and smiled.

I trembled uncontrollably as the placated brute headed for the door and left without another word. Not long after Noah exited, that Reaper fellow returned just as he had the day before. I rushed to my defensive corner as the creepy man entered and stood there looking at me.

He held out his hand full of colorful wrappers as he said, "Do you remember me Christian Axel? If not then surely you recall the kind gifts I give to the good little boys, *ja?" He squeezed the candy in his grip till the wrappers rattled.*

That caused me to perk up my head from behind my leg fortress. He chuckled and scrunched the wrappers once again. My mouth began to water like the Pavlov hund over the memory of the sweet goodness I knew each contained within. I still hadn't been fed much more than a paltry piece of bread that morning.

The Reaper man come a step closer holding the chocolate out towards me. "Which one would you like, Christian? Point at it and it is yours. Then we can be friends, ja?" I licked my lips and nodded while pointing at the red and orange clad candy bar.

He tossed the one I chose across the cell. I whimpered and backed away from it, fearful that he intended to snatch me the second I reached for it. The man seemed to understand my reluctance to accept his offering with him standing there as the witness. Almost in complete silence he rapidly retreated out the door, leaving me alone with his gift.

This time I didn't fool around. I scrambled to the spot where the candy landed and in near insanity ripped the wrapper open. I crammed the luscious sweet into my eager mouth without hesitation. I confess I had every intention of gobbling the delectable chocolate down not leaving even a crumb for the rats to steal.

However, I managed to curb my urge to be the glutton. This pleasure was too wonderful to enjoy quickly. With all the strength I could muster I denied myself a small piece, intending to save it for later. After all, I had no idea if this Reaper man was going to bring me more or if he would stop treating me all together.

I carefully tied off the chunk left in the ripped wrapper. Then I returned to my corner and dug under the straw. Certain that it was well insulated from the roving rodents that often visited my cell, I covered up the chocolate treasure. To be doubly sure nothing stole my wealth, I took up a seat on top of the makeshift bank vault.

I retrieved the stashed wrapper from the candy the day before and began to play with it. It didn't take long for the yawning fit to begin. I stretched and then rolled into the ball over the hidden cache under my straw mattress. There was something about the chocolate that seemed to cause a fellow to need a nap.

I was starting to drift off when I heard the door coming open. That noise sent me on the high alert. I lifted from my comfortable position to hide behind my legs as usual. I found my movements difficult to control. Clumsily I slammed backwards into the wall, and kind of slumped into my thighs overcome by intense drowsiness.

The Reaper man didn't hang by the door but approached me flailing around in the awkward attempts to protect myself. He knelt down, as he had the day before, then grabbed me by the ankle. I whimpered while he dragged me away from the wall. I landed on my back staring up into the darkness of his heavy cowl.

I wanted to attempt a run but my flesh wouldn't mind my brain. There was nothing I could do as the Reaper reached down and rolled my face from side to side. He seemed to be checking to see if I could prevent him from doing that). I heard him let out his breath and then he turned his head as if expecting someone to come through the door.

He kept his attentions on the entry for several minutes then he returned his focus on me. The Reaper leaned in close appearing to be examining my skin. I held still, scared out of my skin hoping he wouldn't hit me or worse take me with him to the land of the dead. This lack of movement on my part appeared to satisfy him.

His cloaked head nodded and I heard his deep voice chuckling as he said, "Ah, you are quiet as the mouse, Christian Axel. You are indeed a handsome creature. I swear to Gott those blue eyes or yours could melt the heart of an iceberg. What a lovely compliment to your mane of spun gold. A true delight to the senses in almost every way. Except someone attempted to spoil this vision of perfection, didn't they? What criminal defiled this treasure? That devil should be strung up and fed to the dogs for daring to cut up this angel. I confess, my bunny, your beautiful flesh is maybe too much a temptation for this lonely old man. Did Noah put these ugly clothes on you little one? Ha. I likely hope such trappings would make you seem less desirable. Well, he's a fucking idiot. you'd be gorgeous if dressed in oil rags and tar. In fact, I believe your far prettier without all these silly clothes. Let's get another look to be sure, ja?" I sucked in my breath, holding still as death while the Reaper man pulled down my breeches.

Once he had those off, he quickly pulled me to sitting by the upper arm. I continued to play stunned as he removed the huge shirt and tossed it into the straw. He then gently lowered my nearly paralyzed flesh back to its resting state on the back. This strange man's actions of desiring to strip me to nude were confusing and deeply disturbing to my underdeveloped mind.

The Reaper hoovered over me, seemingly looking over every inch of my damaged skin. He pulled back with suddenness and sat there next to me in silence. Then I saw him shoot another glance at the door. He watched that entry for several more minutes before he appeared sure whomever he was expecting either hadn't arrived or wasn't coming at all.

Ta my utter horror I saw the Reaper man pull up his robe without leaving his position of crouching next to me. The bottom half of a naked elderly man, not the skeletal remains, were revealed to my stunned eyes. This fellow wasn't the creature that heralded death but an unknown mature man that wanted to hide his identity from me for some odd reason since I didn't know anyone other than that abusive Noah guy.

If that weirdness wasn't enough, his next move really put me into the realm of complete bewilderment. Appearing to keep one eye on the door, this guy grabbed ahold of his manhood. I thought for a moment he was intending to takin the piss on the floor, but that belief was quickly shattered.

Instead of releasing the golden stream of water, this creep began to stroke his cock. I couldn't understand the meaning of that bizarre behavior, until I saw that his pulling seemed to making his member grow larger. I was completely unaware of the functions of the male sex organ, other than releasing water, at that tender age.

Needless to say, this amazing ability the guy was demonstrating fascinated the hell out of me. Sadly, at least at that moment, I didn't know that I should be panicked over what he was doing. I was far too young to understand the dangerous situation I was in, but that lack knowledge wasn't going to last much longer.

The man masturbated there next to me for several minutes. I listened with childish curiosity to his moans of thrill, unsure if this thing he was doing was painful to him or pleasurable. The one thing that wasn't occurring to me was to wonder why he was doing it in front of me, or for that matter at all.

While I was distracted watching him do this cool trick, he had been slowly inching closer to my prone frame. His breathing had become labored and he was rubbing his cock with quickening vigor. Then with suddenness he reached out with his free hand grabbing my own little boy parts. I let out a wail of both surprise and pain as he was squeezing the hell out of my hodensack.

He ignored my cries of distress and started to stroking my member like he was his own. This set off extreme terror within me and something even worse, a nagging feeling of shame. Try as I might, none of my limbs seemed to be working. It was at this point I realized I was helpless to stop this horrific scene.

I began to sob loudly as I wailed out, "Nein, please stop. You're hurting me. Someone help me. Don't. Mommy I need you. I want to go home."

The man let out a loud gasp and then suddenly white goo instead of the yellow water erupted from his penis. He aimed this slimy, warm stuff at my tiny chest and unloaded his pent up tensions onto me. This further traumatized my already freaked out psyche. Focusing every molecule of strength I had within me, I pitched and flopped trying to get from under this monster.

Though that attempt to escape my fate as his sperm dumpster failed, it did manage to alert the fellow that I wasn't as paralyzed as he thought. He finished his perverted misuse of my compromised state. The man let go of me and backed away, rapidly dropping his robe as he retreated.

His ending of that frightening assault didn't calm my weeping nor cries of distress. In fact, by this time I'd worked myself into the fit of desperation. My panicked conduct seemed to cause this fiend stress. I saw him steal another quick glance at the door before he once more drew closer to me.

He leaned down and said in a tone-tinged with fear, "Hush there, dear little one. You aren't injured and I swear no permanent harm has been done to you sweetheart. Your dignity is intact. I merely wanted to have the tiniest taste of you, my beauty, but I swear I didn't take a full bite. I'm not the lucky man that will have the pleasure of getting to have your full skills for my own. The woman that is promised your favors honestly doesn't appreciate the treasure she will hold."

I blubbered out in response, "Please let me go home. Call my mommy. She said she will come get me. Where is my mommy. I'm scared Mister. Don't hurt me anymore or she will put you in jail for it."

The man chuckled bitterly. "Oh you poor thing. You have no idea what's going on or where you are do you? You don't even speak the language. I can only imagine how frightening all this must be for you. Well, tell you what. You stop the crying, and I will give you another piece of candy. That sounds like a deal to you, ja? I think it's only fair to give you a bit of pleasure for the stellar service you just provided to me. If you be a really good boy, one day soon will I take you outside to feed the ducks. Have you ever seen the water birds before?" I shook my head that I hadn't.

This fellow reached out and attempted to pet my cheek. I flinched and turned my head to avoid his touch. He held his hand just beyond reach of my skin and oddly glanced at the door again. Then he reached into his pocket with speed, producing three candy bars.

He held them in front of my eyes as he said, "Dry those tears, Christian Axel. Let's make a deal, ja? If you let me touch you a little, and keeping it a secret between us, then I will give you sweets. I want you to think on this boy. I don't have to give you any candy. You are a prisoner in this cell unable to stop me from doing whatever I wish to you. I could do far worse than molest your pretty skin. I could rape you or even kill you and there's nothing you can do about that. Do you understand?"

I whimpered and sniffed the copious snot that blocked my breathing as I replied in the near whisper, "I don't want to die Mister. I don't want you to touching me either. Please leave me alone. I promise I won't bother you or ask to eat or anything. Just let me see my mommy."

The man made the tisking noise, "You aren't listening to me, boy. Like it or not, you will endure many things you don't want to suffer for the rest of your short life. That silver collar you wear ensures things are going to go badly for you unless you get it into you head that you are no longer in possession of your will. Now I am making my offer to you once more. You refuse me this time, then next we meet I cannot swear to curb the worst of my baser desires. I suggest you take the candy, Christian. I give you the sweets for your silence compliance, but the lesson I teach you by it comes for free. Never forget if you must do things you don't want to do, taking whatever you can get for the pain is better than being used and having nothing to show for it." He put the candy bars in my limp hand then pulled out a handkerchief and cleaned up the mess he left on my chest.

I laid there doing my best to end the waterworks. When he finished his gross task, he looked at me to check that I'd minded his demands to stop weeping. Finding I was no longer leaking he made a guttural sound of approval. I felt *him snatch the candy from my useless hands. He put his finger to his cowl in the signal of be quiet. I watched as he crawled over to a thick place in the straw and buried the chocolate to hide it from discovery by Noah or anyone else that came visiting my cell.*

He barely finished keeping his end of our bargain before I heard the door open. In astonishment I saw another Reaper looking figure come through the open entry. This second cloaked person was holding a large syringe and cupped under its arm was a painting of Felicity with her baby lambs. The three of them were grazing in the Green Fields.

I gasped upon seeing this physical proof that Felicity was real. The robed figure appeared surprised that I made a noise. It shot a glance at the old man Reaper and then approached me appearing curious. I laid there terrified out of my skull. One of these things was bad enough but two, well that blew my tiny mind to bits.

It shook its head and then said in a clearly feminine voice, "What is the meaning of this? Christian is fully conscious. Did you mismeasure the dosage?" She looked to the old man that was slowly taking back to his feet.

He snorted in response, "Nein. I think the boy either spit some of it out or didn't finish eating the laced bar. No worries. He won't remember any of this even if he only ingested half the usual amount. I merely require mild sedation to put a kid this young under deeply. He's eaten enough that he can barely move. I got to hand it to you, keeping his tummy empty was a brilliant idea. So, you go ahead and give him the injection. Soon as you got that out of the way, I'll start the process of opening his mind to your suggestions and commands."

The female nodded and dropped down next to me. She held that needle up to the light tapping the bubbles out of it. I wailed out in fear. I hate shots like most children do. My screams of terror didn't phase her in the least. She pushed that sharp into my exposed hip without any indication of hesitation. Nor did she attempt to sterilize the flesh before giving the injection. Yikes.

Almost immediately after the burning of her stick, I felt sleepy and sick to my stomach. I was quickly drifting off into a peaceful void when I heard her saying to the old man.

"I thought I tole Noah to dress this little brat before all our hard work ends up useless. I hope he realizes I'm going to have his head on a pike when this motherfucker dies of pneumonia. You'd better have a talk with that fool. Sometimes I wonder what will become of the Dungeons once Hemmel is out of the way and we raise him to Headmaster. Seems to me there must be a better replacement than him. I don't give two shits who his daddy it. Noah is soft and not a fucking thing like Bladrick."

I rolled my head to stare at the cloaked woman as shock ran through my veins at the discovery of Noah's paternity. She saw me looking at her and seemed disgusted. I was unable to stop my fast failing neck muscles when she pushed my face to point away from her own.

The old man chuckled. "What did you do that for? Since when does it bother you to gaze into the eyes of your innocent victims? I would think forcing the boy to set his sights upon his creator would make convincing him he's the schizophrenic Priceless easier in the long run. I mean, I know it would drive me insane to realize the most vicious soul that ever walked the halls of Das Kaiser Haus was my mother."

If that information about Noah being Bladrick's son didn't blow my last gasket, hearing this perverted old man refer to this woman in the robe as Agnette completely sent me to hell. Then just when I thought shit couldn't get any worse I helplessly wept while seeing that old man reach into his robe and retrieve a gold watch. Then he approached me swinging it from side to side. His calm, monotone voice began to tell me that I was becoming sleepy and I was. But just seconds before I slipped off into the dark places in my unconscious mind his hood slipped off. He nearly dropped his pendulum tool while attempting to keep his identity from ever being recovered if he was unsuccessful in his hypnotism. Well, his ability may have been exceptional but it wasn't perfect. There before my broken hearted eyes, fumbling for his cowl was the Fur King and my benefactor, Claus, the crossdresser.

Chapter 3: The Last Dance of Santa Claus
Master Mad Maxx and submissive Meine Liebe

Was it just a dream or did Maxximillian just experience a reclaimed memory? There is only one way to find out. Ask the source, and that is exactly what he intends to do.

I spent the next several days in and out of consciousness. Doctor Attila kept me as far as possible from the world of the living without pushing me into the one of the dead. He told me later he did this for two reasons. The first was to keep my overwhelmed mind from suffering the intense pain caused by the many severe injuries. The other was to make sure I didn't attempt to leave his care nor anyone else take me from it.

Ta be perfectly clear, he wanted to be damned sure no one tried to rape me while I was too weak to fight them off. You see, the good doctor was very concerned about the long history of misuse of my flesh for unnatural penetration. He understood all too well that I wasn't always the compliant participant in such perverted sexual practices.

Thanks to the Stasi's brutality, and the sheer number of rapes that night, my uhm, assets were in shambles. The numerous tears had to be stitched and the entire personal area repaired. I was informed that had the situation continued or been any harsher, I'd be looking at a life time passing my wastes through a colostomy bag. Yikes.

Be that as it may, Doctor Attila read me and Mad Lucus the riot act regarding keeping my breeches up until his hard work completely healed. He assumed it would be a full six weeks, but perhaps twelve before I could even consider playing the shameful mare to my many studs.

I have to say this was one of the most embarrassing conversations I'd ever endured, at least at that point in my life. Only sitting through Peter's nasty lessons regarding the use of the enema was close. No matter how delicate one wishes to be when it comes to discussing same sex intercourse from the bottom man's standpoint, it's going to come across as gross because it fucking is.

Anyway, after enduring that hair raising report, I was released from the Haus clinic into the care of Mad Lucus once more. I wasn't able to walk independently yet. That repair job in the land down under was rough, let me tell you. So that royal motherfucker had to aid me the entire way back to the fourth floor apartment.

We traveled up the steps in silence. That lack of verbalization wasn't just between me and Mad Lucus. All around us the silvers, black and even the Dominants and FemDoms knelt or bowed as we passed them by. The usual loud chattering of the residents, high and low, was markedly subdued.

I wasn't sure if this strange lack of commotion was due to my re-appearance in the halls or if this might be the reverent demonstration of universal mourning. Its protocol to demonstrate quiet behaviors for at least thirty days in the effort to honor the lofty dead.

Whatever the cause, not having my ears assaulted by the numerous murmurs and racket was pleasant for a change. Mad Lucus didn't seem to mind the absence of whispers and awkward staring either. He dragged me along quickly. All the while he was panting and sweating under the strain of my weight while keeping his eyes straight ahead. No doubt, we couldn't get home quick enough for the panty waist. Ha.

The second we got through the door, he was ready to yap much to my dismay. "Christian Victor, I realize there is an agreement, but I must insist you mind the doctor's sage advice. I'm asking you politely to remain in our bed for the next three weeks, and then stick around the apartment for the three after. You know, so that you regain your strength completely before well, Jonas and Peter come seeking your favors. I don't mean to offend either fine Dominant, but I honestly don't believe they will be willing to back off their interests in you, not even at the risk of your good health." He pulled me along towards the bedroom as he said that.

I let out a long, tired sigh as I responded, "When are you going to figure out that there is no safe place for me to hide anywhere in this fucking Haus, Lucus? Even if I did heed your advice and attempt to barricade myself in here, if the Vampire or Peter want to attack me, that won't stop them. Gretta survived my attempts to send her to hell. All those perverts have to do is go crying to her dumb ass, and next thing you know I be chained down below, or worse restrained in Jonas's bondage bed."

Mad Lucus opened his bedroom door and struggled to get me to that horrid cock bed as he panted out, "I know you think that Jonas and Peter are unstoppable, and perhaps you think me too weak to stop them or the Council. However, Christian, I assure you this time will be different. Your injuries were life threatening and I dare say still are. The Princes are never going to allow those animals to have their way with a man in your condition. I don't give a shit what their contract with you says or how much pull they believe they have." He carefully helped me onto the mattress and began to pull off my boots.

I glared at the well-meaning but deluded Dominant. "Lucus, playing mother hen is a moot point by this late hour in our association. I'm going to rest a few more days as Doctor Attila recommends, but after that I've got business to attend that cannot wait. I'll follow my end of our bargain to the letter. You will do the same or, well brother, it won't be Jonas or Peter you need to worry about." Mad Lucus stopped his task of stripping my feet to stare at me appearing stunned.

He cleared his throat nervously then said, "I suppose an apology on my part is long overdue to you Christian. When I tricked you into that gold collar and I won't persist in lying about it, I honestly thought I was doing right by you. It was stupid of me to think I'd be able to end the cruelty others chronically have wrought upon your flesh. In my big hurry to play the hero it would seem I've become just as guilty of the crimes I originally set out to end. I confess things got a little out of control. I swear on my life, I never meant to hurt you. I know you have no reason to believe me, but I did and do love you with all my useless heart." Lucus looked at his lap appearing shamed at hearing the words coming out of his mouth.

With a snort I nodded. "Oh, I do believe you believe you love me Lucus. You were almost correct in your confession. The thing you left out is the most important though. You may've entered into the conspiracy with the intent to prevent others from taking advantage of me. Problems is that you didn't care for the competition is all. Be that as it may, in all candor, there is no better option for this worthless man. You, Jonas, Peter, any of the dozens of bastards that have sought to abuse me, what is the difference? Not much in reality. Truth is, you need not attempt to unburden your black soul to me. This Haus never gave me the choice. I wasn't even permitted the smallest of mercies granted even the lowest that live here. My pleas went unheard, and my preference for the female ignored. Now I'm the ruined man. You allowed that bitch Cora to finish what worse men before you started. It doesn't matter anymore that I'm not the natural schwuler bottom. Without the ability to stud, playing the mare is all I'm good for and that is your honest concern now, isn't it? You are afraid that if Jonas or Peter come to drink from my well too soon, they might collapse the watering hole permanently. Ah, and then where will you be my bunny? Stuck forever forcing the blow job or dry fucking my thighs. Now wouldn't that be a bitch for you."

Mad Lucus looked up at me with a startle, "Christian. I resent that you think all you are to me is the fuck toy."

I chuckled bitterly as I replied, "You are the bastard, Lucus. Always putting things in my mouth without my approval. Well, bad enough you force me to suck that nasty cock of yours. I won't tolerate your words too. I never said you believe me nothing but your pleasure hole. I may be the psychotic but I'm no fool. Having the lover that is helpless to stop your darkest desires is only the icing on the cake. If it were just the twisted sex you could get from me, hell I could look forward to you moving on. After you tired of the novelty of your sick intercourse demands, that it. But you're looking to obtain something from me that has long-term meaning for you. It's my ability to make you the most powerful man in the Haus that keeps you buzzing around my head like the moth to the flame. There is your honest love, my sweet. Call me the liar, Lucus, I dare you." I narrowed my eyes and gazed right through the man.

He shook his head mildly and blew out his breath. "Who am I to dispute what you believe Christian? What can I say to change your mind? I've done a shitty job protecting you. I been so busy trying to use your position of power to fix all the ills of the Haus I ignored that you needed me the most. I took it for granted that you wouldn't be offended by being put on the back of that list. Whatever punishment you give me for being the blind idiot, I've no doubt earned it a hundred times."

I rolled my eyes. "Don't patronize me, Lucus. Stop attempting to say what you think I wish to hear. It will do you no favors. I told you there is no better champion for the Mortar Regent. When the day comes that bitch puts me below, it will be your name that crosses my lips. I give you no punishment for lying to me, abusing and betraying me because I understand there is no way to reclaim what you have taken. I could kill you, but then what? I'm left with the harsh choice of who to name Regent? Oh, I know, Matz? Or Roland? Perhaps Jacob? None of them could stand up to

Jonas, Peter, or Gretta. and don't forget sooner or later Claus will take that dirt nap. Then, I dare say, Cora will be looking for the man that taught her empathy for the submissive's childhood in the bowels of this hell hole."

Mad Lucus shrugged his shoulders and shot me a sheepish glance. "So then? I suppose you will entertain my offer to start our relationship over with a clean slate?"

With a grunt I kicked him lightly with my bare foot, "Only if you finish helping me get comfortable, then leave me in peace. I'm in need of a nap and an end to looking at your ugly face. I also need a six week vacation from service, boss. I seem to remember you already have the note from my physician."

He smiled appearing relieved. "Ja, I heard the doctor. You can be assured I won't be asking for anything other than the superficial cuddling till Attila gives you the all clear. I won't mind it a bid either. Not only will the wait help to stroke my desires for you, love, but in reality six weeks is nothing at all. Especially compared to what it could've been had the Stasi been successful." He reached out and gently petted my left ankle.

I scoffed loudly. "With broken hands, I won't be stroking anything of yours or anyone else for far longer than six weeks. Now get the fuck out and let me rest, Gott damn you. I'm already going to have nightmares thanks to your gross cock bed. I need not add depth to them by enduring your foul presence any longer than necessary."

He laughed hard and stood up to leave as he said, "You do realize the more you resist my attempts to woo you the more I desire your affection, ja?"

I closed my eyes and rolled till my back was at him as I replied sleepily, "Of course I do, Lucus. I'm the fucking former Priceless pleasure submissive. My skills at seduction are legendary. I can have anyone in this Haus eating from the palm of my hand thanks to years of painful training. Well, as long as they are the wrong gender to my desires, that is. If you were a woman, then you'd feel for me what I feel for you, disgust. See you later, lover." Slumber quickly overcame me as Lucus left the bedroom laughing like the hyena over the irony of my true statement.

Another few days passed. I was far too ill to make it to the commode without Mad Lucus's assistance. By the next week I'd decided the only thing worse than enduring the torturing of the Stasi was surviving it. Doctor Attila's statements that my injuries would be slow in healing couldn't have been more the truth. Not since the beatings and rapes I suffered at the hands of my father Xavier, and perhaps that dental work of Jonas, had I been more sorry to regain consciousness every morning.

During those days of terrible pain and utter helplessness Mad Lucus loyally stood guard at his bedroom door. I barely arrived home before the first of several visitors came calling, attempting to gain audience with the tormented Mortar King.

Noah showed up with my Lambs in tow. While I was happy to have Felicity and Taube safely returned, I was grateful Mad Lucus forbid that underhanded fucker from breaking words with me.

The next morning, my brute brother Byron come knocking before the cock crowed. Mad Lucus informed me he nearly had to hail Ruslan to get that creep to stop haunting the front door. The misguided Mortar Dungeon Master thick headedly believed no one could protect me better than him. He did move along, but only demanding the promise that the second I was capable of receiving guests, Lucus would let him know first.

The Shadow King also made several appearances seeking information regarding my welfare. To his credit, since no doubt Lucus was still intensely jealous of the man, Mad Lucus was gracious in his refusal to allow Cary to see me. The brute wasn't happy to be sent packing but he, unlike Byron, accepted that I wasn't in the condition to appreciate his presence.

Last, and certainly least, was Jonas himself. That Bat fucker was far more forceful in his demands to check on my health than any of the other men. Mad Lucus told me he did end up giving Ruslan a ring on this uninvited guest. He said the Vampire didn't take nein for an answer. A struggle broke out between the two shady Dominants, that resulted in Mad Lucus being struck in the head with one of Jonas's infamous backhands. That was it. The Haus Captain arrived to break the warring men apart.

It brought me great joy to hear that Ruslan informed the Vampire that further attempts to interfere with the Mortar

Regent's sacred duty to his Gold collar would result in five lashes below. I confess I hoped that Jonas would ignore the Russian's strong warning and return for a second helping of trouble. What I wouldn't have traded to see that motherfucker put in chains and whipped to bloody.

Mad Lucus in the meantime, besides tossing the buzzards that come to circle, behaved like the guardian he swore to be. I didn't have to ask for a damned thing. The man always appeared to know what I required before I had the chance to think of it.

For the first time since breaking my metal, I was fed three squares a day. I even got seconds any time I wished it. My medication was administered regularly and without failure. It wasn't fun to endure his nursemaid skills, seemed he gave me far too many sponge baths, and don't get me started about my painful calls to nature. Yikes! But he did provide perfect service.

More than making sure I didn't go hungry or suffer unnecessary pain, the royal bastard also kept his distance whenever he was not attending to some medical or personal need. He slept on his couch. I cannot tell you how nice it was to be permitted this unexpected peace though it did suck to be stuck in the cock bed. Gross.

It had been a long time since I could rest without the worry of being raped then forced to endure the cuddle of a hairy, snoring, farting bed companion. I wished many times in those bittersweet days that things could remain like this forever, but like most things in my life that was only a fantasy.

In exactly one week, I was capable of mobility with the use of my cane. My inescapable appointment with Claus was approaching. I knew that I could likely claim legitimate illness and avoid his foul interests. That would've been the intelligent thing to do.

However, that bothersome dream prompted me to rise from the sick bed. I knew the Fur King likely was wondering about the results of the wedding party and why Gretta still lived. I had a few questions I wished to ask that Elder Queen myself.

You should've seen the look on Mad Lucus's face when he came into the room with my breakfast tray. His stun that I'd gotten out of bed, dressed, put on my makeup, and managed to pack up the lambs safely in their pocket hideout unaided, was apparent. He stood there at the bedroom door stammering, unable to get a single coherent word out of his mouth.

I glared at him hatefully, "Spit it out, Lucus. Don't you see I'm the busy man? Otherwise put the meal on the end table. I can wolf it down before I go and I have time to take your bloody pills if you hurry the fuck up." I motioned with my cane to the spot where he could place the tray.

Mad Lucus blew out his breath then replied, "Christian Victor, I must strongly caution you against leaving this room. You're still too weak to defend yourself if the thugs of the Haus catch you out and about. Look at you. You're moving slow as molasses and still look like the devil took tap dancing lessons on your face."

I snorted with a bitter chuckle at his likely good advice. "What's that lover? Are you trying to hurt my feelings? I thought you found my blue and black eyes sexy. After I put all this energy into trying to look pretty for you. You're a cad. Humph. Just for that, you can sleep on the couch until further notice. A few more weeks on that lumpy sofa of yours will give you time to reconsider your picky nature, ja?"

Mad Lucus rolled his eyes and walked toward me with the food. "This is no joking matter, Christian. Seriously, I beg of you to get back to bed. Whatever you're off to do, surely it can wait at least a few more days. Or if you insist on leaving, let me call Byron to follow you for your protection."

I sighed and shook my head. "You know better, Lucus. What I do from nine to nine isn't up to you to discuss with me. Look at the clock. In five minutes, you lose all power over my decisions as agreed."

He licked his lips nervously and glanced at the time piece. "Okay Christian, ja, I know what you say is the truth but if you are killed because I let you bully me into keeping that bargain…" I interrupted him with a roar.

"I'm not that pussy little bitch Christian, Gott dammit. If you wish to speak to me, call me by my fucking name. I am Maxximillian. If you ever call me Christian again, Lucus, you are going to become familiar with the reasons I'm referred to as Die Brutale around here. You dig, old man?? My eyes burned with the fires of fury as I stared him down.

The brute's mouth come open and his eyes went wide as he responded, "Maxximillian is your name you say? I, uhm, though, I mean that's the moniker given you when you broke your metal. I called you Christian because that was your honest name, not the one forced upon you by the fiends of the Haus. I meant no disrespect. It's honor I'm granting by recognizing you aren't the person they tried to create in you."

I pushed past him with harshness headed for the door as I replied without looking back, "There is no honor within me Lucus. I AM the monster the Haus built. See you at nine if I survive. If not, then see you in Hell soon enough."

Mad Lucus yelled out after me, "Christ you're bullheaded as fuck, Christia, uhm, Maxximillian. At some point during your travels today, I beg of you to go by and visit your Uncle Leo. He's been worried sick about you. I promised you'd drop in the moment you were able. Swear you will at least consider keeping up my appearances of being the man of his word to that important relative of yours."

I called back, "Sure thing, baby. I've been wondering how his treatments been going. I'll try to fit him into my busy schedule." With that weak promise, I tore out of the apartment fast as my bum leg and cane would carry me.

The stairs loomed before my blood shot eyes, beckoning me to take the trip down them. My appointment with the

96

shady Claus wasn't for several more hours, and I had a list of other tasks to attend before dealing with our meeting that was sure to be unpleasant.

I made a right turn down the hallway. It'd been weeks since my oldest brother said he left my payment in the potted plant outside his former apartment. Worry that the notoriously industrious forth level black collar maids found the cache of his diary and hard on pills pushed me to move at a painful speed.

The object of my desire was within sight when suddenly a loud shriek assaulted my ears. Almost, instinctively, I rushed for the wall and cowered. With suddenness, the door of the apartment that once belonged to the rapist Bartram flew open. There before my stunned eyes, Ivan, the ex-Captain of the guard, came out of it appearing to be fleeing for his life.

He saw me crouched across the hall, with a bewildered look on my face. Ivan shot a frightened glance back at the apartment he now shared with Catarina and Sergie. Then before I could say a word, he ducked and practically slid across the floor. The wall halted his frantic efforts to escape whatever was scaring him as he landed next to me.

I stammered nearly blind in terror over watching the big man's crazy behaviors. "What is going on? Did you bring a pet tiger to live with you, fool?" Another loud animal sounding scream cut through the air as I said that.

Ivan shook his head while keeping a baleful eye on Catarina's apartment entry. "Not quite, your Majesty. I would say if anything the tiger brought me in as the pet." A cast iron skillet come sailing out of the door and slammed into the wall above our heads.

Ivan let out a yelp and snatched me by the upper arm, "Holy hell, run for your life Maxx before she starts tossing the furniture at us. Fuck.!" He took to his feet, pulling me along just as a glass shattered in the very spot we'd just abandoned.

As we rushed away from the kitchenware assault I turned to witness the tiny Catarina come flying out the apartment. She was dressed in a nightgown, and her dark eyes full of demons from the pit. I watched in utter awe as the little woman raised her fist into the air and yelled out in the furious tone:

"Ты грязный ублюдок. Возвращайся сюда и сражайся со мной, как с мужчиной. Я говорил тебе, чтобы ты взял свои мерзкие носки миллион раз. Вы воняете нашей комнатой, как свинарник. Бегите, если хотите, но рано или поздно вы должны вернуться домой. Когда ты это сделаешь, я буду ждать тебя никчемного мужа. Пусть вороны выклевывают тебе глаза за дерзость, которая разозлила твою жену. Я плюю на тебя и твои носки." She spat onto the floor and then re-entered her haus slamming the door behind her while ignoring the mess she made of the floor across the hall, Yikes.

I jerked free of Ivan's grasp nearly insane from wonder as I demanded to know, "What the fuck was that about, Ivan? Did your Frau just throw you out? It's only been a week and

98

already she wishes for a divorce. Damn, you are the idiot brute I thought you to be." I refused to follow him any further till he answered.

The ex-Captain ended his wild run and turned to me with a grin. "Divorce? Nein. You misunderstand, your Majesty. Catarina loves me too much to be seeking the counselor to dissolve our union. Besides, the woman wishes to have the baby before next Spring. That would be kind of hard to do without her Mann there to seed the kid, ja?"

I raised an eyebrow when he said that. "Huh? She loves you and wants to have your baby? Uhm, Ivan, I confess I'm no expert on the ladies but that little scene back there doesn't agree with your claims. I believe Catarina was attempting to murder you. I cannot speak Russian, but whatever she was shouting didn't sound like 'I love you Ivan, come home and make love with me so we can produce a son.'" I turned back to check that the angry woman wasn't sneaking up on the two of us with a second cooking pot in hand.

Ivan scoffed then chuckled with a huge smile breaking out on his face, "Oh that? Hell, Maxx, that's normal behavior for the Russian female, my boy. All girls from the Motherland are fiery by nature. I think it's caused by the long, cold winters. Every Russian man knows he can be assured plenty of heat in the aggressive embrace of the Russian woman. I got to say, she's so much like my first wife, it brings tears to my eyes. I swear to Gott I love that girl more than it's manly to admit. By the way, while we on the subject of happiness. I cannot thank you enough for the favor you gave to me when I certainly deserved none.

Especially from you. The boy Sergie is so sturdy and brave, I'd swear he comes from my own loins. and you see that beauty I call wife. Isn't she something to behold?" He stared at the closed door of Catarina's apartment appearing to be in a trance, swooning with affection.

I did the double take full of shock. "Seriously? You find being nearly clocked in the head by the frying pan a sign of true love? Wow. You know brother, I might have some extra antipsychotics in my pocket. I think you need the medication far more than me." I began to motion toward the hidden inner pocket opposite of Felicity and Taube's hide out.

The Russian startled and pulled his eager eyes off the object of his honest desire as he said with a chuckle, "The only crazy thing about me, your Majesty, is that I didn't attempt to re-marry sooner. I swear I'd forgotten how wonderful it is to have a sweet smelling, soft woman in your arms. My meals are cooked and she keeps the Haus neat as the pin. I've put on five pounds in a week and grown weak from the good living already. In a year, I be useless to anyone but as the door stop or paperweight. Ha, isn't life grand Maxx? Soon you be calling me Poppa Ivan for truth." He slapped me on the back with strength.

I nearly went headfirst onto the floor from that unexpected move as I coughed out, "Ugh, another Ivan the Haus needs like it needs another chapel. Christ, I should've force you to blood bond with the barren woman. Ah, but why am I worried? Catarina will brash your brains in with a kettle before you become the father no doubt. You didn't tell me what she was pissed about. What did she say?"

Ivan laughed hard as he responded, "She told me not to be late for dinner and swore her loyalty to me for all her life. I believe dare was a 'I adore you Ivan. I count the hours till you hole me again' in there somewhere too."

My eyes went wide and I looked back at the spot she'd retreated as I breathed out, "No wonder all you Russians are brutes. Even your words of adoration are rough and tinged with brutality. Yikes."

He cackled so hard he had difficulty speaking. "It is the truth we are a warrior race. But never mind all that. You must forgive me for asking, but what the hell are you doing wandering around the halls? You don't look robust in your health, and traveling without Guardmen watching your back after that shit you pulled last week. Do you really think that wise, your Majesty?"

It was my turn to chuckle as I replied, "Since when do you give a shit about my condition or safety, Ivan? As for my plans, that is no longer any of your concern. I do believe Ruslan is the man in charge these days."

Ivan nodded then said with a twinkle in his eye, "Well, I'm not in charge of your coming and going anymore, that is true. In fact, I was just headed off to see that man that you replaced me with when I ran into your royal Highness."

I put out my wrapped hand in the motion for him to pass as I replied, "Oh don't let me hold you up then. I would not want you getting into hot water or should I say hot with the boss. Be on your way Ivan. I wish I could say it's been a pleasure, but that'd make me as big a liar as you are, ja?"

Ivan winced but kept his silly grin as he responded, "Oh, now that was just mean, Maxx. I never lied to you. I merely withheld certain facts is all. Anyway, it doesn't matter anymore. You got your revenge, or at least I hope you feel secure that you did. If you are done kicking me in the hodensack for fun, I really must be going. Ruslan is indeed a harsh taskmaster. One more thing before I leave you to whatever deviltry you're doing. I believe the Fur King been seeking audience with your Majesty. If I were you, I'd make my way down to his apartments and see what's bothering him. Sergie told me that old bitch is pitching a fit demanding to speak with you."

I nodded. "I have a standing appointment with him today at one, but you already know that. Everyone knows that. He can wait a few more hours to gripe me out." I started to take off back toward my original goal of that potted plant.

The ex-Captain snorted loudly as I began to leave. "Perhaps he can and maybe he cannot. Sergie also reports Claus's ailing pretty bad the last few days. I'm not a doctor but it seems to me when a fellow is as close to the Reaper as he is, nothing can keep for even a few more minutes. Not my business, I know, but thought you should know. I see you later maybe if you don't fall down the stairs, or accidently get shot, or fall on a knife."

I turned around and glared at him full of fury. "I'd be careful imagining the death of a King if I were you Ivan. You may believe I cannot injure you without bringing down the KGB or Stasi on my head, but I've at least a couple of ways to make you wish I'd killed you. You digging what I'm saying to you brother?"

The burly Russian shot an anxious glance at Catarina's apartment door and gulped as he replied, "Surely you're not that evil. Nein. Your heart is too soft to carry out such a soulless crime."

That caused me to break out in wild laughter. "Is it Ivan? Are you sure you know me that well? Piss with me and I'll make a believer of you twice over. Better get to work. You're already late, pal." I left the brute standing there with a far more frightened expression on his face than when he come rushing out of his wife's door.

When I arrived at the plant Justus identified as the one holding my payment for his rise, I leaned into the wall. The traffic in the hall was light, but I didn't wish to have any prying eyes witness me digging around for the coveted items, you know. Several moments passed before I was absolutely sure the coast was clear.

I didn't have to search hard. To my relief the thing was made of plastic, and therefore the diary and pills under its fake roots weren't full of water damage. Plus the objects promised were still there thankfully) I quickly snatched up the dusty old notebook and the wrapped package of hardening pills.

It took a bid of work but I managed to stuff these treasures into my empty inner pocket. Broken hands are a bitch. Without another second of lingering I bolted off headed back for the staircase. My next intended destination was the Haus gym. I expected my older brother Byron to be there working out, as he was most mornings.

Forcing him to recant that uneven contract between us wasn't something I regretted. That said, I knew my life in the Haus would be unbearable unless he continued to provide his pain killers and cigarettes. I had by that time come to view smoking as one of the few pleasures in my shitty life. I wasn't looking forward to renegotiating with that brute, but like it or not it had to be done. All I could do is pray this time our agreement could be something I'd be capable of tolerating.

Ah, you maybe wondering if I still believed Byron intended to get us an escape out of the Haus. Well, sure I wished he was being honest in his boasts that he could and would do such a thing.

However, I now understood the Haus was the least of his hurdles to jump. Byron is the native of an occupied country with strict rules regarding immigration and heavily guarded boarders. Like me, he had no proof of his identity or even the legitimate birth certificate. While Christian Axel had been reported to the Danish and East German government as dead and buried, Byron's existence was never recorded at all.

No matter how much money he poured into his black-market contact, I doubted he'd be able to gain the proper documents. You see at that time, the border guards were working hard to curb the stream of people escaping the cruel government regime.

The rumor was that every few days the legitimate mark on the immigration papers were changed in the effort to prevent forgeries. This meant that whomever he was paying may provide him with forms but by the time we managed to slip past the Haus guard and make the long trip to the checkpoint they would be fucking useless.

My unfortune familiarity with the brutality of the Stasi and complete understanding of their undisputable power thanks to it, had crushed all my illusions. I still held out the weakest of hopes that Byron would manage the impossible but I was slowly coming to terms with the horrific truth. It was becoming pretty clear that the Palace prison cell was the likely future for Maxximillian. That really sucked but there wasn't shit I could do about it.

Well, being completely helpless isn't entirely factual. If it turned out that I was doomed to be held in the foundation of Das Kaiser Haus for a lifetime, however long or short that may be). I understood that what I did for the next five months mattered a lot.. The only way I could hope to improve my pathetic lot was to change the way things were run above the Dungeons. The hope being that what happens above will eventually trickle below.

The first move towards this was seeing my sadistic brother. His aid was paramount to my plans. With his useful tools I was sure I could bare the terrible things I needed to do. Otherwise I was looking at far worse than the terrors I'd endured during my initial introduction to life as the Mortar King. Yikes.

That trip down the steps was painful and not just because of the inner turmoil at where I was headed. The cane digging into my very tender palm added insult to the griding agony of dragging a near useless leg downhill. The reverent kneeling of every damned person I come across threatened to make Ivan's predictions of me falling seem a distinct possibility.

I think it's likely I would've slipped to my death, but Ruslan happened to cross my path before my knee failed me. The huge Russian saw that I was in peril and come running. I let out a reflexive yell of surprise just as the Captain grabbed me around the upper arm to offer stability.

He shot me a sheepish smile as he said, "My sincerest apologies, your Majesty. I thought you saw me. I beg you allow me the honor of aiding you on your journey. I thank you for the mercy of it." He sucked in his breath appearing worried I would be angered by his rash behavior.

I glared at him with irritation, mostly because he had frightened me for that moment, as I responded, "Slipping up on a man like that will get you murdered, Ruslan. What is wrong with you, fool? I would trust that my pretty sister is keeping you well sated. I think she should be ashamed that she leaves her Mann so deficit in affection he feels the need to go around touching other fellows."

Ruslan chuckled and dropped his sights to his boots but refused to let me go. "Matilda is the dream come to truth for me, your Majesty. I tell you I've no complaints in her services to me both in and out of our private bed chamber.

Honestly, I'm the happiest of men. I cannot thank you enough for all that you've done for me. Correct me if I'm wrong, but I'm guessing gratitude wasn't what you were seeking. I've a more important reason for being at you side at the moment then merely keeping you from tumbling down the steps."

I narrowed my eyes at him. "Oh? Pray tell what would that be, dear Captain?"

The Russian glanced around us at the kneeling collars and then leaned in close to whisper, "We cannot speak openly with so many ears listening. If I could be so bold as to ask you to meet with me later. You select the time and place. I'll be there, Sire."

I nodded and whispered back, "I will meet you alone at five o'clock in the Haus pool area. Almost anyone of worth will be in the Great Hall for their supper. We should have the place to ourselves for at least an hour or so."

Ruslan smiled. "Ah, that's true. Consider it done. Oh, before I forget to tell you I think you should know the Fur King been seeking audience with you, your Majesty. He's ailing pretty bad, Sire. I wouldn't wait too long to drop by to speak with him."

I rolled my eyes and blew out my breath in frustration. "This again? Ruslan, I've already heard this bullshit. For your information, I run into Ivan a bit ago and he said the same thing. Is the old toad really that close to croaking that you fucking Russian's believe he cannot wait till this afternoon to cuss me out?"

Ruslan frowned and his expression went serious as he said, "Ja, his health is failing fast according to Sergie die Silent."

I startled for the second time since the Russian's appearance. "Sergie die Silent? Who the fuck is that?"

The Captain chuckled low. "Oh, that's the pet name Ivan's stepson has acquired. The boy cannot speak well because of, well you know."

I nodded and grunted with disgust. "Shit, are the people around here such simpletons that they need to point out every unfortunate's disability by calling them by it?"

Ruslan shrugged as he responded, "I'm not sure that's what the intention is, your Majesty. Sergie doesn't speak often but when he does it's important you can be assured. I don't believe they call you Die Insane do they?" He began to cough nervously appearing to realize that last thing he said maybe wasn't wise.

I halted my travel abruptly, mostly because we'd arrived at the first floor. "Excuse me? Did you just say something, Captain? I certainly hope that I was having a hallucination but I thought I just heard you refer to your King as crazy." I glared at him with fury rising within.

The Russian looked around the hallway trying to seem distracted. "What is this you saying? Ah, nein, you misunderstand. Oh hey, you, ja you. You hold up right there Borya. I've been looking for your sorry ass. You left a mess in the barracks. Uhm, I must beg your forgiveness, your

Majesty. There are a few important matters for me to attend at the moment. I see you at five as we agreed." The brute tore off in the direction of his unruly officer as if his ass were on fire.

I stood dare watching the Russian beating a hasty retreat. It was a tough call, trying to decide if my plans to find Byron should be put on temporary hold. The idea that Claus could die before I got the chance to speak with him about that disturbing dream. Well that pushed me to head toward his apartment rather than the gym as planned. It really didn't matter what time I kept our weekly appointment. Nine-thirty or one o'clock, it was still Thursday.

I arrived at his door and took a deep breath to brace myself. Dealing with Claus's lustful interest all those years had never gotten easier. It wasn't that the man was twisted, or even terribly harsh when takin his sexual favors. That didn't change the fact that I honestly found his interest in me repulsive.

Not just because he was old enough to be my great grandfather, but he also demands to kiss and cuddle while raping me. Believe me when I say that was gross beyond imagination. Bad enough to put up with his horrid intercourse without having to endure his nasty fondling before, during and after it.

As usual, I shook off the rising feeling of despair. I knocked forcefully, secretly hoping that I'd arrived one second too late. To my dismay, Sergie answered before I could fully enjoy that fantasy of being free of Claus's claws for the rest of my life.

He smiled as he motioned that I was to follow him. I grimaced and hobbled after the tiny boy. The entire apartment smelt of urine and bile. While it was clear the Elder hadn't succumbed to his cancer yet, the aroma in the air seemed to indicate the Russians warning weren't that far off the mark.

When we arrived at Claus's bedroom door Sergie halted. He turned to me still smiling and hand gestured that I was permitted to enter.

I nodded at the grinning boy as I said, "You look famished Sergie. Why don't you head down to the Great Hall for breakfast, ja? I will keep an eye on the King during your absence. If his condition takes a turn, I know how to dial the Haus doctor." The Ukrainian shot a nervous glance into the room as if unsure what I suggested was permissible.

Claus's raspy voice called out from beyond my view, "Sergie darling. I believe I hear the Mortar King giving you an order. It's bad manners to ignore the words of a sovereign. Do as he suggests. I can assure you, I'm in the best of hands till you return. Get going boy." Sergie smile got wider as he bowed before he ran for the door.

The wooden barrier barely slammed shut before Claus called out from his bed again, "Come in, Maxximillian. Let my tire old eyes take in the glory of my beautiful boy while they are still capable of reporting such splendors to me."

I stepped into his room and was immediately struck by his greyish pallor. "I hope you are alright with me moving up our scheduled appointment today. It seems you've fooled everyone in the Haus into believing you're so close to the abyss they are expecting to be digging your grave by one this afternoon." I chuckled bitterly but could understand why that rumor was circulating. Yikes, he did look bad..

Claus shot me a weak smile and struggled a bid as he sat up from his prone position. "I'm not dead yet, my beauty. Bring that gorgeous ass of yours over here and sit with me. If the buzzards are truly about to feast on my flesh then I would wish for them to find their dinner resting in your arms." I nodded and limped to join him on the mattress.

The lusty old bastard reached out to caress my cheek the second I took a spot next to his withering frame. "Ah, you are like the tonic to this dying man. I swear no matter how many times I see you, it still takes my breath away as if it were the first."

Stifling the urge to gag I cleared my throat and said in the near whisper, "With eyes so blue they could melt an iceberg, ja?"

Claus startled and pulled back his caressing old paw, "What did you just say?"

I glared at him unblinking. "How long we known each other Claus?"

He shrugged his shoulders and licked his lips nervously. "Why are you asking such a silly question, Maxx? You surely haven't forgotten when I saw you at the Haus Theater. You were wearing that horrible silver collar of Peter's. Remember, you couldn't takin your pretty eyes off me. I know no matter how addled my brain gets I cannot forget it. Best day of my life." The Elder gently took my bandaged right hand into his and smiled as if enjoying the image of the seduction that had been forced on me by my Master.

With a snort I pulled from his grip. "You sure that was the moment you and me were first introduced, Claus? Because I'm not as positive of that as you seem to wish me to believe you are."

The old man shook his head appearing bewildered. "I can tell you one thing, my boy. I've known you long enough to know better than to try to argue with you. What's all this about? Stop stalling and say what is on you mind. Out with it."

I sucked in my breath and stared into his watery grey eyes. "I wish to hear a secret about a little boy that didn't eat all his chocolate one day and saw something he wasn't supposed to remember, but suddenly does."

Claus's expression fell and his mouth went ajar as if hit by a baseball bat as he whispered, "Surely this is not happening. Dear Gott not now, not ever."

I nodded and leaned in close to his face and growled. "It wasn't a fucking dream was it, you fucking pervert. You did take advantage of me when I was a frightened kid chained up to the wall in a dungeon cell. That's pretty low Claus, but in this Haus, not the worst thing that's ever happened or even unexpected. Misuse of the virginal silvers is common as the snowy day around here. Molesting an eight year old is illegal but as the Elder you could've easily paid Noah to look the other way. What I honestly wish to know is what the fuck you were drugging me up for? Not like I could escape your foul lusting and no one could understand my language down there. That leads me to wonder why you needed to attempt to buy my silence with chocolate in the first place. There was a woman with you. She spoke Danish. You were afraid I might tell her what you were doing to me, ja? Why would she care if you were touching me? Who is she? Answer me damn you, or so help me I going to make your final moments on Earth more painful than you ever imagined in your worst nightmares." I moved with speed and straddled the ailing Elder's heaving chest ready to carry out my threat to completion.

Claus gasped and struggled weakly under my weight as he rasped out, "Maxximillian, stop this insanity immediately. Please think for a moment. If you kill me, the Haus will burn you at the stake for murder of the Fur King."

I chuckled bitterly while nodding but didn't remove my flesh from his. "They won't even know your life was ended by me Claus. Cough up the truth and maybe I won't choke out the tiny bit of life you have left."

The Elder groaned from the agony of my slow crushing of his frail flesh, "Okay, I will tell you what you want to know, but only if you get the fuck off me, dammit." He attempted to push me as he gasped for air.

I laughed hard and squeezed him lightly with my thighs before dismounting. "Alright if you insist on breathing a bid longer who am I to argue. Now start spilling the beans old man, before I start knocking a few holes in you to release your foul fluids." I took a seat next to the wheezing Elder.

Claus caught his wind and with a look of remorse said, "Before I say anything Maxx, I have to know. Do you intend to withdraw your promise to give me a taste of your affections weekly?"

I rolled my eyes and let out a small yelp of frustration. "Seriously Claus? I'm quite ready to end your life and all you worried about is whether or not you still get to fuck me every Thursday at one? Gott dammit, you are more the pervert then I ever realized. Whatever! Speak the truth without fear that I'm gonna welch on our prior contract. that's if you still around to enjoy your end of it."

Claus nodded slowly while takin a deep breath. "You've always been a good boy Maxx. Nein, the very best boy. That said, I admit I will die with regret for my part in the damage done in my effort to hold you in my arms even if only for a moment in time. Be that as it may, there is no taking back my misuse of your poor lot in life. I won't lie. If given the chance to do it all again, I cannot swear I would do anything different. You're the only thing in the world that ever brought me truthful joy, and one of only three people I've can say I honestly love with all my heart."

I scoffed loudly. "There is that word again, love. I hear my name used with it coming out the mouths of many monsters since I was only the child. I suppose masturbating and raping my helpless ass for all these years is your demonstration of such a lofty emotion. Perhaps there is a better definition for the thing you feel for me, Claus. I do believe the correct term is pedophilic."

The Elder chuckled bitterly and nodded. "Ah, there you go Maxx.. Always cutting right to the chase of a conversation. Well, if you wish to believe my desire for you is some twisted lie I tell myself to justify lusting after a beautiful boy young enough to be my own grandson, I won't try to change your mind. That doesn't change the fact that love comes in many guises. Not all them easily definable or even recognizable to the average person. I've not always told the truth, and on many occasions I've actively set out to deceive others. Hell, most of my life falls into the category of cloak and dagger, false tales, or contrived illusions. That said, when it comes to loving you, it's maybe the most honest thing I can claim."

With a glance at his clock I bellowed, "You're wasting my time old man. Get to speaking about the things I wish to hear and let cupid have a coffee break. I could give a fig less if you the biggest fibber in the entire country as long as you tell me the truth about what you and that woman were up to all those years ago when I was little."

Claus stared at me as if surprised. "Ah, but you see my adoration for you is part of what I was up to my boy. If you would allow me to explain, and from the very beginning, I think you'll agree. But you must understand I can only tell you what I know about this. There is a great deal that I was never given information on."

I put up my hands nearly ready to burst in frustration. "Fine, fawn, slobber and pluck the harp all you like Claus. Just get on with it already. Fuck."

The Elder chuckled at my obvious irritation, then began to speak of many things, some that answered burning questions and others that raised many more. He looked at the ceiling as he began his long tale:

"I was born in 1890 to a family that at the time wasn't as wealthy as it eventually became. My father was a hardworking man in the mercantile business, and my mother was a beautiful seamstress. Their love affair was epic I'm told, but by the time I was born it'd fizzled to one of convenience.

You see I was the last son of many my mother bore for my father. I came along late in life for a woman of that era. The aging lady had long since lost her youthful vigor and figure. My father had taken up with a series of mistresses, leaving my mother's bed empty and heart broken.

If this wasn't cruelty enough, I, her final child, was a disappointment right from the start. You see my mother had eight pregnancies in all. Five of them resulted in live births, but all were male. As you know, as it is today, boys were the preference in gender of any baby. Sons were expected to follow in their Vater's footsteps and carry on the family name. Girls were viewed as the liability. Girls were to be married off with speed the minute she was of age to produce more male children.

For the lonely Frau, if isolated from her kinsmen as my mother was, her only hope to break the hours of loneliness was to manage a girl somewhere in between production of the aloof male child. It was my mother's deepest prayer that I would be born female, but to her utter despair she delivered a fifth healthy boy.

By the time I was born, my older brothers were already over the age of ten. Back then, male children were expected to work as soon as they were able. Every day all of them would leave with my father to work in the stores he managed. This was yet another reason my mother craved producing a female. The girl wasn't allowed to leave the haus of the middle class German home until given over in the care of her Mann.

So, that was her lot in life. My depressed mother, left alone with a baby that the minute she'd grown attached to it, would abandon her like all the other men in her life to that point. This understanding, and the looming emptiness of her middle age, caused a mild type of insanity within her.

In the effort to alleviate her fear of being alone, she began to put her baby boy in the pretty dresses she sewed for the daughter she never bore. Of course, she only did this when the men of the Haus we at work. That calmed her terrible sadness for a bid.

However, one day my father came home from the shop early. He eyes come upon his toddler son twirling and parading around proudly in a gown my mother had made for me. I had no idea prancing around in a girl's attire was wrong. I was only four years old but that didn't matter to my father.

His rage reaction was over the top. He come at me with the devil in his eyes. I can still recall the beating I received over it. The shame of having that dress practically ripped from my battered flesh while he did it hurt even more than his blows ever could've.

My mother heard my cries of distress. She came running to defend me from her furious husband. He gave her a fist sandwich for daring to interfere with his correction of her errors with his son's gender identification.

To make matters worse. When my brothers got home I was subjected to hours of ridicule, merciless taunts and full on bullying by the lot of them. When all the males went to bed that night, my bruised mother snuck into my room to do her best to sooth her grieving daughter.

During this bonding cuddle, my mother decided she'd had enough of my father's isolation tactics and cruelty. Without explanation of our behaviors, the woman held me tightly to her bosom as she fled from our home into the darkness.

There was no such thing as the car in those ancient days. My mother was forced to run on foot, as far as she could hoping to escape the clutches of my cruel father. That was an impossible task for a woman of that day, much less one without the means to support herself, not to mention being with a baby too.

Needless to say, after a week or so of hiding out in ditches and hovel sheds, a local villager spotted us. He reported our whereabouts to the authorities. We were quickly rounded up, and I was sent home to my father's haus. My mother, on the other hand, wasn't welcomed to return.

I was too small to understand why my mother had abandoned me to endure the cold environment of my father's home. It would be many years before I saw her again, and everything was explained to me, but I will get to that in the story shortly. For now, just know life for me was harsh, and my brothers blamed me for our mother's disappearance.

I was endlessly taunted about the dress incident, and often the victim of vicious beatings from all four of them. The years were hard and believe me when I say nary a night went by that I wasn't drenching my pillow with my tears of grief. It wasn't the brutality, but the empty hole in my heart left by losing that special soul that I knew as my mother.

When I was eight years old, I was sick with an illness that was common among the young at that time. It wasn't that I felt that bad, but I couldn't work due to being contagious. My father and brothers went on to the shop and left me alone at home.

During the long hours of boredom, I decided to sneak into my father's room and pick the lock for my mother's old closet. I thought maybe a clue as to where she'd gone was hidden in dare. Why else would the old man go to such lengths to keep us boys out of there, ja?

Well, while I didn't find the clues to her location that I hoped I would behind that door, I did discover something almost as wonderful. All her dresses were hanging there, as if any minute the woman would return to wear them. To my delight, I could still smell her scent on them. When I closed my eyes, I could almost believe she was right there in the room with me.

I couldn't resist the urge to take one off the hanger and put it on. The feeling of the material on my skin and her smell brought on a peace within that I hadn't experienced since that terrible day we were parted. I paraded around the room, twirled and curtsied.

Ah, the rush of excitement made my heartbeat race and blood boil. That little moment of crossdressing may have passed into my history without going any further but it turned out I wasn't as discrete as I thought I'd been.

Not long before I came down ill, new people had moved into the haus next door. The coming and going of the other people in our neighborhood wasn't really of any interest to this deeply depressed boy. I hadn't even noticed that a young man around my age was among the family members that could call themselves our neighbors.

Apparently, he'd come down with the very same sickness around the time I did. He likely caught it at primary school like me. He'd also been left home alone, and unlike this idiot had been aware a potential playmate lived in close proximity.

This precocious young man saw my father and brothers leaving that morning. He recognized that I wasn't with them. With intelligent deduction he assumed I'd stayed home, and hoped I'd be willing to make a new friend. I didn't hear him politely knocking on the door while I paraded around my father's room in one of my mother's beautiful gowns.

When no one answered, the boy became concerned that I'd maybe collapsed or was too injured to come to the door. No one locked the doors back then, so without any effort or fear he'd let himself inside to check on my welfare. His worry that I was in trouble was quickly calmed the minute he cracked open the bedroom door and saw me spinning around with a grin on my face.

I didn't realize I had an audience for Gott knows how long, while the boy got to enjoy this most unexpected show. If he hadn't coughed, sick remember), it's possible he'd have snuck out before I discovered his voyeurism.

His noise caused me to startle. Besides my mother's dress, I'd donned her fancy high heeled pumps. I was far from graceful in these shoes to begin with but the fear my father or brothers had caught me sent me sprawling to the floor at speed.

The boy come running into the room when he saw me take that rough spill. He first checked to see if I was all right. When I said I was fine, he offered a hand to help me regain my footing and introduced himself as Keifer. His concern that I'd been severely injured, instead of teasing me about wearing a dress doubled my surprise in the situation.

I took his offer for aid and did all I could to hide my shame over his catching me in drag. Keifer seemed unconcerned about my strange attire. He asked several times if I was sure that I didn't break a bone, and then to my shock wanted to know if I'd be interested in hanging out with him.

Well, there was no way I was about to tell this boy nein. He was privy to my secret for starters. More than that, he didn't seem to mind that I was prancing about in the woman's dress. I told Keifer I'd be delighted to act as his playmate for the day. His smile lit up the room over my agreement to be his buddy.

During the next many years, me and Keifer were inseparable. He was the only son of a poor family, and I was the overlooked spare of one that was driven to become rich. The friendship between us couldn't have been cemented with a stronger adhesive.

Honestly, I wasn't ashamed even back then to admit Keifer was my rainbow in a world of bleakness. No matter how bad things were going, I could count on him to be there to dry my tears. Not since my mother had I felt as close to anyone. Thick or thin, he was always at my side.

Then when my puberty came into full blossom, I found that I wasn't interest in the girls like all the other boys around me. That strange lack of urge to chase the female, bothered me a great deal. I did all I could to hide my apathy at courting but my best buddy Keifer wasn't fooled.

One day in our sixteenth year he asked to meet me in an old barn we often haunted when planning some childish deviltry. I arrived expecting that he'd greet me with a bit of liquor he'd managed to swipe or perhaps have some elaborate practical joke he wanted to plot. Well, to my surprise Keifer had far more exotic things on his mind that day.

I found the boy sitting in a pile of straw with a beautiful white gown and matching ladies shoes laid out next to him. You know like a Frau had been there but somehow melted away leaving only her clothing behind. That scene was weird in itself but the way he was dressed really added mystery to this odd vision.

Keifer was wearing a man's fancy riding outfit. He looked every bit the part of a gentlemen that was headed off to the stables, including the fine leather crop. I stood there staring at him unsure what to make of what I was seeing. He was known for pulling crazy pranks all around the town. I shrugged off the feeling of unreality and joined him on the hay assuming these were items he'd snagged for yet another of his infamous gags.

I barely sat down when Keifer suddenly turned that crop on me with vigor. I let out a yelp of pain and demanded to know what the hell had possessed him to be hitting me with a horse tool. If I thought that was a surprise, his next move floored me.

Keifer stood up, looked me right in the eyes, and without a word put his lips to mine. I was so stunned by it I

123

didn't attempt to stop his advances. Before I could protest, I found myself the object of Keifer's inexperienced attempts at necking.

His clumsy mouthing went on for several minutes. I still didn't push him off and punch him out for daring to kiss me. I honestly was unsure what to do, or what to think about Keifer's behaviors. At least, not right away. When he finally pulled up for air and asked me if I wanted him the way he wanted me, that was the moment I finally realized he was all I wanted for the rest of my life.

Keifer had known I was gay, long before I knew or at least admitted it to myself. I felt an inner peace I'd never known when I told him that I loved him. He of course smiled with thrill that his affection for me wasn't misplaced. I started to attempt a re-engaging in the kissing when he pushed me back and said, "Put on the dress Claus. I want to be with the girl I've been dreaming of since I first laid my eyes on her years ago. You can say nein but if you do I fear I may have to spank you. He grinned and swatted me on the backside with his crop as he said that to me."

With a groan I interrupted the reminiscent Elder. "Christ, what the fuck does any of this shit have to do with what happened in the Dungeon, Claus? I don't want to listen to your perverted tales of romping in the hay with your old boyfriends. Gott Dammit, tell me why did you drug me up and who was that with you when you did it?"

Claus glared at me, then said in the angry tone, "If you'd be patient and listen you'd realize I am answering your fucking questions, boy. Now, are you going to let me finish or are you determined to go ahead and murder the only person left on earth that knows the truth about who you really are?"

I startled when he said that. "Huh? You're speaking nonsense, Claus. What I don't know is the identity of the woman in the hooded robe. I already know who the fuck I am."

The Elder narrowed his eyes at me then said, "Do you Maxx? Then why are you asking me who that woman was?"

I rolled my eyes. "What the fuck are you babbling about? Are you trying to tell me it was Agnette? I know that bitch is capable of it, but I know the voice of my own fucking mother Claus. That woman wasn't her. If you seeking to protect this woman by laying false blame on Agnette, you can cut the crap. I'm not falling for it."

Claus chuckled with a bitter tone as he replied, "Once again I say to you, Maxx, you don't have a clue about a thing until you allow me to enlighten you. That means you'll either have to hear all the facts of your existence I can tell you or you will be left believing only what we wanted you to believe."

I nearly choked as I blurted out, "Wait a minute, what do you mean by that?"

The Elder nodded and flashed me a diabolical smile as he replied, "If all a human has to rely upon to tell him who he is and where he is going is his memories, what happens to the real fellow if those memories are corrupted, supplanted or even replaced by the tampering of an outside force Maxx?"

A tremble of fear began to tiptoe down my spine as I responded, "That guy would be the slave to the one fucking with his head. Is that what you and that woman were doing to me, erasing my mind and replacing it with lies?"

Claus blew out his breath, then slowly said, "I guess you will have to sit there, like a good little boy and listen to find out. Tell you what Maxx. Go to the kitchenette and look in the cabinet. I had the black collars put some candy in there yesterday. The sweets are all yours, my beauty. I think we both know you tend to obey better when given incentive to."

I started to come at him with rage running through my veins but was halted mid-attack when Claus calmly said: "You'll never complete the mission if you don't follow the lamb. Felicity knows the way."

Chapter 4: Is There a Twin
Master Mad Maxx and submissive Meine Liebe

I wanted to murder that old pedophile but when he said that it was as if I were paralyzed in the spot. Claus laid there smiling at me while I struggled to get my limbs to mind my commands to strangle him. The look of shock that come over me must have been the comedy to that bastard because he began to chuckle.

"What's the matter Maxx? Don't tell me your interest in the sweets has subsided since you become the man. Why the boy I remember would be practically ransacking the cupboards seeking those delicious treats instead of sitting here next to the smelly old Fur King." he hand gestured me a release and suddenly I was able to move once more but not towards his throat as I wanted.

I couldn't stop myself from getting up and hobbling right to his kitchenette. Sweat poured from my brow as I began to tear through the cabinets trying to find the candy he promised would be there. The moment my eyes lit on the handful of chocolate bars in the brightly colored wrappers, I let out a gasp of delight.

A madness overtook me with vigor. I snatched the entire batch of sweets and fell to the floor ripping them open fast as I could with my teeth. I crammed them into my eager mouth so quickly I nearly choked to death trying to swallow the sugary goodness.

Euphoria filled me to the point of ecstasy with each bite. It took less than three minutes to devour the entire cache of candy and lick the paper wrapping clean. I leaned back into the wall and took deep breaths, glassy eyed and spent. If you'd been there to see me, you'd have the hard time telling me from the drug addict that just had his fix.

This weird behavior would have continued unchanged for some time if it hadn't been for Claus yelling out, "Maxx. I know you finished the sweets by now. Get your pretty ass back in here like the good little boy you are. I want to finish the story I started. You can never say that I'm not a man of my word." I groaned with misery rising within as I realized I was already limping toward the sound of his voice incapable of halting my journey.

I took a seat on the mattress next to the Elder right where he pated and commanded me to. My skin felt hot and my eyes started to go blurry from the grief sweating behind them. I felt my lips begin to tremble. There was no doubt, I was about to break down into the crying jag over my sudden understanding I was nothing but Claus's puppet.

The Elder looked at me with pity in his expression as he said, "Ah, no tears my beauty. It breaks my heart to see you cry. This discussion was never supposed to happen, but you always were the precocious child. It was one of the things I loved about you the most. It reminded me so much of Keifer. Unfortunately, it's the very quality that's gotten you in a world of shit on more than one occasion. Tell me something I've always wondered. That incident you recall, the one that brought you here with questions, I didn't find any place where you spit out the chocolate, but clearly you didn't consume the entire dose. How did you manage that?" He reached out and caressed my cheek gently.

I blinked hard fighting to hold back the salty flood as I responded in the hollow tone, "I wanted to save a piece for later. I hid it in the straw. Like you did the ones you gave me to keep the secret of your molesting me."

Claus pursed his lips and nodded. "Ah, I should've guessed. I assumed you'd be incapable of denying your commands to eat all the candy. It was so early in the sessions. I suppose the prompts weren't solidly set within your subconscious just yet, ja?" He shot me a glance that seemed full of shame.

I took a deep breath to brace before I asked, "Claus, you and that woman did something to my memory didn't you? That's why I didn't recall your touching me. Did you do more than that touching I remember and why did you mess with my mind? To give me the schizophrenia? That's what you did isn't it? You induced madness." The first tear flowed down my cheek as I slowly began to come to grips with the horrific truth of my mental illness.

Claus lightly wiped the wet trail from my face as he said, "Please Maxx, don't stress yourself thinking I stole your dignity before that bastard Peter got the chance to. I know you may not believe it, but I swear on my beloved mother's grave I never did anything other than touch you a little, well and touch myself. I didn't even enforce oral or manual services. What you recalled that day, is as far as it ever went until you were ordered to seduce me."

I gasped when he said that. "You knew Peter sent me to seduce you? What about the schizophrenia? Did you and that woman put that disease into my head?"

Claus chuckled bitterly. "Ja, I was aware of Peter's designs. We will get to that situation and discuss it soon. As for your other question. Oh my beauty, you were already quite mad by the time me and Ingrid began our attempts to unlock your mind. We were trying to cure your mental illness, my, love not cause it."

That really sent me reeling. "What? Justus's mother was the woman with you? Why would she be there helping you to, wait, why did you two think my mind was locked? What information were you trying to get out of me? Claus, Gott dammit. You're not making any sense. Stop messing with my head and tell me the fucking truth. Don't you think you owe me that much for all the lies you've told, and raping you done to me all these years?" The water spilled down my face like a levee had broken as I yelled that out.

He grimaced and let out a frustrated sounding sigh. "If you'd be still boy like I told you, I was trying to explain everything. Now if you are ready to hear the truth or at least what part of it I can tell you, then I will get back to my story. After that, you'll have to figure out the rest of it on your own. There are many things that no one but you can know the answers to. Believe me, Ingrid and I did our damnest to discover them but no matter what we tried, you kept your secrets well, Christian Axel or Maximillian, or whoever the fuck you really are."

My eyes went vide as terror unlike anything I'd ever known before, that I could recall anyway, filled me, "I'm Maxximillian, Claus, don't you see that?"

He flashed me a smile that appeared full of fatigue as he replied, "Are you? Or are you Christian Axel? Maybe today we finally are going to find out which boy you are and which one is the illusion, ja?"

I nodded and sucked back my tears as I whispered, "I'm listening, Claus. I thank you for the mercy of it."

Claus shook his head and laid back on his pillow as he began his tale anew. "Mercy? Ah, that's not something you would know much about, my beauty. Now where were we? Oh, ja. My beloved Keifer had just put the move on this old fool, and I fell for him harder than the first freeze of the Russian winter.

Anyway, Keifer may've been sloppy in his delivery of kissing but with that riding crop the boy was a fucking pro. The idea of putting on that gown, even if he wished to see me in it, brought back too many painful memories. I balked at his demand and he tore into me with his thudder till I was begging for mercy.

Needless to say, he promised to relent his punishment if I'd hurry up and make myself beautiful for my man. I didn't feel humiliated over wearing the gown and shoes, but his referring to me as the woman, that's a different story.

I complained enough that Keifer decided I hadn't learned my lesson about denying him what he wanted. I was again assaulted by his well-honed skills with that blasted crop. By the time he finished, my ass cheeks likely glowed red through the backside of that white gown.

Well, that added to my appearance as the crossdresser drove Keifer near insane with lust. That very afternoon Keifer and I became more than best buddies. We became the honest lovers. Though the sexual encounter with him was overeager and clumsy, we managed to figure out what went where.

Hahaha. What I wouldn't give to be the innocent and inexperienced youngster basking in the delight of my beloved Keifer's eyes once again. Ah, but that's the trouble with anything. The first time you do something and find it amazing, you spend the rest of your life trying to recapture that feeling of excitement and thrill. Only to be left with the 'second best or third or so forth.' But never mind, that shit has little to do with what we are here to discuss. It is just this old man doing as you accuse me of, reliving the joys of my past life.

The truth is Keifer's affection allowed me to admit that I was schwuler, but I also needed his rough handling to accept my honest identity. Crossdressing in that white gown and being adored by my male lover was like releasing a genie from the bottle. My dark nights were over at last, because Keifer's light chased away the gloom within me.

The story should've been the gay boy's fairy tale that took on reality, and for a time it was. In those days public opinion was far harsher on the male that found attraction for the male then even it is today. Getting caught in the arms of a same gendered lover often resulted in far worse punishment than shunning. Many homosexuals were murdered by the people that grew up in the same damned villages and knew them all their lives.

Keifer and I weren't stupid. We knew it wasn't likely the people around us would understand our situation. His fetish for the crop and mine for the crossdressing only assured complete disaster if anyone found out about our secrets.

So, for the next few years, we played it close to the hip. Each day we went to our classes and jobs behaving as the normal rambunctious young men. He and I would pretend to chase the girls, but oddly never caught any, worked hard and drink harder.

Then, when no one was looking, he and I would sneak off together to the old barn. In those glorious moments, I was his beautiful girl and he was my handsome Dominant man. Getting away in the beginning was easy, but as time wore on, responsibilities of our outer appearances made it harder to escape unnoticed.

By the time I turned nineteen, it seemed we barely got to be with each other at all. Then one night as we laid in each other's arms lamenting that our dreams were being consumed by duty, Keifer told me something that would change our lives forever.

He said that he had a cousin that was a few years older than us. Keifer and him got along famously. In fact, this was the fellow that taught my lover how to wield a crop like he was born with it attached to his arm. My beloved went on to say this cousin wished to move into a special place where people like us were not only accepted, but even celebrated.

I, of course, laughed my ass off at such fantasy. I'd never in my life heard of any village, town, or city that would be thrilled to call the crossdressing schwuler boy a star. Keifer insisted such a place did exist and to prove it, he wanted me to come with him to speak with his cousin about applying to becoming a member.

Well, much as I loved Keifer, this idea of living in a fringe community was a real turn off. I politely declined his offer and to my surprise Keifer immediately broke up with me. Oh, my Gott was I ever devastated. I couldn't believe this man that I'd loved more than even my lost mother was able to toss me aside with such ease. I simply wouldn't believe it.

Well, Keifer wasn't kidding. He left the barn with haste and for the next several weeks refused to even walk by me on the streets. He returned all my letters and stubbornly refused all other attempts to communicate with him.

I suppose it goes without saying I was broken hearted and completely inconsolable. I'd not only lost my lover, but my best friend too. When the end of that horrible month came up and he still was refusing to see me, I decided I would rather be dead than go on without him in my life.

Since Keifer was blocking every attempt I was making to beg him to takin me back. I went around the man. Keifer had given me enough information about his cousin that I was able to locate his address without too much effort. I contacted him and asked if he would mind if I dropped by to speak with him about Keifer.

Well, I lied to the guy and told him something was wrong with his favorite cousin that I needed his advice about. Without hesitation he invited me to come to visit with him. He was happy to do whatever he could to aid his troubled cousin.

He had no idea when he agreed to meet with me that I was coming to kick his ass. I honestly believed it was his fault Keifer had left me. I thought if he'd kept his mouth shut about that community none of this would've happened. I wasn't a burly fellow nor even the experienced fighter, but with my blood boiling I made the long trip to Saxony to confront this man.

When I arrived at the address he'd given me, I was shocked to discover his haus was huge. The mansion and grounds, however, didn't belong to Keifer's cousin. Nein. The truth is, I'd just set my eyes for the first time on the place Keifer had been trying to coax me to join, but didn't know it.

So, in the Spring of 1909, with awe in my heart, I walked up and knocked on the door of Das Kaiser Haus. A brute of unusual size answered and bid me entry. I had no idea that the second I stepped over that threshold, nothing in my life would ever be the same.

Back then, the country's life blood hadn't been sapped by crushing wars yet. The wealth and opulence of the people was just beginning to reach an apex that to this day has never been achieved again. Despite this fact, I being the simple middle class man from a small village, was blown away by the amazing sights that greeted my provincial eyes. I confess this wasn't the scene I was expecting when Keifer's cousin said to come see him.

The brute lead me through the winding hallways which were quite the vision. He was dressed in a fancy black tuxedo, and around his neck he wore the oddest necklace I'd ever seen. It seemed to be made of metal but was black in color, reminiscent of a collar one put on the pet dogs. This fellow was polite, subdued and more strangely had told me he'd been informed to be expecting my arrival.

That completely caught me by surprise. I wasn't a man of importance or means by any stretch of the imagination. It seemed to me my appearance at the door of this lofty place shouldn't have even raised the most curious of eyebrows. Yet here I was being let up a set of fancy steps like I was the son of the fucking Kaiser himself. To say I was impressed is the gross understatement.

Our trip ended on the fourth level of the staircase. This black collared Haus man ushed me down the richly decorated halls crowded with heavy dark wooden doors.

There were many people of each gender and various ages dressed in fancy ball gowns, fine silks, and expensive suits crossing our path all along the journey.

That was striking enough to cause me to gawk in shocked silence. There, however, were other far more interesting folks rushing about among the obviously overly enriched. My stunned eyes come across numerous incredibly beautiful young boys and girls dressed slightly less ostentatiously. It was a curious thing to notice that like the fellow I was following, these youths also wore weird pet collar necklaces. Only instead of theirs being of the black metal, the color was shiny silver.

I noticed these 'silver collared' young people appeared to be of great interest to the men and woman of immense wealth. Of course, I need not tell the legendary ex-Priceless pleasure submissive of the functions of those teens that mingled, loitered and scurried in every direction.

We reached our destination before I could gain the bravery to ask the attendant any questions about the magnificent things I was seeing. I stood behind the brute while he rapped on one of the hall doors. I was frightened out of my mind by this point.

It goes without saying I had lost all interest in demanding this fellow duel with me. I assumed all the people in the place were his loyal employees. There was no way I could hope to win a war with such a prosperous man. I wanted to run away like the coward and find a quiet spot to lick my wounds and of course to shed many tears.

Keifer's cousin answered his door to find me resolved that I was never going to bask in the glory of my lost lover ever again. The weight of that understanding caused me to keep my eyes to my shabby boots as his relative invited me into his apartment.

I entered his home feeling damned low. I was doing all I could to come up with a reason to excuse myself, and run away, but before he even shut the door that plan changed. There sitting on the man's couch with a wicked grin on his face was, ja, you guessed it, my beloved Keifer.

There sharing the couch with him was the woman I recognized as his younger sister. At only sixteen Ingrid's physical beauty had already become the talk of our village. With long blond hair and eyes of blue that rivaled the clearest of skies, she was truly an angel fallen to Earth.

Even I, the very gay Claus, couldn't deny the Danish roots of the Reinhardt clan had blessed both Ingrid and her brother Keifer with coveted attributes most rare. You see, Ingrid was the spitting image of my boyfriend, only in the female form."

I gasped. "That's why she could speak my language. She was Dane by descent, and that's how you learned it, ja? Keifer taught you didn't he?"

Claus growled with an irritated tone. "Ja, I thought I told you to be still Maxx. You need to let me tell this story or are you planning to keep interrupting me? Not like we have a whole hell of a lot of time here, boy. Haven't you heard the

138

rumor? My system could fail at any moment, you know." He reached out and lightly swatted my leg.

I dropped my gaze to my lap and mumbled, "I beg your forgiveness, your Majesty."

He chuckled bitterly and nodded. "Ah, now there's my good boy. Let's see where the fuck were we? Oh, ja, so there was my lover Keifer and his pretty sister Ingrid sitting their grinning like the cat that ate the canary. I couldn't believe my fucking eyes. Before I could ask what the hell was going on. Keifer stood up and approached me. I was frozen to the spot both from shock and I suppose fear that he was going to order me to leave immediately.

Instead, he took me into his embrace and leaned into my ear and said, "Sure took you long enough you hardheaded fool. Welcome home, baby. I've missed you more than you can ever know." He kissed me on the neck with gentleness.

I was completely taken off guard by this unexpected behavior. Not only did Keifer not appear afraid to demonstrate his affection for me openly, with his family sitting right there watching, but his words confused the shit out of me.

I pushed him off me with reflexive vigor and yelled out, "What the fuck is going on, Keifer. First you tell me you never want to see me again. Now you greet me like a lover? Someone better start talking or so help me, I'm going to crack some heads."

My sudden rage outburst shocked the fuck out of me. I'd never been a violent man but this situation set off something deep and dark within me. I swear to Gott, I believed with all my heart, I could've murdered the lot of them that very second if none had worked quickly to quell that furious tempest of anger.

Keifer giggled like the silly schoolgirl as he said, "You sure are the sexy beast when you're pissed, sweetheart. Well, while I would love to explore this vicious side of your nature till we both collapse from fatigue. Business must come first. I'm not the only person that has been waiting with bells on to set eyes upon your beautiful face. Take a moment to freshen up in the washroom then I asking you nicely to follow cousin Bladrick. He's gonna take you to meet someone that can answer all your most burning questions far better than I ever could. I believe the current owner of this Haus has been patiently awaiting your arrival for far longer than this worthless man." I glared at my lover unsure what to make of his words since I could claim no association with this kind of wealth in their pocket.

The cousin – which you now understand was the late, great Bladrick himself – put his hand on my shoulder and said, "Claus, please do as Keifer suggests without offering further argument. I swear on my honor if you can control your temper a little longer, you'll be the blessed man for it."

I nodded slowly. "Alright, I suppose I've come this far already. However Keifer, if I discover this is one of your stupid practical jokes, I might do far worse than beat the shit out of you. Bladrick, lead the way. I'm right behind you. One question though. When I'm introduced should I bow? Surely the title holder of this Haus must be of royal blood or damn close to it, ja?"

Bladrick shot Keifer a humored glance as he replied, "Ja, the owner is indeed a Monarch of a type. Normally I would advise you to bow, or kneel but in this case, perhaps a curtsey is more appropriate." He chuckled lightly.

My rage nearly boiled over as I stared at Keifer. "You told your cousin about my secret didn't you? How could you do that to me? I thought I could trust you."

Keifer continued to smile appearing unruffled. "Claus baby, I tried to tell you but you wouldn't listen. Outside these walls you must hide your truths, but in this Haus, your fetish for the crossdressing is accepted and celebrated. Bladrick doesn't pass judgement on your preference in dressing any more than he is upset by my carnal interest in you."

I stole a glance at Bladrick that to my shock was smiling with a nod. "You really mean that?"

Keifer nodded hard. "Ja love. Bladrick and everyone that lives in Das Kaiser Haus wouldn't give a damn if we were to fuck right in the middle of the busy hallway. Here we are free to be ourselves. We can love who we want and do as we please without fear of reprisal or punishment."

I shook my head and said, "You misunderstand. I'm not questioning that these people living here are the horse of a different color, that's pretty obvious. I meant, do you honestly still wish to be with me as my lover?" I held my breath scared of what he might respond.

Keifer's beautiful eyes lit up with the fires of passion as he replied, "Claus my love, with you by my side, I can never be the unhappy man. I love you today more than I did yesterday and tomorrow I will love you even more still."

Ah, I could've died the most thrilled man on the planet when Keifer said that. Only the day he announced his affection for me was a sweeter one in my memory. He sealed his vow that he meant what he said with a deep kiss, and for the first time ever, I didn't care who saw us doing it.

Bladrick ended up having to break up this overzealous lover's reunion. If he hadn't it's probable Keifer and I would have tested his theory about fucking there in the hall for all to witness. Hahaha, okay that's not important to the story but it's the damned truth I tell you.

With some regret at leaving Keifer behind, I was fearful he wouldn't be dare when I returned, I begrudgingly followed Bladrick out of his apartment. He let me back to those fancy stairs. We went up them another two levels. I noticed immediately not only did the foot traffic thin out as we ascended but the decorations became even more stunning to behold.

Then we traveled down a hallway devoid of any living soul. There were doors lining the walls on that level like the one Baldrick's apartment was on but here I counted only five in total. It was pretty apparent that whoever lived up here were very important persons, with huge spaces to call all their own. Bladrick took me to the very end of this area of affluence and to my surprise we began to climb up another set of steps painted the color silver hidden behind a richly decorated pillar.

The staircase was so narrow we had to walk in single file, unlike the other one. If that wasn't odd enough, the next sight really set off my anxiety. At the end of our hike there was a huge dark oak door, edged with what appeared to be precious jewels. I swear that vision took my breath away.

Bladrick knocked on that entry, while I braced myself to be introduced to a King, sultan or some other powerful man. I assumed the fellow had to be royal in some way given the opulence on that door alone. Yikes.

That bejeweled gate opened and a beautiful girl wearing one of those weird silver collars stood there with her eyes caste to the floor. Bladrick calmly informed her that Claus Albrecht had arrived as requested by her Majesty. I nearly fainted when I heard him saying the Queen was seeking audience with me, the no account Claus.

The young girl nodded and stepped out of the way as she replied, "My Mistress has been eagerly awaiting Master Claus's arrival Master Bladrick. My Mistress respectfully requests that she be granted privacy for her meeting. I've been commanded to escort you and your honored kin to the Hall of Records for your swearing in ceremony Milord. Follow me please, and I thank you for the mercy of it." She kept her face bowed in a display of respect I'd rarely seen granted a man of little worth as Bladrick, and his entire clan, was.

Bladrick slapped me on the back and took on a serious expression as he said, "Good luck in there Claus. I wish to thank you for your part in the improvement of my family's poor lot in life. As far as I'm concerned you're welcome to visit my home anytime, and I'm proud to call you brother. See you later." With that he took off with the pretty girl leaving me their trembling in my boots at the mouth of that massive royal apartment.

I stood there unsure what the hell to do next when I heard a woman call out from within, "Why do you hesitate Claus? Come inside and give your beloved mother a hug. I've waited forever to hold you in my arms once more, my beautiful little girl." My heart stopped in my chest and blood froze in my veins as I recognized the voice of my long lost mother, Felicity Albrecht."

I sat there staring at him realizing that his use of that name wasn't related to my precious mother lamb but to his own mother. With a bit of relief filling my chest, over that explanation, I shifted my position.

I really wanted to leave because his reminiscing about the old days was getting on my nerves. I assumed he was intentionally irritating me by evading answering my questions, hoping I'd lose interest and give up. I decided to stick it out for no other reason than to prove to myself I wasn't Claus's puppet after all.

Claus shot me a look of caution and paused a moment as if gaging my reaction, then continued with his long winded story.

I was beyond overjoyed to rush into the awaiting embrace of my beloved mother. She plied me with her grateful kisses and washed away all the years of pain with her tears. We held each other in silence for many sweet moments, allowing our strong bond to re-strengthen in that palace at the top of this Haus of wonders.

When at last she'd calmed herself enough to speak, she told me of the forces that brought about our glorious reunion.

Felicity said that the day my father discovered our hiding spot, he'd told the authorities she was suffering from madness. He immediately filed papers to have her put away in the hospital for the mentally incompetent. Back in those days divorce was difficult to obtain, but sending an unwanted wife off to the loony bin was quite easy, and I dare say fashionable.

So, without any recourse to defend herself, she was promptly arrested and hauled off to Irsee Abby. By that time this old monastery is where many Germans claimed mentally ill were sent for treatment. There she languished for a year without access to communicate with anyone from the outside. She told me this was the hardest time of all her life. Her grieving over the loss of her freedom and the belief of never getting to hold her baby girl again nearly drove her to ending her life.

Before she gave up all rays of hope, she met and fell in love with an orderly called Friz Altergott. The two of them met in secret whenever possible, but the chances of their forbidden romance getting caught was high. Friz knew it was only a matter of time till the hospital administration would split them apart.

The thought of losing Felicity broke his heart. He decided the only way they could be assured to be together was to break her out of the hospital and find somewhere to hide where they wouldn't be found. Friz knew just the place they could go. His family clan had a long history with a Haus few in all the country, or world for that matter, were aware existed at all. All his youth he'd listened to stories of the Das Kaiser Haus, and her ability to make people disappear from the public eye.

The trouble was that neither he nor my mother had the cash to gain membership to this very selective club. Luckily, thanks to my father's name being among those believed to have ties to the founding fathers of Das Kaiser Haus and Friz's family's good standing within it, his request to the Fur King of that time was accepted with conditions. Without hesitation nor regret, Friz snuck Felicity from under the hospital guards noses. They ran as fast as possible to the Haus, and once they went through the front doors they called it home forever.

Because neither of them could pay even the lowest rental amounts, both were given the option to serve in the Dungeon. The idea of being forced to train orphaned children as servants to the wealthy of the Haus was a harsh fate for my kindhearted mother. She really had no other choice but to accept this condition set on her by the Fur King though. It was do the job or go back to the horrible Abby. She choose wisely to take up residence within the stony cells in the bowels of the mansion.

Well, back then the silvers were not treated nearly as poorly as they are today. It was still the fact that young children from hard luck backgrounds were exploited without earning a true wage, but they weren't thrown away once they weren't fresh anymore either. Silver collars could expect, like impoverished German, a life of hard toil doing shit they didn't enjoy. Yet they also were granted access to good food, a beautiful shelter over their heads, modern medical treatment (do remember this was before antibiotics) and most lived longer than the average life span of that era. Same thing was true for the people wearing the black metal.

Still, correction techniques employed to train the young men and women in their assigned services were often brutal, even downright medieval. Felicity entered her career as the Dungeon Mistress full of disgust at the deplorable conditions her wards suffered.

Like the angel she honestly was, Felicity decided if she was unhappy with this situation, it was up to her to change it. I can only imagine the joy on the faces of the many tormented little silvers and blacks when the mother first arrived in their lives. It took that amazing woman less than a month to clean up their hovels, lobby to have their rations increased, and end the worst of the torturing practices they endured on the daily basis.

Within the year nearly every submissive in Das Kaiser Haus had a picture of Felicity in their hovels to worship as their Goddess on Earth. She became known to all the residents, great and small, as Mother Felicity thanks to her legendary gentleness and tireless compassion for all souls, no matter what their rank.

The more celebrated she became, the more Friz and all the residents grew to love her. Over the next five years, her work with the submissives yielded the finest crops seen in anyone's memory. This skill at producing loving, happy, talented, and well-rounded servants assured Felicity wouldn't be kept down in the darkness for much longer. When the third Prince of the Fur took ill and passed away. Felicity was unanimously voted right up to the sixth floor by the Elders.

This wonderful windfall assured that my beloved mother was no longer in danger of exile from the Haus. Mother Felicity had managed to rise from the Dungeon hell right to nearly the top without skullduggery, manipulation nor aggression. Such a rise hadn't been recorded in many a generation. It goes without saying as the first and then the second Fur throne became vacant, Felicity climbed the seventh-floor steps. Amazingly, this woman without prestige, aggressive ambition nor wealth became the Queen of the Fur, the owner of Das Kaiser Haus.

Ta say a worthless son was proud of his mother's achievement would be redundant. I was far too stunned to even know where to begin with the questions. My mother, ever the wise soul, didn't leave me to struggle with words or query. She quickly informed me that the moment she'd arrived at the Haus, she'd began to devise a plan to bring me home to her.

I listened in pure awe as Felicity told me Friz knew of a family that could claim status as founders but like him couldn't afford the membership fees. He went on to inform her that these people would do anything to gain entry into the hallowed halls of Das Kaiser Haus for their young sons and daughter. With that knowledge in mind, Felicity went to great lengths to become familiar with the patriarch of this lost clan of Haus natives.

Over the next three years, she managed to save enough money from the Dungeon work to pay the rent on the haus next door to her husband's. She gave all of it to this family with the assurance that they would find a way to look after her youngest son for her. By this time, you realized of course, Keifer was the one selected to do the job.

While the love a mother demonstrated for her useless son was touching, hearing that Keifer was being paid to find me and become my friend hurt more than you can imagine. Mother Felicity, always the wise one, saw the pain in my expression upon hearing the truth of my lover.

I will never forget how she reached out and softly petted my tear strewn cheek as she said, "There, there, my little lamb. I merely sent the Reinhardts to seek you out. None of them were aware of our association and they never need be made privy to it unless you wish it. The relationship you developed with their youngest Keifer is not corrupted, I swear it. Whatever that boy's words to you are from his heart innocent of any conspiracy to obtain a position of power within this Haus."

I sniffed back my anguish and replied, "I wish to believe that mother, I really do, but why didn't Keifer simply tell me a woman called Felicity was behind his family moving next door?"

Mother Felicity chuckled as she responded, "Claudia, my beloved daughter, he was only eight years old when he met you. His father didn't tell him anything other than to make friends with the beautiful young girl next door silly. In the Haus, children of the Dominants and FemDoms in good standing must be absent from her halls by that tender age or they are put into the service cells of the Dungeon. They cannot apply for entry as the honored member until the age of consent at sixteen. Keifer became your friend, then your lover with honesty. Only within the last few hours have any of them been notified that the fourth-floor apartment is theirs the second they take the Das Kaiser Haus oath. I can assure you, I've watched you grow up through Keifer's eyes, but the boy never knew I was looking through them."

Well, that was all I needed to hear. I believed Mother Felicity because I wanted to with all my heart. Truth is, I needed to trust her. Without her and Keifer's help, I would see everything through rose colored glasses, I knew my life would return to the sawdust floors and choked existence of gloom of my father's world.

I embraced her explanations as factual and agreed without hesitation to join the family Reinhardt in the Hall of Records. That very afternoon, I stood before the leaders and swore my allegiance to defend Das Kaiser Haus's secrets to the grave.

Before the sunset, I'd become a full-fledged life member of the Haus. I'd reunited with my beloved mother and reclaimed the lover I'd thought I'd lost forever. The headiness of so many blessings at once was further improved that very night.

There, with my proud mother and the beautiful moon watching, Keifer got down on one knee and asked me to join him in the sacred blood bonding. Once that ritual marriage rite was explained to me, you can bet your gorgeous ass I gave him a resounding hell ja.

Like any good girl of that day and age, I told Keifer I needed to be courted properly first. He was happy to play the good fiancé, while Mother Felicity enjoyed the thrill of planning a huge wedding party for us. Bladrick agreed to being my husband's best man, and Ingrid graciously accepted my offer to make her my bride of honor. Our date of union by blood was set for the next Spring, twelve months exactly from that day as was acceptable protocol back then.

For the next twelve months, life was a whirlwind of pleasure so magnificent it still takes my breath away to think of them to this very day. Keifer and I spent the days enjoying all the wonders the Haus could offer, and each night we partied in the Great Hall with Bladrick, Ingrid and all the other young Dominants and FemDoms our age.

When we tired of our decadent attendance to all our baser urges, we'd crash in the Fur Queen's ostentatious apartment. Ingrid and Bladrick were rarely out of our company. Mother Felicity always welcomed me, Keifer and all our best friends.

Ah, if there is a heaven Maxx, then I would believe it looks a lot like the Haus did in 1909. Mother Felicity's generous nature trickled from the top down. Everyone loved her, no matter what their status. Thanks to our close proximity to the beloved Fur Queen, Keifer, Ingrid, Bladrick and I were automatically the most popular people in the Haus, next to the Mother of course.

Because Friz had saved Felicity, she had repaid him and all his eligible kinsmen to the Elder level. The Voters were controlled by the Wagner faction. The Altergotts were known for their severe nature, and the Wagner's for their lack of interest in any kind of morality as a general rule. None of that mattered to me, or my buddies. We'd barely reached our minorities. We viewed politics, even with the Haus, as best left to the stodgy old folks. That was perhaps our first mistake but it certainly wasn't our worst.

The four of us partied the year away, never once considering for a second our futures other than over the next few days. Mother Felicity had granted Bladrick and his family the most coveted apartment, aside from those of the leaders, in all the Haus. It was the fourth-floor corner apartment. When we weren't getting drunk in the Great Hall, swimming in the pool, raising hell in the gardens or hanging out on the seventh floor, you could find us their plotting some juvenile deviltry together."

I blew out my breath loudly and exclaimed, "Holy hell, that apartment your mother gave to Bladrick is the one Rolf gave to me, isn't it? Oh Christ, I am never going to be able to sleep in there again. How the fuck will I get the image of your nasty bastards' doing Gott know what out of my head. Yuck!"

Claus glared at me appearing ready to burst from fury as he snarled out, "Ja, that apartment that idiot Lucus took from you is the very same one Mother Felicity gave to the Reinhardt's for their aid in bringing me home to her. Now, do you really think it wise to hurt my feelings with cruel statements, Maxx? I think boys that behave badly don't get treated well. I was about to call the black collar attendant to bring you more candy before you leave, but keep acting the little brat, and you will talk me out of it."

I sucked in my breath with sudden apprehension filling me. "Nein, I'll shut up and be good for you, Claus. I swear it. I want the sweets. I thank you for the mercy of it."

He nodded and chuckled low as he said, "That's better. You be still and listen. I will call the attendant when I'm nearly finished with the story. Now where were we?

Oh ja, so that fourth floor apartment of the Baldrick's became yours, and was taken over by that fool Lucus is where we often plotted silly pranks or spent quiet moments reading each other poetry or stories. I tell you, if my life had gone on in the repeat of 1909 without a single change to it, I'd be far more regretful about saying goodbye to life than I honestly am.

However, things didn't continue to remain beautiful nor peaceful. That next year, 1910, began the same as the year before it. Things were wonderful, and no one in the Haus had any serious complaints, not even the submissives. Under Mother Felicity's rule, all residing within the walls received their fair share and benevolent treatment. The dungeon was not filled with the sounds of children screaming or flooded with their tears. Even the torture chambers grew a layer of dust thanks to lack of use while the loving Fur Queen reigned.

The day of my blood bonding to Keifer was approaching faster than I believed possible. Everyone in the Haus was invited to attend the wedding party, regardless of their level or status. Ja, even the submissives. I need not tell you this was an event the great and small were looking forward to with great anticipation, but no one more than Keifer and me.

I'd just celebrated my twentieth birthday. My mother presented me with a beautiful white bridal gown she'd handmade for me, intending that I honor her by wearing it to the wedding. Of course, I was delighted by this unexpected luxury and quickly agreed to do as she asked. She then informed me that there was another item that she desired I wear when I became Mrs. Reinhardt but that this gift she had for me was to be given before the ceremony itself.

I had no idea what this item was but knowing Mother Felicity it was sure to be something very special. I confess, I was nearly as excited to see what she'd gotten for me as I was to finally become the legal life partner, at least by Haus law, of my lover Keifer.

That night of my union with Kiefer was a flurry of anxious activity. It seemed no matter how long we'd had to prepare for that wonderful evening nothing was going right. That would've been a clue to a more superstitious lot. But to the headstrong, self-important four of us, no one considered it a sign that the winds of our good fortune were going stale.

Keifer and I were granted permission by Bladrick to use his apartment for the enacting of the sacred blood coupling. He was chosen to act as the witness, and Ingrid granted permission to watch over his examination of the newlyweds.

That sexually explicit part of the story I'm more than a little aware you not interested in hearing about. So I will keep that beautiful memory all for myself. I will only say it was second to no other intercourse experience I've ever had save one, the one I shared with you. I glared at Claus stifling the urge to puke as he stared at me dreamy eyed for a moment.

Once Bladrick formally announced Keifer and I were the honest couple, the Haus shook with hundreds of cheers, whistles and clapping of all the residents. It was the wedding of the century of two of Das Kaiser Hauss most beloved sons coming to completion at last. Everyone was beside themselves with excitement. Especially since now that the formality was out of the way, the party could commence.

I should've been as full of celebration as everyone else, but something was wrong. I'd not expected Mother Felicity to make an appearance at our bloody bedside, but when we emerged from our ritual I still didn't see her among the many happy faces.

Despite his protests, I was hell bent to hang around to receive both her blessings and that rare gift she'd promised. When she still didn't appear after half an hour, Keifer practically had to pick me up and drag me down to the Great Hall. I finally gave up arguing with him, thinking that maybe Felicity got caught up making sure everything was perfect in the Hall for her daughter's big night.

We arrived to find almost every soul there ready to gorge and drink themselves senseless. Keifer gave the go ahead to begin the festivities, while I fretted over still not finding my mother's face among the many in the crowd. I spent the next hour watching the Hall doors like the nervous animal, feeling my heart fall further to the floor with each person that came through it that wasn't Felicity.

I finally could take the anxiety no longer. I politely excused myself from Keifer's side and tore out of there heading to the top of the Haus. I think deep inside, I already knew something bad had happened, but I wasn't able to deal with the nightmarish idea of it.

Sadly, the son's gut instinct was soon proven correct. I found Felicity collapsed on the floor. She'd been in the process of donning her best gown for her daughter's wedding when tragedy struck her. I let out a wail of terror and fell upon her prone flesh checking for signs of life. I found them, but barely.

The Haus doctor was called to attend the ailing Fur Queen. He arrived and upon careful examination it was determined she'd suffered a catastrophic stroke. It wasn't expected that she'd survive, but he told me that anything was possible.

For the next two days, the Haus was assaulted by the whispered prayers of a people begging Gott to spare the beloved mother of each of them. Above them all, was the sobbing voice of a devastated son.

I never left Felicity's side during her last forty-eight hours on Earth. By the second day, I realized Felicity wasn't going to recover, but I was hoping against all hope she would regain consciousness for even a few moments before she shed her skin to become what she'd honestly been to so many, an angel.

Keifer was as always my rock in the storm of misery that engulfed me. He sat there helping me watch over my dying mother, holding me when the grief was too much to bear. I don't think I could've handled that horrible situation had he not been there. It's no small thing to understand even the mercy of have someone to share my heavy burden was thanks to that glorious woman that bore me.

Sadly, Das Kaiser Haus's Fur Queen Felicity the Benevolent passed away without ever opening her eyes even for a second. I was inconsolable over my not getting the chance to tell her how much she'd meant to me, nor how grateful I was that she'd been my mother. I tell you Maxx, not saying those things to her every single precious day I had with her was one of the biggest mistakes I've ever made. Believe me I've no small number of things on my list of regrets.

Perhaps the only person who was more broken hearted than this idiot son of Felicity's was her lover Friz. That cold rainy afternoon they buried Mother Felicity, the man promptly went to his Elder's apartment and slit his wrists. The residents were so deep in mourning over the loss of their beloved Queen no one found the poor man's corpse for a couple days.

And so, it was that in the Spring of 1910, Das Kaiser Haus said goodbye to it's beautiful moment of peace and tranquility. A new era of darkness was rushing in with speed to erase all evidence that at one time, this place was Heaven with a real life angel running the show.

Unfortunately, and I say this with great shame, I was part of the faction that rote the next segment of Das Kaiser Haus's history in blood.

A week passed before the Elders were able to come to an agreement on the naming of a new Fur Monarch. I was contacted by one of the sitting Fur Princes and asked to see to the packing up of Felicity's effects. With a heavy heart, I hurried to do as they asked. I told Keifer to stay with Bladrick and Ingrid. It was my belief, this final kindness I could offer the woman that had done so much for me, was something I needed to do privately.

In the rush to save her life, and the terrible grief in the days to follow, no one had noticed what had been in Felicity's hand the moment she faltered. That day I come to pack her away into anonymous boxes, I discovered this overlooked item.

There on the floor where her near lifeless hand come to rest was a blue velvet box. I reached down and picked it up with wonder. I'd never seen it before that moment but clearly this was of great importance to her. She'd appeared to have been trying to regain a grip on it when she collapsed instead of trying to pull herself back to her feet.

I took a seat on her bed and with a deep breath I opened the box. Inside I found an expensive, custom made cameo set. To my astonishment there was a note contained within the silken inner folds. My hands trembled as I fought back that sudden surge of grief as I realized the handwriting was Felicity's and that letter was addressed to me.

Carefully I opened it and could hear her voice as I read her final words to me:

Ta my Beloved Lamb, Claudia.

I wish for you to know that you've made me very proud. Keifer is a fine man to call your Husband. It's always a mother's worse nightmare and sincerest dream to watch her little girl grow up into a woman. This is the day I've both feared and prayed for all your life. That said, I'm eager for the two of you to start making me many grandchildren. I hope it's not too much to ask but I would like to request you remember to produce at least a single daughter. I know that sons are important but it will be your little girl that will bring you the most joy in this life. I say this from experience, my lamb. The girl child will always be there to love her mother when the boy has already forgotten her sacrifices for them. I want you to know I love you more than I ever could any son. Bring me a granddaughter Claudia soon as you can. Then I can rest knowing that you'll never know what it feels like to be alone. I've had this cameo set made as the family heirloom to be passed from daughter to daughter in honor of this auspicious occasion. It is my sincerest wish that it never rests for long in any mother's hands for as long as the Earth continues to turn.

With love and respect, Mother Felicity.

I closed the note careful to keep it from being soiled by the flood of tears that erupted upon my finishing it. My poor deluded mother went to the grave still denying that I was her son but her daughter. I suddenly realized Felicity never stopped suffering from that deep loneliness that seemed to hold her hostage all her life.

That cameo set is in the top drawer of my dresser Maxx. I know you'll recognize it the minute you see it. It is the one you insisted I wear with the gown you selected as your favorite the night you ended Drexel's life. You know. I've always found it curious that you chose the wedding gown mother Felicity made for me out of all the beautiful dresses you demanded I try on for you that night Peter leashed your collar to me. It was as if, well never mind, that's not important. There is a good reason I tell you where it's located.

I wish for you to take it with you when you leave this apartment today. I know you have some place safe to hide it a way. It's worth quite a bid of money, not just because of its age but it's metal is precious. I don't give this one of the most valuable things I own for you for sell though.

I want you to keep it with you until the day you select a bride for your own. When the girl becomes the mother to your daughter give your Frau mother Felicity's cameo set. Tell her when her daughter becomes the mother of a baby girl to relinquish her gift to your daughter. The same instructions hold for your granddaughter and all females of your line till time ends.

Promise me you will do this task for me Maxx. I know I've no right to ask you for favors, but this one I don't request for myself. I never was able to be what my mother needed me to be for her. She intended for me to give that to my daughter, and for my daughter to her own daughter. I've waited a lifetime to have the chance to pay Mother Felicity back for all the love she gave to me, and to the others of the Haus in her time.

Hurry up and swear it to me, and I will give you anything you ask for doing this task for me, boy. With your vow, I can face her and tell her that her worthless son did do at least one fucking thing correctly.

I nodded trying hard to knock the expression of shock off my face as I said, "I'd give you my word to do as you ask Claus, but I'm not, I mean, Nestor neutered me. I cannot do what your mother wanted any more than you were able to."

The Fur King scoffed loudly then responded, "Look Maxx, I've no time to try to argue with the delusional. I will only tell you I happen to know you will become the married man to a lovely girl one day soon. Take the cameo set and give it to her anyway, even if she never delivers a single girl or kid of either gender. I suspect that any female that selects you will be of rare intelligence. I know deep within my heart she'll find a way to make Mother Felicity's dreams come to truth. Now what do you request in exchange for this service?"

I shrugged still thinking he'd gone insane like some do before the Reaper takes them home. "Uhm, I'd like some more candy. Oh, and forgiveness for not destroying the Silk Queen like you wanted."

Claus rolled his eyes and let out his breath as he replied, "The sweets are a done deal. If only all the agreements I've had to make in my life were so damned cheaply obtained I'd be dying with a far cleaner soul. As for that other thing you ask, I was informed by a little birdy that Gretta managed to save her worthless hide by getting pregnant. You did the right thing allowing her furlough on the death sentence. It's enough that you set it down in the record. She cannot remain with child forever. When she is not hindered by an innocent, finish the job. If you promise me that you will, then I know I can trust it'll get done. You're a man of your word, ja?"

I nodded vigorously. "Ja, I am a man of my word. But what about that chocolate? Can I have that now?"

Claus laughed hard as he yelled out, "Damn, you are still as greedy as you have ever been. I swear to Gott that every time I would visit you and your brother at Ingrid's haus, I'd have to bring four times the treats to keep up with her ever hungry grandsons."

My heart skipped several beats and my breath felt like it was barely entering my lungs. "What did you just say? What the fuck are you talking about Claus? Me and my brother at my grandmother Ingrid's apartment, are you demented? I don't have a brother and Agnette's father was married to a woman named Annika. Gerard told me and I saw it on my fucking birth certificate enough times to know that much of what you are saying is a bold attempt to screw with my head."

The Elder sat up with unexpected speed and stared right into my stunned eyes. "Are you sure about all those details you claim to be truth? Ah, part of your memory is accurate. Agnette is indeed your mother, and you did live with my older brother Gerard for a time, but there is something missing in your story. Well, someone to be exact. Tell me something boy. Which one are you? My beloved Golden Hund Maximillian or my precious little lamb Christian Axel? Think hard. There was two beautiful boys that were the spitting image of their great Uncle Keifer. Which one of them are you?"

I stammered and saw a sudden flash of red before my eyes as I whispered, "I had a twin is what you're saying? Nein, that's a fucking lie. If it were true then where the fuck is that guy, and for that matter why the hell have I never met him? That's what you and Ingrid were doing down there in the Dungeon wasn't it? Trying to get me to believe Ingrid is related to me, and Gerard is related to you. Why the fuck were the two of you trying to give me an imaginary twin brother? Gott damned that's insane. What's the point in all this bullshit? You better stop lying and tell me what I want to know," I yelled out suddenly feeling that the walls were closing in on me.

Claus didn't takin his ailing eyes off me while I sat there nearly ready to flip out on his ass as he said, "You know where your brother is boy. In the green fields, remember? Follow the lamb, he knows the way."

My throat seemed to close so tight I couldn't catch my breath. I stared in horror at the scene of Gerard coming through the barn door. He was carrying a knife on him. I couldn't stop him as he grabbed up the little golden hund that nice lady give to me. I forgot to hide the toy. With an evil grin he picked up the tiny stuffed animal.

His voice shock my brains as he said, "Which of you figured out how to pic the locks? Neither of you willing to fess up? Oh my, that's not good news for you fellows. You know what? It makes no sense to feed an extra mouth. One is all that's desired, so one is all that is required. Say goodbye to each other boys. This brat is going to make for fine fertilizer. Come the Spring the fields will sprout green and be the finest of feed for the baby lambs."

I wailed out helpless to stop Gerard, "No, please don't kill him. Don't put him in the green fields for the lambs." I continued to scream at the top of my lungs while he plunged that knife into the toy, then tore Der Hund's stuffing out onto the straw.

A stinging pop awoke me from this horrific memory of seeing my stepfather destroy my only company in that isolated barn. I blinked rapidly trying hard to re-gain my location. The image of a stern appearing Claus came into focus, just as I realized I was on the floor next to his bed.

The Elder shook his head with an expression of deep pity on his wizened face as he said, "Are you the brother Christian Axel or are you the brother Maximillian? Think hard boy. There were two of you at one time but my brother Gerard kidnapped the both of you. Only one of you survived the years of savagery while held as his hostage. Which of the Agnette's twin boys are you? Do you even know?"

I whimpered at his feet and responded, "Why are you doing this to me Claus? Haven't I served you well all these years? I swear I never tell anyone about your molesting me in the Dungeon. I will take that cameo of your mother's and give it to my imaginary wife to pass on to my mythical daughter as I promised. In fact, I will do whatever the hell you want until they bury you without quarrel, but please, I'm begging you, mercy. Stop messing with my mind. I don't think I can take anymore. You already gave me the schizophrenia. What more could you possibly want from me?"

Claus sighed and gently petted my anguished face as he replied, "Ah you poor baby. You honestly think I'm making all this up or maybe that's the only way you can avoid the horrific truths that blew your mind to kingdom come in the first place? Well, that's fine with me if you never want to recall that unbelievable trauma that you've endured. However, I will have to end my story if you insist on accusing me of attempting to tamper with your understanding of reality."

I sniffed back my tears, appearing to regain that feeling of numbness as I responded, "I only wanted to know why you and Ingrid were drugging the candy and what you were doing to me when I was little. I still want to know that answer Claus. I need to know it."

The Elder shrugged his shoulders and very slowly climbed back into his bed. "Alright Maxx. I think we are playing with fire here, but I won't go to my grave with you believing that I denied you an explanation that you're correct, you've certainly earned many times over. Get off the floor and return to your spot next to me, my beauty. We will get back to the story where I left off and perhaps when you obtain the answers you're seeking, then you will return the favor by giving me the one I've asked you."

I closed my eyes and took a deep breath before attempting to rise. I snuck a quick glance at Die Brutale holding up the back of the wheelroom wall. The boys saw me looking at them.

Christian and Mad Max shrugged their shoulders and said in unison, "Go ahead and listen to what the old goat has to say, Maxximillian. Just make sure you remind him he promised to give us candy before we are released."

I nodded at the triple shard with a chuckle. "Will do brothers. Guess one thing he says is the truth of it. We are some greedy sonofabitches. Hahaha."

Without another word I sat back down next to the Elder. After he took a deep breath he began his story anew…

As I said, it was a real mistake to ignore the men and women holding positions on the thrones of leadership while Mother Felicity lived. Not even two weeks after she'd left the four of us to fend for ourselves things quickly went from horrible tragedy to utter catastrophe.

Chapter 5: An Intimate Betrayal
Master Mad Max and submissive Meine Liebe

We still have several decades to cover in Claus's story of Das Kaiser Haus and ultimately the story of Christian Axel/Maximillian.

The Elder Altergott relatives of the late Friz come together only a few weeks after they buried Mother Felicity. A kinsman among them by the name Amos was the lucky one to be granted the vacant throne of the Fur. The Haus people celebrated, while still mourning their mother, the rise of a new King.

I was grieving too deeply to care when Keifer and Bladrick told me of the Elder's election. In fact, I'd fallen into what today would be called a clinical depression. No matter that I'd just married the man of my dreams and enjoyed the finest lodgings besides the leaders' apartments. All I could do is cry and lay in my Mann's bed with the curtains drawn. Life, for me, seemed without luster. I didn't comprehend how I was to go on without the only woman I'd ever loved.

Well, perhaps had things continued unabated like this I'd have done something stupid. Like the fool I've always been, I'd been seriously considering committing suicide. Ja, can you believe that? I still had an adoring husband and two of the best friends a fellow could ever ask for in Ingrid and Bladrick.

Yet there I was feeling as lonely as I did back when my mother first disappeared from my world. But father time kept marching despite my heart feeling that he'd been paralyzed to the standstill.

About a week after Amos Altergott was crowned King, a large crashing noise stirred me from my darkened room. I come running into the living area of the apartment to find Bladrick throwing the fancy furnishings into the wall while hurling curses nearly unintelligibly. Ingrid was hiding behind the couch in an obvious panic and my Mann Keifer was doing all he could to calm his furious cousin.

I had no idea what the fuck was going on, but it didn't take long for the reasons for Baldrick's fit of rage to be determined. A black collar messenger had approached him and demanded that month's rent payment for the apartment granted him by Mother Felicity.

Of course, not a one of us had a damned penny between us to pay the preposterous fee demanded by the sitting Fur King. Keifer finally got Bladrick to cool off by assuring him this request for the rent must have been sent by mistake. All the boys needed to do is gain audience with Amos and this misunderstanding surely would be cleared up in no time.

Ah, that is what we all thought was the problem. Amos was the first cousin to my mother's late lover Friz. None of us met the man before, but like the dumbasses we honestly were, we assumed the fellow would honor the arrangement Bladrick made with Felicity. After all, it was the Fur Queen he owed his rise as Elder and ultimately to King.

169

So, me, Keifer, and Bladrick asked politely to speak with Amos. The King was most happy to receive his elite guests and at first, it did appear this man seem willing to listen to our argument. The idea that Amos was as benevolent as Felicity was quickly dashed the second Bladrick finished giving the fellow his pitch. I cannot forget the horror that filled my heart when at last the realities of Das Kaiser Haus came to slap all three of us right in the face.

Old Amos leaned forward on the golden throne and with a wicked grin said, "Well boys, seems you have one hell of a problem. You've got no proof the late great Felicity made any arrangements with you, do you? I've seen no contract in the Hall of Records with her seal upon it stating that apartment was to be yours for life. As it is that near palace your worthless asses are sitting in is of great value to a man in my position of power. Becoming the King is almost impossible but holding on to the throne is exactly that. The man or woman that holds the Fur Throne must have ways to pay for protection against those looking to take his seat. You will either pay me the monthly fee that fine apartment historically reaps or you will vacate it immediately. You can go willingly or I will have you removed right over the banister. It's up to you. Not a bother to me whichever way you choose."

Me and Keifer stood there shocked into silence while the headstrong Bladrick replied, "You know we cannot pay you that money, honorable Amos. If we are to leave the apartment where the fuck can we go? You should at least show a little mercy and grant us another place in the Haus? We aren't picky. Surely there is something on the third, second or even first floor you can spare to four paupers that are loyal to your family and throne."

Amos chuckled bitterly as he responded, "Loyal to me and mine you say? Ah, now how do I know that Bladrick, my boy? You are the head of the family Reinhardt, who are the long term enemies of the clan Altergott. The way I see it, sending you, your cousins and that fucking Albrecht back to the streets is one bid of protection I can get for free. Felicity was a Gott damned idiot. She wasn't satisfied that the Wagners were a big enough threat to our family's continued good health. Nein, it was in the time of my grandfather that your debouched kin were ejected from the hallowed walls. Das Kaiser Haus has never been more at peace with your people drowning in the mire where you belong. The insane woman tempted fate by dragging through the dregs till she mined out what remains of your monstrous families." He angrily slammed down his wrinkled fist on the throne's arm.

I thought for sure Bladrick, he was very hot headed in his youth, was going to blow as he said through clenched teeth, "The way I've heard it told, the Altergotts aren't exactly without a few stains on their souls, your Majesty. Be that as it may, I'm not here to defend my relatives actions or misdeeds. Me, Keifer, Ingrid and Claus here aren't cut from the same cloth as the ones that come before us. I'm not a man that will lower myself to begging. If you cannot see it in your heart to allow us to haunt even the shoddiest of apartments in the Haus for free, then that's your right as the owner of all within the walls. Perhaps, you will instead consider that our back are strong and none among us afraid of hard work. I'm asking you politely to grant us a job that pays enough to cover at least the lowest of rents."

That old buzzard smiled with suddenness and blew out his breath as he replied, "You don't listen very well, Bladrick. I said kicking you and yours to the streets is smarter than allowing your clan to retaken root like the life strangling weeds you honestly are. However, I'm not a man that is completely unreasonable. Tell you boys what. If you can prove your words of loyalty to the Altergotts and at the same time demonstrate your honesty when you claim no allegiance to you own family's brutal reputation. Then, I will consider allowing you to stay and even offer you legitimate work that pays enough to afford to remain within Das Kaiser Haus."

Keifer nearly tripped over his words as he eagerly responded, "Name the way this can be completed to your satisfaction and consider it already done." Bladrick shot my Mann a glance of caution, but he nodded in agreement with his statement.

Amos nearly split that mummified head of his in two with the nasty grin on his face as he said, "The most dangerous man in this Haus to my continued reign is the Silk King, Samuel Wagner. You find a way to eliminate that motherfucker and I swear you boys shall find your place here in the Haus assured."

I couldn't believe my fucking ears. Amos was essentially telling us that if we killed Samuel then he'd allow us to gain employment. Then we could pay rent in some hovel on the first floor. I shook my head when Keifer raised an eyebrow and looked to me for my vote on this horrific request.

My Mann shrugged at me and Bladrick cleared his throat as he responded, "Just so we are clear on this, your Majesty. You want us to murder the Silk King? I don't mean to sound ungrateful but that's a pretty hefty price for the deal you offering in return. I mean we are speaking about ending a man's life that's never done a thing to us to deserve it. You're the Fur King. Why not simply find a reason to exile the honorable Voter?"

Amos chuckled with a diabolical sound. "Bladrick my boy, I'm a bit more inclined to believe your saying that you are nothing like your kinsmen. There's never been a single Reinhardt I've met that wouldn't jump at any chance to color his hands red with blood. That said, you best be careful what next you say to me about how I rule from my throne, little man. You either take the offer I give you or you pack your shit and get the fuck out. No other options, for any of you."

Bladrick shook his head with a sigh. "We must accept your offer when you put it like that, your Majesty. We thank you for the mercy of it." He motioned me and Keifer to follow him as he tore from the room.

The second the three of us were far from the King's chambers, Keifer rushed up to Bladrick. "Forgive me for asking this cousin, but why did you agree to kill this man? I have no intention of becoming the murderer to obtain a job in this Haus or anywhere else for that matter. I know Claus

173

won't do this horror either. You didn't even find out what work Amos give to us if we did do this terrible thing he asks for us to do. What if this is a trap. Did you consider that? We do what he wants, and then he points his boney finger at us. That crime will earn us a place on the stake. Or perhaps Amos lets us do his dirty work and he keeps us drowning in the blood of men that get in his way."

Bladrick halted his fury filled marching and glared at Keifer angerly as he responded, "I'm fucking aware that Amos could be setting us up cousin. That's a distinct possibility. Unless you or Claus got a better idea I don't see that we have any choice but to do as he says. There is nothing left for us outside of the Haus but a life of near starvation and degradation. You and Ingrid were assisted by Felicity. You never suffered the realities of the poor man on the streets. I for one refuse to return to that nightmare. If Samuel is the man standing between me and a chance to become the men of untold wealth, you can bet he's dead already."

I gasped full of fear over his cryptic words. "Bladrick, please listen to Keifer. You aren't a killer. Let's just leave this place. There is plenty of work out there that don't expecting a fellow to go murdering people."

Bladrick shot me a glance full of disgust as he replied, "Sure is Claus. Nothing stopping you and your husband from applying for the plentiful jobs you speak of either. God luck being together as the couple. But you can bet outside Das Kaiser Haus's walls, the outsiders sure won't have the same moral conflict as you boys seem to about ending a man's life the second they discover the schwulers among them."

Keifer dropped his face to stare at his boots as he said, "Like it or not Claus, Bladrick speaks the truth of it. I cannot stomach the idea of returning to that life of sneaking around and constant fear that we endured before coming here. Okay cousin, no matter what happens you can count me in. I don't dare to put words into my Husband's mouth, but I pray he wishes to come with us."

I stood there feeling a sense of unreality as Bladrick and Keifer looked at me for my answer. I wanted to argue further that this request from Amos was insane, but my throat seemed to choke off all my attempts at sounds. I felt my head nodding that they could count me among their numbers in this conspiracy to put the Silk King to the yard.

I won't get into a lot of details regarding this first of many assassinations of a powerful person in the Haus. I think it's enough to say that the second Bladrick managed to talk me and Keifer into plotting with him, Samuel's days were short.

It's enough to say old Samuel was an easy mark. though the fellow prided himself on being the clever man regarding guarding against attempts on his life. He wasn't expecting a bunch of kids to be seeking his demise. It only took two days of quietly observing his every move for the four of us to contrive a brilliant plan. We told Ingrid of the deal and she was in without near the arguing me and Kiefer gave to Bladrick.

You see, we discovered every morning at the crack of dawn Samuel and his huge trusty silver went to swim in the pool room. The night before the deed was to be done, Bladrick hid out in the locker area. No one spotted him as the black collars locked up the place for the night. At six the next day, as always, Samuel and his submissive headed down to do their work out. Me, Keifer and Ingrid followed the two of them at a safe distance.

Once the black collar servant unlocked the door, Samuel hurried into the room, but his silver was held up. Ja, you guessed it, the three of us tried to enter behind the pair. As was his job, the pleasure submissive attempted to block our path to takin a dip of our own. We stood there arguing that silver, loudly demanding to know why the pool was off limits to us. The fellow was near red faced trying to explain that for security reasons no one was permitted to use the water at the same time as the Silk King.

Well while this staged bit of distraction was going on, Samuel may or may not have decided to carry on with his daily ritual. Whatever the man was up to as his silver did his duty to block out interlopers, only Bladrick ever knew. He never said a word of the happenings that led to the Silk King's corpse being discovered by his loyal servant only fifteen minutes later floating, lifeless on the surface of the water.

Because we had witness of our whereabouts when the King found his grave, and Bladrick wasn't viewed leaving the scene of the crime, no one suspected any of us. Well, none of the Haus residents, that is. Amos was quite aware when the four of us showed up at his apartment the very afternoon Samuel 'drowned' that we'd successfully held up our end of his bargain.

He didn't attempt to weasel out of our arrangement by claiming there was no proof we did as he commanded. Samuel was an expert swimmer in excellent health. The Haus doctor's claims that he'd tired and sunk to the bottom was more than a little unbelievable. To our relief Amos didn't even ask us for details about how we'd managed what seemed to be impossible. I told you Samuel was paranoid and extremely careful, but not enough. Hahaha. That anxiety calming was doubly amplified when the Fur King didn't immediately order our arrest for doing the job he'd insisted we do.

But that initial feeling of respite was quickly dashed when the old bastard said, "I knew that brutality still resided within your veins, boys. You're honest Reinhardts and Albrecht right to your oily heart. While I may one day regret ever making deals with the likes of your kind, I do believe the skills each of you possess by heritage could be useful to me. The Dungeons have been misused for far too many years. My predecessor, may Gott rest her soul, was far too reserved in her training techniques. I need strong men and woman that have the lust for conquest down dare breaking the wills of the fresh crops. You boys, and my Lady are granted permission to remain in Das Kaiser Haus. I even give you the good paying jobs and apartments free of fees. That is IF you prepared to remove yourselves with speed from the honorable resident and head below to the bowels of the Haus where I dare say you fucking belong."

Bladrick's face turned seven shades of red he was so full of fury as he yelled in response, "You want us to live like paupers in the Dungeons? Are you fucking joking? This is your idea of reward after honest service we have done for you? Well, you can go to hell, Amos. I didn't commit the most horrible of crimes only to end up in a worse position than if I'd left and sought my fortune elsewhere."

The Fur King narrowed his eyes and leaned forward as he growled, "You will mind your tone and keep that temper of yours in check when in my royal presence, boy. If you dare to speak to me insolently again, I can make better use of your skills by seeing your flesh feeds the gardens. If you don't find my offer to your liking, fine by me. Pack up and leave while I still feel some affinity to allow it. Now what about the rest of you? I offer you the chance to prove your worth to the Haus as the Dungeon Masters and Mistress. Report to the Headmaster before the sunrises or join Bladrick because if I see any of the four of your faces again in this lifetime, I promise you, Samuel will get his chance to have revenge on his killers."

That was all Amos needed to say. The four of us hightailed it out of his presence, three full of fear and one full of fury. We went back to the apartment on the fourth floor for the last time. Bladrick railed and threw things, while Ingrid sat on the couch sobbing uncontrollably over our terrible situation.

Me and Keifer stood there in the corner of the living area holding each other in silence. He didn't have to say a word for me to know he wanted to accept the deplorable conditions Amos offered us.

I, of course, agreed with my husband. Not because I was submissive to him in our relationship but because Bladrick's reminder that we couldn't be free outside the Haus had taken root deeply within me. You see when you honestly love someone, even hell would be an acceptable address. Just as long as the two of you are able to be in each other's arms while suffering. It's a good thing Keifer and I had such strong feelings too, because the Dungeon, even way back then, was comparable to Satan's lair.

Bladrick finally calmed after he'd stomped, shattered or tossed most of the paltry things the four of us owned. He sat down next to his weeping cousin and pulled her into his embrace. His attempts to reassure the broken hearted girl weren't of any use. She more than the rest of us was in real danger. A young, unmarried woman, particularly a very handsome one, was a target for ill treatment both in the Dungeon and outside the Haus walls.

You see back then, females weren't permitted to obtain honest work or live without male aid anywhere in the country. Even in the Haus, being a woman was a real liability to obtaining any position of power. Mother Felicity was a rare exception to the rule.

A girl was expected to marry the moment a worthy match could be arranged, usually by age sixteen to eighteen. She was essentially viewed as the property of her father until she became the ward of her husband Nothing had changed for the female from the time of my mother's unlucky fate in marriage).

In the Dungeon where the males were strictly separated from the females, Ingrid's hope to be courted by a man of wealth or power, which for an impoverished woman of that era was the best case scenario, was dashed. Her beauty would be of no use to her in this bid for a desired suitor when wasted upon the grey stone walls of that horrific prison-like environment.

If she were to leave the Haus, things could go even worse for her then that. Without a dowry to offer, she'd be lucky if the lowest brute from the class of paupers that was common in the country was willing to call her wife. The fate of a gorgeous, intelligent, and gentle natured young girl's prospects in town would go to shit in only a matter of hours. I can only imagine the gut wrenching fear that must have been driving her cold tears of despair.

Thankfully she'd always had her brother Keifer there to make everything seem better. He broke from our unspoken agreement to try our luck in the Dungeon and went to her side. I didn't say a word as my husband promised her no matter what came she could count on him and me to defend her honor and do all that is possible to gain her a husband good enough to father her children.

It was breathtaking to watch that beautiful girl's blue eyes full of tears shine with the light of trust in her brother. Keifer was always capable of making the darkest night seem brighter somehow. She dried her face, braced her resolve and agreed to come with Keifer and me to our new lives at the bottom of the Haus.

Bladrick on the other hand wasn't having it. He was the straight man and not a small-framed fellow. Not many months before Mother Felicity went home to heaven he'd met a girl in the village not far from Das Kaiser Haus. Quietly, the brute been wooing that pretty lady. She'd told him on a few occasions if he wished it, her father could get him work at the local factory.

Initially the concept of breaking his back doing twelve to eighteen hour shifts in some dangerous industry turned him off. That all changed when faced with the Spartan lifestyle expected of all Dungeon Masters and Mistresses.

He was already twenty-one years old and like Ingrid unwed. The man was ripe for a chosen mate and starting a family. We were all aware it would be many years before Amos took the dirt nap and we could emerge from the hell hole. Bladrick wasn't as willing as Ingrid to put his interest in family aside for Gott knows how long.

So, with much regret, Bladrick said his goodbyes to the three of us and lit out. It was truly devastating to watch helplessly as he returned to the life he'd even committed murder to escape. Me, Keifer and Ingrid swallowed our tears and hand in hand walked down the stony steps into the darkness that awaited us. It would be a decade before any of us saw the world above again.

Once settled into our new home, it didn't take long for our mistakes at ignoring Haus politics to come crashing down upon our ears. Ingrid was separated from Keifer and I to be placed among her sister Mistresses. The two of us were given a meager cell to share with the Masters. Within the hour of the arrival of the new recruits our baptism of harsh hazing at the hands of our brothers began.

Relentlessly, Keifer and I were subjected to verbal bullying, backhands, and random thuds from every seasoned Master we encountered in the halls. By the time chow was served in the Dungeon dinner hall, both me and my husband were nothing but walking bruises. I confess, if the sight of our bare stone hovel hadn't near broken my spirit, the cruelty we endured from our co-Masters sure did.

I was near tears and unable to eat the single bowl of tasteless porridge that sat in front of me that night. Keifer, ever the optimist, saw my depressed state. He leaned over into my ear and kissed me while promising things would get bedder. I wanted so badly to believe him as I always did, but this time things seemed gloomier than I'd encountered before.

It may have been that I'd given up had it not been for Ingrid. You see while Keifer attempted to sooth my wounded heart, she managed to slip past the Headmistress. She caught our attention from her hiding spot as we slowly limped back to our room after that unappetizing meal. The other Masters were not far behind us, so with a nod that we heard her calling the two of us we went on with our journey. She understood and carefully watched to see which door was the one to our cell.

We didn't have to wait long for the clever girl to come knocking, begging us to let her in. She entered the room full of useful information regarding our best chances for survival among men that obviously were seeking to see us retired with speed.

While the Masters were brutes of the highest caliber, the Mistresses turned out at be a far softer lot. Ingrid's assigned trainer had, like most that met her, taken a real shying to this pretty teenager. The woman happily told Ingrid the history of Das Kaiser Haus during her work at introducing her to the duties of the Mistress. It was through this long winded descriptions of this closed society's belief systems that Keifer's little sister realized remaining neutral wasn't a wise option.

Both of us sat there stunned to stupid as Ingrid told us that the Haus was nothing but a bloody battle ground of family feuding. The Altergotts, Wagners, Reinhardts, Schmidts, Albrecht, Krauss, Herz, Finck, Wobben and Haas had been killing each other off for more than two hundred years. What's more was that over that span of two centuries, there was a predictable cycle in the rise and fall in power for each family.

As it was explained to her, the original founders were close friends that came from the peasant class. One of them, named Joseph Schmidt, come into a bid of luck. His Master died and left to him a small plot of land. This area the man inherited was secluded but boasted a beautiful view, with great potential.

Joseph was a brilliant and well liked fellow in his tiny community. He come up with a plan that was sure to improve the lives of him and all his friends if they would be willing to work together. His idea was to build a fancy palace on the land.

In this Haus he and his partners would provide services fit for a monarch to only the wealthiest in the land. They would charge high fees to these rich persons with the assurance that whatever 'off colored' interests they were seeking would be provided discreetly. Of course, the nine other families readily agreed to see Joseph's vision come to fruition.

At first, without real funds to work with, the Haus was not much more than a couple of rooms in cabin in the woods. However, as the word got around of the unusual entertainments provided in this hidden get-a-way, the clientele list grew larger. The ten families re-invested their ever increasing earnings until after only a decade the tiny shack grew into a proper mansion.

It wasn't clear, no one bothered to write it down if Joseph and his friends were the ones servicing the Lords and Ladies themselves. Or if the families were using the local orphans, and impoverished villagers to attend them. Whichever was the case, over the years Joseph and the nine other clans became men and women of means.

Anytime there is vast wealth and untold power to be claimed, friendships are sure to suffer. The Haus and her ten founders were no exception to this dark truth of humankind.

Even before Joseph and the original founders found their graves, feuding had broken out among their kinsmen.

Fearful that the constant squabbling was going to tear their legacy to bits, each of the ten families elected a speaker from within their ranks. These ten men and women met at the top of their hand built palace and drew up a series of laws to govern their growing community. They then fashioned a way to rule over all of it.

First they created ten thrones to represent the ten founding families so that each had voting power. They separated these thrones into five that would be controlled by young, strong persons. These five Princes or Princesses were to enforce the laws written by the founding group.

The other five they decided would be the seats of older, wiser Princes or Princesses. These men and woman would advise their younger counterparts. They were also assigned the sacred duty of collecting fees to pay the debts or services for the Haus, along with gate keeping against riff raff.

Obviously, these ten thrones would require someone to oversee that the duties were done to perfection. The ten founders constructed two monarchs to rule over the rulers. The younger would be known as the sovereign of the Silk and the Elder the King or Queen of the Fur. The reasons for choosing these two objects wasn't recalled but it has been assumed that the two things were very precious and rare in that era.

The founders assumed that their dare descendants would always agree as to which among them was best suited to fill these coveted positions. Well, either they were ignorant or honestly neglectful in their reasoning. As you well know, almost immediately the fighting broke out among the ten families, all them trying like hell to claim every throne for their own clan.

The rest was history. Ingrid was told that through the years, a cycle of blood shed repeated itself about every generation. Two or three of the original clans would gather enough family members to overtake the Silk and the other the Fur. Then like clockwork, the Silk would try to dislodge the Fur, and vice versa. All the while from the fourth floor two or more of the other clans would try to sabotage those above.

Anyway, I won't bore you too much with details you already have surely discovered this during your own journey through the Haus. I will only say that this information came as quite the shock to me and Keifer and obviously Ingrid. She told us that placement in the Dungeon was at the sole discretion of the Fur Throne. Amos had put us down there because it was traditionally the only sure way to prevent a rival clan from rising.

This was because the ruling clan of that era often kept their spare kinsmen safely stowed away. When one of the thrones above became empty due to death, natural or unnatural, the Silk and/or Fur Monarch would raise one of their awaiting people from the bottom. As you know, in order to sit on one of the Fur Thrones you must serve first in the Dungeon. Well, even if you're hoping that your relatives from the Silk will raise you eventually, one may as well use that time getting that five years requirement out of the way, ja?

That was a second reason people were sent to work the Dungeons by the Fur monarchs. Once one of the ten had gained the seats of power they weren't capable of holding them forever. It wasn't that they didn't do everything possible from quickly reproducing with each other to murdering of anyone from rival clans they could. No matter what had been tried over the years, staying at the top with so many pulling at you from below was simply impossible.

When a ruling family's numbers dwindled to a low number, they would be thrown out by one of the awaiting clans. The next to take possession of the thrones were usually the founders that recovered enough of their blood ties to overwhelm them.

This constant struggle to remain in power was historically how the original ten families managed to survive all those years. Otherwise, like the Reinhardts, they were condemned to wallow in the mire of abject poverty. It turned out that the Haus was the sole income source for all our ancestors.

As the leaders, the families amassed a mild fortune from the collection of fees from the wealthy residents. They funneled that cash to their non-ruling relatives. When they fell from their place of easy money, the kinsmen that never held a place of power could often afford the rents on the first or second floor apartments for a single generation.

After that, the next crop would be left destitute. Often instead of accepting eviction, these youngsters would takin their vows of loyalty and be forced to accept jobs in the Dungeon to survive. This unlucky situation on the surface actually was historically the source of the next crop of leaders. At the moment, we'd been sent below, a large group of awaiting Altergotts and Wagners claimed residence with us.

However, they were scarce in number compared to the growing faction of Schmidts and Krausses. It seemed that at every turn, the man me and Keifer encountered claimed roots to one of those fellow clans. I'd noticed that the surname of Altergott or Wagner wasn't nearly as prevalent. In fact, Ingrid been told they'd been shrinking in population for almost three years prior to our arrival.

It didn't take the genius to realize the vicious Schmidts or notoriously cunning Krausses were on their way up. In fact, everyone in the Haus was expecting that to happen the second the Altergotts and Wagners managed to eliminate each other.

So, why would Amos put us, his natural rivals, down there where we would rack up points needed to be a threat to his power in the future? The answer Ingrid found out was real easy and explained our less than kind welcome. He was hoping that either his people would murder us, or that the overabundant Schmidt and Krauss faction would do it for him.

This bothersome news caused my husband's usual alabaster pallor to take on a whiter shade. Without any protection against the vast number of blood thirsty Schmidts and Krausses, we were sitting ducks. It was at this moment that all three of us regretted letting Bladrick leave. Our only hope to live long enough to escaping our time below ground was to surround ourselves with as many family members as possible.

Ingrid left before she was found missing only after Keifer assured her he'd come up with a plan to keep us safe. The second the girl was out of earshot while sneaking back to her barracks, I turned to my husband near ready to run screaming right out the back door of that horrible place.

To my shock Keifer smiled when he saw my expression of terror and said, "Why so glum lover? When will you learn to trust me? You may be thinking what Ingrid found out is terrible but if that's the case, I must say you need to look at this situation from a different angle. If what she said is the truth of it, then one day we will all be rich beyond our wildest dreams."

I shook my head nearly dumbfounded as I asked, "How the fuck do you figure that? Keifer, didn't you hear a word she said? The damned Altergotts or Wagners, or shit the Schmidts, are going to kill us in our beds. Ingrid said the only way a family clan can win the thrones is through brute force and large numbers. There are twelve thrones and three of us. Even if we did survive assassination and fight our way to the top. We got nine other motherfuckers who will put a knife in our backs to put their brothers in our spot."

Keifer chuckled "Ah, you think me, Ingrid and Bladrick are the only Reinhardts looking for a better lot than lady luck gave us? I will write a letter to my Aunt Muarl and Uncle Jorge tonight. I'll ask them if maybe they can spare a few of their many sons. At the moment, they're suffering hard luck in the farming of that rock we call our motherland. I think cousins Kristian and Max are old enough to be enrolled as the members. Then there is Bladrick's half-brothers Barnham and Drexel. I believe Barnham is nineteen and his little brother Drexel just turned sixteen. Thats another four of us right there, lover. How about you? I seem to recall you have four brothers yourself. Think any of them would be willing to join us in seeking our fortune?"

I nearly fainted when he said that "Hell nein. I wouldn't invite those rat bastards if they were the last blood ties I had on this Earth. Think, will you Keifer. They would murder us both if they knew, well you know about us."

He frowned,. "Oh ja. Sorry baby. I wasn't thinking. But if not them, surely you have other relatives that may be looking to improve their finances?"

I shook my head with a sigh. "You'd think so, but nein. The only other family that carries my father's name is his youngest brother. I've heard tale from his wife that he's become independently wealthy. His daughter Sofie is only two years old and their son Leo was born only last month. That pretty much sums up the extent of my kin."

Keifer's expression turned to one of pity as he said, "My poor Claus. No wonder you are always so blue. Well no worries, my love. Me and Ingrid have more than enough relatives to spare. You will never be alone again. Not since you are officially one of us. The Reinhardts are like cockroaches. We breed in mass and are hard as hell to eradicate. You stick with me, and I'll make you the rich woman with tons of people to call brother and sister, baby."

Well, that's a promise Keifer was hell bent to keep let me tell you. Before the end of the next week, Das Kaiser Haus increased its population of Reinhardts by four. Kristian, Max, Barnham and Drexel come running the second they learned of the prosperity that could be had if they'd be willing to suffer a few years of harsh living.

Kristian and Max were a lot like their cousins in looks and personality. I liked the two teenagers the moment I was introduced to them. Kristian was the elder barely turned nineteen with white, blond hair and the same clear blue eyes the Reinhardts were known for. His brother Max was younger by two years and his blond locks boasted golden highlights. His eyes were also blue, but oddly they had flecks of green mingled in them. This unusual color combination caused everyone to do the double take. I confess, they were almost as breathtaking as the icy hue of his brothers.

Barham and Drexel on the other hand, I disliked from the very start. These two fellows carried the same hot temper of their brother Bladrick but neither had his good sense of humor to go with it. Barnham had a habit of making snippy comments even when such a thing was uncalled for. I found him to be too rude, crass and downright mean to find any interest in getting to know him better.

Drexel, that boy, well what can I say about him that you don't already personally know? The word weirdo doesn't begin to describe my first impressions when we met. He didn't speak much and his gaze made a fellow feel creeped out. I mean you look into his eyes and there didn't seem to be anyone staring back out at you. Like he was alive but not, or something like that. I admit, I wasn't too damned shocked years later when I was told of his affinity for the statue. It seemed to me predictable that the guy would gravitate toward the thing most like him.

So, there we were, seven Reinhardts strong. It was no small thing to notice the minute the other boys arrived, the brutal treatment from our brother Masters cooled off substantially. I thought this was a good sign, but not more than another week passed before once more Ingrid called out from the shadows begging audience.

This time we were horrified to hear she'd learned of a plot by the eldest Schmidt brother to start picking us off one at a time. The only reason we hadn't been taking the dirt nap yet was that the Schmidt brothers Bernt, Derbeck and Xavier were blocking their elders from smiting us. The reason for their interference she'd been unable to ascertain.

This wasn't good news to say the least. The minute Ingrid slipped off to return to her cell, Keifer called together the brute Danes Kristian, and Max. I was a bid concerned when he warned only these two of what we'd learned but left Barnham and Drexel in the dark. His reasons for that he never told me, though I believe he already knew day weren't to be trusted.

As the four of us prepared for battle, the intelligent Ingrid was conceiving a plan of protection of her own. It became the open rumor within the week that the pretty teenager was being courted by all three of our defending Schmidt brothers.

Though we didn't know it at that time, she'd been cleverly using her strongest weapon to keep her brother and cousins alive. Without hesitation Ingrid wagged her beautiful assets before the coming of age young brutes. While I believe her original intention was merely to outfox them by playing the fox, in her game of seduction, she fell into her own trap.

Not too much time passed before it become clear that the oldest brother Xavier had captured the ripe girl's heart. Pretty soon you never saw one without the other close by. I initially hadn't paid any attention to any of the vicious members of the prolific Schmidt clan. It was only after Keifer became concerned about his sister's good welfare that I bothered to take a closer look at these men.

Bernt was the youngest and seemed to be the dourest of the three. He never smiled and was the tallest of these giant fellows. I immediately disliked him. It was far more than his foul attitude that turned me off to ever considering association with the man. During that time of my observations of the Schmidt brothers, I'd more than once witnessed him abusing one of the children wearing silver that we were supposed to be training.

I don't mean he was heavy handed with his tawse either. You see back then, the virginity of a male pleasure submissive wasn't as coveted as it was during your time. That's because despite the acceptance of the schwuler male in the Haus culture, catamite boys were not in high demand. The male silver was expected to be sold off to the FemDoms and Dominants as bodyguards or to stud their favorite silver females.

Therefore, the boys selected to wear the silver collar weren't chosen for beauty but for assumed size, intelligence and strength. Sex with the male pleasure submissive enforced by a Dominant wasn't forbidden, but it truthfully was frowned upon. If a boy silver was discovered to be behaving as the catamite, he was viewed with disgust and often considered ruined property. That means their collar wouldn't bring much on the market. So, keeping such a thing from occurring in the sexually repressive Dungeon was of paramount importance to the Headmaster.

The female silver's virginities were fiercely guarded by their Dungeon Mistress trainers. A girl that was auctioned but found to be not fresh was taken as an insult. Any case of such a thing being reported was investigated with vigor. The guilty Dungeon Master would be accused of stealing from her wealthy owner. Since the item couldn't be replaced, the offender could face fines equal to the purchase price of the pleasure submissive he dishonored, or even find himself exiled for the crime.

As it stood, punishment for raping a girl was stiff. Raping a boy though, the burden of shame fell on the soiled male's shoulders. This belief system that a boy was useless when proven dominated by another male was already ages old when I was the young man.

In fact, this terrible thing was often employed by the battling clans against the sons of rivels in attempts to gain revenge. You see, if one clan was insulted by another and they were either denied justice or felt not enough punishment was given for a crime against them, it was common practice to attack the offending clan's young sons and gang rape them with witnesses to the crime.

Once the non-collared boy was rumored as being misused like that, the entire Haus population no longer viewed him as a viable Dominant. He'd be publicly shunned and universally viewed as submissive for the rest of his life. The family wouldn't be capable of obtaining him a marriage of any worth within the Haus population. These young males often were sent away to live out their lives in disgrace far as possible from those that knew about his dishonor.

Now back in those days such a thing as breaking your metal was unheard of. A pleasure submissive was the life-long servant by definition. As I told you, their lives were no harsher than any low incomed German citizen of that age. They weren't killed without proof of a grievous crime. This meant day followed the same laws and were held up to the same social morals as all non-collared residents. That included a male's dignity that he'd never been dominated by another male.

That brings me back to Bernt Schmidt. While it was Dungeon policy to keep it in your pants when dealing with the silver and black children. It also wasn't that uncommon for the half-starved, overworked youngsters to be willing to sell their flesh for any favor they could buy with it.

Most of the Dungeon Masters understood this temptation to take them up on such desperate offers wasn't acceptable. Well apparently Bernt wasn't among that number. To my absolute horror on more than a handful of occasions I walked in on the man soundly fucking some obviously unwilling boy. He'd throw the abused child an extra bowl of mush for not screaming too loudly while he raped him to near unconsciousness.

I will tell you I reported that bastard every time I caught him. I sadly must tell you since the Headmaster at that time was a lazy Altergott, no punishment was ever handed out to Bernt for his crimes. The boys he injured were not so lucky. I stopped telling on that bastard after I discovered each one I'd named came down with the worms right after my report. I never knew for sure, but I must assume Bernt murdered them to assure no one ever backed up my claims of their abuse at his hands.

Needless to say, Bernt and I were enemies over that alone. Now I mention this man in particular because his actions and attitude matter to you more than you realize. This man was to become the father of two sons. both of them you had the bad luck to become familiar with. The cruel Peter and simpleton Friedrick call this beast their father.

The middle brother was named Derbeck. This was the only one of the three brothers that I cannot say anything bad about. He was not overly cruel to his wards, nor did I ever hear even the rumor he misused any of them. I've spent many years wondering how different things might have turned out for all of us, including you, had Ingrid chosen this brother to love rather than the one she did.

I only mention him at all because he was to become the father of the Voter you know as Rolf, and his older brother Oliver. You never met Oliver because he escaped the Haus long before you were old enough to recall him. However, I can say he was of the same fine personality as Rolf and their affable father Derbeck.

That leaves me to describe the object of Ingrid's true desires. The man that tried to kill you and found his grave for it. The infamous child killer Xavier himself. I assume by this point you've realized this fellow is your own father. Don't attempt to deny you've discovered this well guarded secret boy. I may be an old coot but I didn't live to be that by being stupid. There are very few things that happen in this Haus that I don't eventually get wind of. I happen to know Rolf stupidly told you that Peter couldn't possibly be your father. I also am aware you always knew Gerard wasn't that fellow either.

I'm aware you are a bright boy. Without a doubt Justus's sudden rise to the empty Elder's seat by your order come over a secret he told you. I told Ingrid to keep Agnette away from him. She didn't believe me when I warned her that he was in love with the girl. I've no doubts that your mother

197

blabbed to that fool of the paternity of the contents in her belly. "

I shrugged my shoulder and glared at Claus, "I won't deny a damned thing, your Majesty. However, I wish to know why you are giving me the history of the fucking world when all I wanted to know was of your actions in one instance."

The Elder stared hard refusing to break from my hateful gaze, "In order for you to understand the answer to your fucking question, I must explain to you the reasons the Princes of Das Kaiser Haus existed in the first place and why they were kidnapped by my brother."

I shook my head with a frustrated sigh, "You already told me why there are Princes of Das Kaiser Haus, Claus. Damn, you're getting the dementia most encounter as they are dying, ja? I don't give a shit about any of the Silk or Fur Princes of ancient times being taken hostage by your brother either. That hasn't a thing to do with you fucking with my mind or stroking your cock over me in the Dungeon. Stop trying to distract me from my purpose. It's not going to work that I can assure you."

Claus rose up from his pillow and backhanded me with force which caught me off guard big time. "Enough. You will be still and fucking listen to my explanation. I'll be dead soon. Then you never have to hear my voice again in this life. Until then, you must show me the respect I've more than earned." He laid back down while I rubbed my smarting cheek.

He took a deep breath and said, "I've told you about the Silk and Fur thrones, but the Princes of Das Kaiser Haus are not the same creatures, boy."

I whimpered a bit as I replied, "You didn't have to hit me, Claus. In all the time we've known each other I've never denied your commands. If these Princes are different than the ones I'm more than a little aware of, then why the fuck have I never met them or hell even heard of them?"

Claus's angered expression soften as he replied, "Honey, you have met them and are more familiar with them than anyone in this Haus could ever hope to be. You see one of them in the mirror every time you look into one. The other was murdered by my brother Gerard long ago. I know if you think on it hard, you'd recall that since you sadly were there when it happened."

That caused me to gasp as I whispered back, "There you go with the attempt to convince me I had the twin brother again. Why do you keep on trying to twist my mind with such bullshit, Claus? That is a bold faced lie and I will never fall for it. Even I'm not that crazy."

Claus frowned. "My boy, I never said this brother I'm claiming you had was a twin, not once. Yet somehow you made that inference. Ask yourself how you come to such a conclusion when I could've been claiming the boy was older or younger by years than you."

That caused me to startle a bid. "You did say it was a twin. I distinctly recall you did."

He shook his head while tisking. "Nein, I didn't. However, you are correct. The Princes of Das Kaiser Haus were a pair of beautiful twin boys born to the dishonorable Agnette in June of 1957."

With that nervous feeling coming over me once again I replied, "You call me the Prince of Das Kaiser Haus, but I wore the collar of the Priceless pleasure submissive. If me and this imaginary twin brother of mine were called that why did you Elders put that fucking collar around my neck, Claus? And for that matter, what the hell is a Prince of Das Kaiser Haus? Is there another blasted throne I've never heard of? Gott I pray not. I already wearing enough crowns as it is. I don't want the three I got."

Claus groaned and blew out his breath. "Gott dammit you trying my patience boy. It is only because of the knowledge that you suffered nightmares so terrible I cannot fathom them that I don't have you takin below and whipped for insolence. That said, I will repeat I'm trying to explain to you the factors behind your Priceless silver and horrific journey to this moment. I assure you, this wasn't what me, Bladrick nor Ingrid wanted for you or your brother. However, thanks to forces beyond our control, it is what was to be. For a bit longer I demand you give this old buzzard your full attention. When I finish this story of your creation, I will entertain further questions if you still have any. I doubt you will have any though. While the twists and turns that led to the birth of Ingrid's plan to set Das Kaiser Haus on the path to peace are complex, the honest desires behind it are not. The answer to both your original questions and to why you are here today is simple. We were trying to undo the damage we'd caused in our haste to become the most powerful in the Haus history. Now where were we? Oh ja, Ingrid and Xavier had become the unexpected lovers.

It seemed the impossible love affair. Relationships in the Dungeon were usually forbidden among the Masters and Mistresses. As I told you earlier, the reigning Headmaster at that time wasn't too interested in running the bowels of the Haus. All he was doing was passing time while waiting for his kinsmen Amos to raise him to a throne. It goes without saying that this gave Xavier plenty of opportunity to tempt the pretty young Mistress Ingrid into his bed.

By all accounts, Xavier was as smitten with Ingrid as she was with him. I don't believe the love affair was less heated on either side of it. If that bastard was playing her for ignorant, he sure was doing a fine job with the acting he'd been hit by cupid's arrow.

His younger brothers were jealous of his good fortune to have landed the woman of their dreams. In their irritation they dropped their interests in destroying their Reinhardt rivals. The random hazing ended not long after that, and for a few months a cautious truce appeared to come over both families. All eyes were on this union of Schmidt and Reinhart blood. The sneaking around to engage in the act of lovemaking became the open gossip heard in every corner of the men's barracks.

Back then birth control was a thing of science fiction. A girl that slept with her man took the chance each time that a permanent trophy could be made in her womb. As was all too common at the time, Ingrid didn't stay without a bun in the oven for long. By the fourth month of her triste with the burly Xavier, her monthly visitor took the sinister holiday.

Terror gripped the girl as she come to discover Xavier's seed had firmly taken root within her. She told him of her delicate condition sure that he'd turn her away trying to claim he wasn't responsible. To everyone's surprise, the brute not only laid claim to his actions he happily begged her to marry him.

So it came to pass that the first and only, that I've ever heard of anyway, union between an active Dungeon Mistress and Master was permitted to happen. Keifer gave his blessings to his thrilled sister despite his misgivings about the identity of her unborn kid's father.

I never heard tale of the expression on Amos's face when he received the news. I spend many a night cuddled with Keifer smiling as I imagined it. I hoped with all my soul it caused that old geezer sleeplessness over the realization he was the cause of that union between two of his most hated rivals.

Immediately our conditions improved in the Dungeons. We'd also increased our number of allies by volumes. That didn't change the fact that all of us were still were trapped in that Dungeon hell. Amos refused to die, even though many of his kinsmen were falling from the banister.

In fact, over the next several years two things became constant. Ever other year Ingrid and Xavier welcomed another son or daughter into our underworld. Meanwhile the Wagners and Altergotts buried one or two above us.

Slowly but surely, the families that held the Silk and Fur Thrones numbers shrank and their power weakened. In the Dungeon the exact opposite was happening. The rise of the Schmidt/Reinhardt was becoming more the reality by the month. It was also becoming pretty clear that the family clan likely to be our strongest opposition to maintaining our hard earned power was going to be the Krauss.

The men and woman that would eventually become the mothers and fathers of Julius, Fiona, Stephan, Grisham, Gustov, and others you never met were growing in might almost as quickly as our clan was. The battle lines were already being drawn in the Dungeon dust with several brawls breaking out between various overeager members from time to time.

By the Spring of 1914, Amos had taken serious ill. The doctors didn't believe the man would live much longer. The years of assassinations carried out by both the Wagners and the Altergotts had left the clans stripped of fresh relations to keep their thrones secured. Our rise from the bottom seemed to be imminent.

The only news we were listening to more closely than that of the happenings of the Silk and Fur was that of the country. Tensions were high between Austria and Serbia. Germany was an ally of Austria, and we were all hopeful the countries would come to a peace treaty. But by late summer of that year, it was clear war was coming to our country.

Amos managed to hold on to his life and throne during this time of anxious waiting. Nothing seemed to move and the days melded together into a blur. It seemed the only thing worse than keeping down the utter frustration at having to endure more years in the darkness was the fear that soon enough things like Fur and Silk would be the least of our problems. Keifer, me and all our kinsmen that served with us were the proper age to be called to arms if war broke out among Germany's allies.

After the assassination of Archduke Ferdinand many men across German began to kiss their loved ones goodbye. By September the first World War began. I cried for many hours after the declaration was broadcasted across the radio. I was sure me and Keifer would be separated and very likely killed over arguments neither of us could understand.

As it turned out, being trapped in the Dungeon, terrible as it had been, was our saving grace. While many men in the Haus were called out by their kinsmen to serve their country, the ilk below the foundation may as well not exist at all. No one realized there was a group of strong young men hidden away below the ground. The war raged on above, but in the Dungeon life went on as it had for the hundred years before.

In 1911, Ingrid gave birth to their son Xavier the second. In 1913 she had a daughter they named Christina. Then as the war raged on another son Henson joined their growing family in 1915. 1917 saw yet another blessing added to Xavier's brood. A healthy son day named Lars come into the world.

I must say, Ingrid wore motherhood well. She loved her children more than any woman I'd seen before save that of my mother Felicity. Spending a few hours with the bubbly Ingrid, prideful Xavier and playful children was one of the only bright spots during those hard years of the Great War. I still hold the memories of their happy family dear to my heart. If only that scene had been permitted to exist in its natural state, well, never mind. No sense in wishing for things that were not to be.

Keifer and I had reached a place of settling in with regard to our passionate love affair. It wasn't that he or I didn't feel completely adored by the other. I mean we'd become comfortable in each other's company. The raging flame of lust had calmed to the glowing ember of caring affection. I didn't complain that our bedroom wasn't the place of unbridled carnal desire it once had been. No relationship can maintain that level of hunger forever.

That said, the seven year itch seemed to have affected Keifer even if I seemed immune to such drivel. The first of many heart breaks in our families occurred the summer of 1917, when I returned after a long shift to find my husband absent.

At first I thought nothing of it. I started to go to bed to catch a few winks but my stomach was aching. I'd missed the noon meal, and assumed this pain could be calmed with a bit of a snack. I headed down to the mess hall without any intentions to go seeking the whereabouts of my wayward lover.

Until I realized something was amiss when I sat down at the dinner table. At that time there was a pretty young silver trainee called Vern that was to serve all the Masters there meals. Normally I wouldn't notice the identity of the pleasure submissive that brought me food but this boy was unusually handsome. though I would never consider it, I did enjoy looking at him. I didn't realize it, but apparently so did my husband.

The thing that caught my attention was that Vern wasn't the boy that rushed to put the plate in front of me. I glanced around the near empty room and noticed his face wasn't anywhere among the boys serving the few Dominants there to eat. I pulled the kid attending me to the side to question him about Vern's whereabouts.

I was concerned Bernt was up to his old tricks and the idea of his ruining Vern caused me great dismay. The young silver was terrified to be questioned by a Master of my experience level. He trembled and wept as he pointed down the empty hall towards the closed pit door. His lack of being capable of speech told me that my worst fears were realized. A Master had coaxed the innocent boy into giving up his dignity for a price surely unworthy of the gift being taking.

I hurried for the Pit hoping against all hope that I'd be in time to prevent Bernt from ruining the gorgeous kind. If I was lucky all that been taken was oral services and he could still claim usefulness as the honorable silver. That wishful thinking drove me to near madness as I ripped open the door ready to beat the pulp out of that shady bastard for daring to harm the boy I liked to dream about.

Well, you already know that when I come raging into that torture room it wasn't Bernt I found deflowering the pretty Vern. Nein, it was my own husband plunging deep into that boy's coveted assets. I need not tell you the pain of my heart splitting in two was sheer agony. I ran from the room, my eyes so full of tears I nearly slammed into the door before opening it.

I didn't halt my crying flight until I arrived back at our sparse barracks. I took to the bed sure that my life was over. Without Keifer's love, I didn't believe life wasn't worth living. As luck would have it, Ingrid arrived soon after I retreated into my bleak place of despair. She'd been dropping by to get a break from her rambunctious brood. When no one answered her knocking she'd let herself in to find me, laying there wailing like the lost banshee.

After a bid of work she was able to get me to tell her what caused me to grieve like that. Being the wonderfully caring soul she truthfully was, she listened quietly while I poured out my pain.

Once I'd related to her my tale of woe she sucked in her breath and said calmly, "Claus honey, did you ask the boy if he was being raped by Keifer before you jumped to conclusions?"

I couldn't believe my ears as I sobbed in response, "Does that even matter, Ingrid? Vern is the pleasure submissive. He must do what he's told or be punished for it. To be honest that isn't the issue. Even if the boy is the raging homo extraordinaire, I just caught my husband cheating on me. If you walked in to see Xavier fucking another woman wouldn't you feel betrayed?"

She smiled bitterly and nodded then said, "Honey, I have caught him fucking other women several times. Sure it hurts but the idea of not having him in my life is far more painful. Sex is not love Claus. He might fuck another female but it's this one he sleeps with. Before you think to throw away seven great years of friendship and truthful love, at least agree to speak with my brother. Believe me Claus, Keifer loves you with all his being. He's nothing without you as you are without him. Don't allow this little bid of fluff to come between the two of you. You'll be sorry for all your life if you do." With that she kissed me on the forehead and let herself out.

I laid there dinking about her confession of finding Xavier in the arms of other women. She seemed so confident that his trysts didn't dimmish his deep love for her. I thought if she could bear the burden of such betrayal then the least this man could do is confront Keifer. After all, I couldn't allow Ingrid to be the bigger woman than me. Hahaha.

Keifer come crawling home in about an hour, his head bowed low and tail between his legs. I sat there on the bed glaring at him angrily in silence for many minutes. I could tell this lack of verbal assault was making him uncomfortable. That made me feel some better, so I maintained my stance of quiet observation.

Finally he couldn't stand it any longer and he blurted almost too fast to understand him, "Listen baby, things got out of hand. I never meant for it to go all the way with Vern. He was just coming on so strong and well, I let my baser urges take me someplace I should have never been. I understand if you hate me. I deserve it. However, I want you to know that what you saw never happened before. Not with Vern and not with anyone else. I've been the exclusive lover to you all these years. I swear it on Mother Felicity's grave."

I drew in my breath then replied, "Do you love him? That boy, Vern?"

He shook his head without breaking his gaze from my own. "That's what's so shitty about this situation. The answer is nein, I don't even care to know him despite having just taken him intimately. I threw away the man I love more than my own life for a tryst that means no more to me than takin the piss."

That bothered me more to hear his response than if he'd confessed to being passionately in love with the boy. "So how am I to trust my husband if he can stick his cock in a boy almost half his age without any more care than relieving his water? The man I come to love all these years would never use another human being as you just have done. Do you realize Vern is ruined silver? Does it matter to you that he will be tossed out of Das Kaiser Haus to starve in the streets? Christ Keifer, who the fuck have I married?"

Keifer flashed me a bitter smile as he responded, "I may be the home wreaker but I'm no monster. Vern is not going to be tossed out of the Haus. He come to me at the evening meal to confess he's discovered his gender preference is that of the gay male. I was caught off guard to be spoken to by one of our boys so openly about such a thing. I took him away from the other guys to try to talk him out of taking the path of the catamite. He wouldn't hear of it, and before I could stop him he threw himself at me. I pushed him off several times, but I won't lie. I'm weak and his favor was too much to resist. Before I knew what was happening, well you saw so I won't go into details. Anyway, seeing the pain in your eyes killed my lust for that boy. It ended the second you left the room. I took Vern to see Derbeck. I made him confess to the man his words to me and even with that man's caution Vern insisted he's schwuler. As is Haus law, Vern has been sent above to be sold at the next auction to a gay Master seeking the company of a pretty young boy."

I let out my breath in mild relief to hear Vern was safe, well as much as any catamite of that era could be. "Okay so you did right by Vern, but what about your injured husband. How you gonna undo the damage you've done to him?"

Chapter 6: Slaughter at the Haus
Master Mad Maxx and submissive Meine Liebe

Remember when Claus is telling his story in 1975 he is eighty-five years old. Claus is a wealth of information regarding the history of Das Kaiser Haus, Germany, and human nature in general. We return to the year 1917. The Great War rages on, and Claus has just taken another big bite from the bitter apple he called his life. But his journey has only just begun to go sour.

I glared hard at Keifer as I replied, "For starters I wish to make it clear to you husband. If I ever catch you or even hear a rumor you are thinking of fucking around on me. We are over. I refuse to put up with a cad with the roving eyes and hands. You got that?"

Keifer nodded eagerly. "Ja, baby I give you my word. I will never stray from you ever again. I've learned my lesson well."

I let out my breath as I then said, "Not so fast. This hurt you caused me tonight is going to take time to heal. I expect for some time I will require much special attention to convince me I'm still the only man you honestly desire. You always played the Dominant in our love life. Well, you demonstrated that your unfit to be trusted in that position of responsibility between us. Until further notice, I'm submissive to your authority no longer. You will bow to my words and act as the wife or I will find a fellow that is more capable of meeting my needs."

Keifer grinned wickedly as he replied, "Why Claus, I thought you'd never ask me for such a delectable change of pace. Hell, you making me the lusty man just hearing you speak to me like this. Keep talking dirty to me and I may have to misbehave until you are forced to spank me."

It took all I had not to bust out laughing when he said that, but I wasn't finished being pissed. "So be it. I'll whip the flesh off your gorgeous ass when I'm done correcting you, little brat. Last thing I require to allow you back into my bed is a promise. You will swear to me this minute that you will remain so loyal to your Husband that you won't even die unless it's in his arms."

My beautiful husband dropped to the kneel at the side of our bed and with his blue eyes glistening he responded, "I swear to you my love, the day the reaper come for me. I'll hold that bastard at bay until you can get your arms around this worthless Mann of yours."

How could I remain angry with him? It simply was impossible. Keifer always had my heart from the second he reached down to help me to stand. You see, that was why I loved him in the first place. No matter the depth to which I tumbled. My Husband was there to pull me back to my feet.

Despite that little slip he had with Vern. I didn't turn him away. We made up that very night. Loudly and with renewed vigor. Hahaha. Okay there I go again telling you things you surely don't wish to hear. Too bad for you though. I'm an old fart that has nothing left to make the dark less fearsome than a few beautiful memories. So, you will sit there and put up with them.

So, as for Vern. The boy managed to find a buyer in the Auction. Derbeck told Keifer and I his beauty and youth come in handy since it was hard to unload catamites, used or fresh, back then. There simply wasn't a market. If one did get lucky like Vern had to capture the attention of a wealthy Dominant, he could only hope to hold that fellow's attention till he outgrew his pretty boyish stage.

By adulthood they were often abandoned by their Masters who then went seeking fresh game. That's the reason Keifer and Derbeck attempted to talk the boy out of his insistence to play that role. It sucked to counsel a silver gay male to pretend to be straight, but that was the sad truth of those days. If he wasn't discovered to be schwuler he could expect to be cared for all his life rather than tossed the second he wasn't cute anymore.

Well, Vern didn't listen to Keifer and Derbeck's wise advice. His handsome features were of use to gain him a ticket out of the Dungeon but for how long no one could say.

As 1917 drew to a close, word come to us that the Dominant that bought his collar had fled the Haus taking Vern with him. We never heard of his fate after that news. To this day I've often wondered if he is out there in the world somewhere or if like so many others before him he found his grave the second he become a man. Of course, there is no way to ever know.

The sorry situation of the catamite male wasn't the worst that could be encountered by a silver back then. For any submissive or impoverished kid death was a constant threat. Common childhood sickness, starvation, war, those were not the only monsters lurking under their beds.

This was the times before modern medicine and antibiotics. Finding a doctor that could do more than tell you what disease was killing your loved one was unheard of. Cures employed by them were about as worthless as the home remedies and prayers said over the ill.

Diseases of particular interest to those at Das Kaiser Haus were of the sexually transmitted kind. Syphilis and gonorrhea are easily eradicated in this day and age, but for the people of my youth acquiring one of them was the automatic death sentence. Worse, the death you gained was a very slow, ugly and painful one. Sometimes it takes many years to rip the suffer asunder.

I'm not sure when the rumor began, but many believed syphilis could be cured by deflowering a virginal girl. That bullshit wives tale was a horrific tragedy I've never heard anyone say much about in the history books. It's a sad thing no one wishes to confess to the cruelty this error caused untold numbers of young women, some before they ever reached their puberty.

Often the wealthy men came from all over the country the second they heard a new crop of worthy silver females were up for bids. Sometimes the brutes would get into brawls trying to be announced the winner of some pretty virgin.

This confused the Haus people. The silvers were trained in the art of pleasure services. Yet a girl that had no honest skills in lovemaking wasn't considered as valuable as the experience ones. The residents didn't wish to deal with a crying, quivering lover that didn't know her way around a cock.

Well, it didn't take long before the leaders of the Haus discovered the reason their virgins would sell like hot cakes to the outsiders. The next morning after the auctions, many of the silver virgins sold off would be discovered wandering about the halls of the Haus. When questioned, these little ladies always told the same tale.

The man that bought her, took her to a room and forced quick rough sex. Then the brute would excuse himself telling her he'd be right back to collect her. Of course, that monster never returned, having gotten the cure he'd come to take. The poor baby would be left deflowered, abandoned and worse, cursed with a terminal and painful disease.

That kid could never became a mother or enjoyed the pleasures of sex ever again without passing on the STD to another. This happened so regularly, the Leaders decided to try to quash the practice of it.

They met and made a rule that no virginal girl could be sold at auction for less than a minor fortune. This idea did almost nothing to curb the issue, but it did increase the amount of money secured for that ruined silver's care.

The sum of the cash collected by the sale of the unlucky girl's collar was used to grant her the only mercy available to her in that time. If a silver female was found to be riddled with syphilis and abandoned to the care of the Haus because the asshole that bought her only wanted to attempt his cure. She would be painted black immediately. She would then be removed to a special apartment built to haus these ruined submissives. There she would be permitted to live out the years, or months depending on how bad she was infected, in peace without being forced to serve ever again.

The ruined black collar maids were given ample food and weren't treated with disrespect. There was a law that anyone found to be harassing or taunting these women would be severely punished. No one ever dared that I'm aware of, but I was told to be found guilty carried the punishment of being forcibly infected with their disease. Yikes!

Furthermore when the disease the ruined maid suffered became too painful for her to wish to endure. She was given the right to demand the Haus Doctor give her a concoction so that she could end the agony before it progressed to the horrific state of insanity paralysis.

Now I tell you all this because though STDs were a problem at the Haus in the years before my time. They were never at a horribly high level thanks to high prices for virgins and strictly enforced medical exams of year round residents. When the Great War began, however, that all changed.

The German soldiers were returning for holidays or as hopelessly wounded in droves. Many of them fooled around with the prostitutes of the regions in which day were stationed. This led to an epidemic of all the nasty STDs that began to plague Germany. Then it trickled into the overly promiscuous Haus residents very quickly from there.

The fear of becoming the place of disease caused the Leaders to take immediate actions. Without quarrel the Wagners and Altergotts created new laws regarding the sexual behaviors of all those living within the walls full time. Sex with the outsiders was banned until further notice, and every resident was commanded to submit to medical checkups once a month. They included all diseases, not just the sexually transmitted kinds.

From that moment on if you wanted to sleep with anyone that lived at Das Kaiser Haus, you had to produce a card with the doctor signature claiming you were clean of disease. Being caught fooling around without this clearance carried the punishment of immediate exile without question.

If you were found ill with any disease, you were to be removed from the Haus immediately. No one was allowed to enter or re-enter, if the illness was curable, without an intense medical exam and the doctor's authorization. This law was extended to include the submissives, visiting and ruling classes within thirty days of its original passing through the Council.

Now back then by tradition submissive collars were volunteers obtained free of charge. The lands surrounding the Haus were home to many small villages and towns full of impoverished families. Due to disease, hard luck, the high rate of death during childbirth, or random crop failures, there was never a dearth of the orphaned or the relatives who couldn't afford to support their children.

Every morning for over a hundred years, the Headmaster and Headmistress would go to the back door of the dungeon. There he and she could more often than not expect to find a handful of children aged eight to ten years old milling about.

They have been left abandoned there in the night, or they found their way there through rumor, by their own kinsmen. It was the open rumor around the land that a kid of this age could be assured a better existence than the one they were facing because of the factors I stated.

These children would be examined by the reigning leaders of the Dungeons. Those that showed potential and were found to be in at least decent health were taken in to be trained as submissives. The unfortunate that were ill, weak, or otherwise damaged were taken to the local monastery and turned over to the church to deal with.

This practice had always assured Das Kaiser Haus had a solid supply of collars. Back then the submissive class was grateful to be granted this second chance when otherwise their doom was assured.

I tell you these two bits of information, about the laws on disease and how submissives were obtained, because both of them have much bearing on the rest of my story. In fact, I can safely say, it's the reason me, Keifer, Ingrid, Xavier and eventually Bladrick evolved from the kind hearted, well when compared to most people of our era, merciful souls we were into the monsters each of us became. That may seem strange to think either of those things could be so important to the fate of the four of us, and therefore you and Das Kaiser Haus herself, but believe me it's the truth of it.

So, it came to pass that 1917 came to an anxious close. Nothing could've prepared us for the darkness that was to descend upon us for the next two years. As it was, all of us in the Dungeons celebrated the start of the New Year with great hope in our hearts.

The war still raged outside the walls, but inside, Amos and his faction's fall seemed assured. We all believed, Schmidt/Reinhardt and Krauss alike, that before the end of the spring, our stony cells would turn to golden palaces.

Xavier and Ingrid had double reason to be overjoyed. In the rare incidence of quick recovery, the beautiful mother of his children announced she was once again expecting. Keifer and I spent the entire first night of the year 1918 drinking toasts with the proud pappa to be.

Xavier wasn't bashful about bragging of his good fortune either. There wasn't any doubt that man honestly loved being the father and husband. He was a well-known womanizer but as she'd confessed to me after Keifer's indiscretion, this unsavory behavior didn't dimmish Ingrid's love for her husband. I can say other than that single weakness for chasing tail that didn't belong to him, Xavier was actually a pretty decent fellow, at least back then.

His attention to detail, fairness when dealing with the trainees, and strict adherence to Haus laws had earned him much respect both among his brother Dungeon Masters as well as the submissive trainees. He'd been the trainer of many collars that had risen to legendary status once they'd ascended to serve above. No one could deny, Xavier knew his shit and was a man you could trust to get the job done.

Ingrid also had earned herself a reputation as the perfect Dungeon Mistress. She was renowned for gaining the trust and love of the submissive girls through the use of a gentle hand. It was often said her skills at obtaining the undying loyalty of those wearing the metal was comparable to that of the late great Mother Felicity herself.

The pair had become such a powerful force within the dust and stone halls, that even the top of the Haus couldn't deny them. As the first month of the year came to an end, the lazy Altergott Headmaster finally got his call to rise. He was to fill the recently vacated third Fur Throne, after the former owner accidently slipped down the stairs.

While that useless bastard packed up his harness, Amos sent down word that his choice to replace his Headmaster was, ja you guessed it, Xavier Schmidt. This news came as no surprise to most, but it did cause much resentment. Not just among the ever increasing Krauss faction that shared the Dungeon with us either.

Bernt, though the youngest of all the Schmidts of age, had gotten it into his head he should've been named instead of his oldest brother. That sibling rivalry wasn't brought out by Xavier's rise.

Bernt always had hated his two older brothers with a passion. This discord had been deepened by Xavier's capturing of the pretty and fertile Ingrid, but now he was nearly insane with jealousy over what he viewed as yet another slight.

I believe more than any ding, Bernt's wounded attitude of unearned entitlement is the catalyst for the beginning of the end for all of us. But it took a series of unfortunate world events for the worm of discontent to advance into the moth of evil beyond imagination.

The rise of Xavier to Headmaster and the sudden disappearance of all surnames of Altergott and Wagner among us seemed auspicious. Everyone believed that Amos was finally ready to accept his time in power was up.

Only the large group of Krauss stood in our way of a quick takeover of all the thrones of power. Though they were a worry, most of them were younger than the youngest of our clan. The best they could be towards even the weakest of our factions, at least for a few more years, was a nuisance. For that moment in time, all our futures seemed bright.

These peaceful and hopeful spring months brought about a renewed vigor for me and Keifer and all our kin. The Dungeons practically sung songs of happiness. All of us were ignorant that while we rejoiced, outside the walls things in our country had taken a sinister turn towards disaster.

The first signs that things were amiss come at the end of April that year. Word came down from above to Xavier and the reigning Headmistress, also a Schmidt, that they were forbidden to accept any new submissive prospects.

While that was concerning news to be given, the rest of the message put all of us into panic mode. The doors of Das Kaiser Haus were to be sealed, and every resident was confined to the Haus until further notice.

A lockdown of this proportion could only mean one thing: Plague had descended upon the land. Through careful listening of the radio, it finally became clear a pandemic of horrific proportions had taken hold of the world. They were calling it the Spanish Influenza.

For that entire Spring, the Haus held her breath while the news of death was heard all around us. though the numbers succumbing to this new plague weren't terrible as they were to become, the reports heard of the illness's progression were frightening.

It was rumored that a perfectly healthy person could awaken in the morning feeling fine. Then be stone cold dead by dark fall. No one seemed to know how to stop the disease from spreading. The ongoing wars assured even if they wanted to isolate the virus, it wasn't possible.

By the summer the numbers of ill and dying began to calm. It seemed the illness had run its course and Das Kaiser Haus had weathered the storm without a single casualty. All the residents have been holding their breath for many months. This news that the sickness was retreating was wonderful.

However, by then that Influenza wasn't the only devil threatening Germany. It was at the beginning of the summer that rations started to shrink in size. It didn't take long for word to reach our ears that Germany and her allies were not faring well in the war. Our countries enemies had successfully cut off the routes that were used to bring in supplies and food.

Many worried that the plans to starve our people was an indication that the war was in her final stages. Worst, there were strong rumors that we were losing. Suddenly, finding a way to escaping the Dungeon hell wasn't the most important thing on me and Keifer's minds, or anyone in Das Kaiser Haus. Fear at what horrors the victors would do to Germany and ultimately us, gripped every heart big and small.

As the month of September began, two things consumed our every thought. The nearly non-existing rations coming down to the Dungeon, and the rumor that the Influenza had returned to the land. Only this time, the illness wasn't playing around. It had briefly subsided and returned in a form so deadly few that became ill were surviving its ravages.

Ingrid and Xavier had been suffering more than anyone during those months of scarce rations. The two doting parents divided their meager portions among their growing children. Keifer and I became alarmed at the sight of the beautiful mother, as she began to whittle away at an alarming speed. Without a word of discussion between us, we began to insist she share half of all the food we managed to snag.

Things were hard, but we knew if we worked together, somehow we'd survive this trauma. The war couldn't last much longer with most of Germany starving to death, and our best men already long since killed in battle. To be honest, no one even cared if we were the losers anymore. We just wanted this nightmare to be over. Damn the consequences.

Amos had ordered another lockdown of the Haus. Everyone knew this was a wise thing to do. Without quarrel all residents, great and small, locked their doors and isolated themselves away from the crumbling world outside Das Kaiser Haus.

It was at this moment that Xavier youngest sisters wrote to their favorite brother Bernt and requested sanctuary. These girls were twins that you knew as the violent Heidi and Helga. They were just three months from sixteen years old and wanted their powerful brother to pull strings to get them membership in the Haus. They been suffering, like all in the country, harsh living conditions with scare food. The Haus seemed to them to be the beacon of plenty and a safe port in the coming storm of occupation due to Germany's defeat.

Bernt took this request to Xavier because only he had the key to the Dungeon back door. Xavier knew that Amos ordered no one was to be permitted entry for any reason. He wanted to help his sisters but knew that the Law forbade it. He told Ingrid of his moral dilemma at turning his own blood away.

Ingrid wisely pointed out that Xavier's first duty wasn't to obscure sisters he'd barely knew, they didn't grow up together, but to his own children. Ingrid reminded him her situation of pregnancy during a time of famine had resulted in even Kristian and Max giving up half dare rations to her. All her cousins, her brother and me were already sacrificing everything possible to protect his young.

Therefore there was no possibility that his sisters could fare any better among our number. She then cautioned him against taking the chance that his disobeying Amos would go unnoticed. Punishment was exile and because of this, his second loyalty must always be to the Haus. Without it he had no opportunity to improve the lots of them or their babies. Her words seemed to harden the man's spine.

He returned to Bernt and told him he'd considered their request and was forced to respectfully refuse. This infuriated his younger brother who had grown up with Heidi and Helga. He called Xavier a Judas to his kinsmen and attempted for the next few days to turn anyone and everyone against him that he could. This public display of disloyalty appeared to embarrass the strong Headmaster. It also must have pulled on his heart strings to take pity on his desperate sisters.

However, a case could also be made that Xavier's next actions were solely based upon his lust for power. The addition of two more Schmidts, and females that could increase their numbers at that, could've pushed him to go behind everyone's backs and break the lockdown law.

It's as probable that the support Bernt was amassing worried him as well. Many of his kinsmen viewed his refusal of his own baby sisters pleas as cold hearted. They assumed if he was willing to turn a blind eye to the plight of his closest blood, then surely none of them would receive any favors.

In fact, several of the Schmidts and many of the Krauss had joined up with Bernt. The Krauss were more than happy to fuel any discontent within their more powerful rival clan. A few even voiced demands that he hand over his title of Dungeon Headmaster to his suddenly more popular younger brother.

Whatever the reasons, Xavier stupidly planned with Heidi and Helga to slip them into the Dungeon. He allegedly asked the girls to confess to any associations they had prior to their arrival at the back door of the Haus. Of course, the bitches bold faced lied to him.

They claimed they had honestly observed his requested ten-day quarantine in a hotel room in the village. That later proved to be bullshit. Even back then, the twins were fiercely competitive. Young, pretty, ja do recall they were only girls at this time, and full of the Schmidt promiscuity they used their access to full benefit.

They'd taken up residence in the local village hotel Xavier paid for, but they did anything but remain isolated. The two teens made great sport of the many returning soldiers that got off the trains. It was said Heidi and Helga managed to amass a great deal of chocolate, cigarettes and other hard to obtain items by selling their sexual skills to the woman starved, traumatized young men.

Well as you may have guessed, these war hardened fellows were the ones spreading the influenza like wildfire across the lands. That night Xavier snuck down to the back door and ushered his little sisters inside to the unused cells. Well thanks to their games, both girls were likely infected with the dreaded flu.

For five days, Xavier slipped past everyone's radar in the night. He visited their hiding spot with a small portion of his own pathetic rations to make sure his sick sisters didn't starve to death. This was source of the end of the story for many souls that resided in the Haus in 1918.

Xavier managed to contract the illness through these brief meetings with Heidi and Helga. On the sixth day after his betrayal of all the Haus people, he collapsed during one of his regular training sessions with his collars.

Me and Keifer were called to help carry the huge man back to his cell. The Haus doctor was called to attend him. No one knew the cause of his sickness. We all assumed he'd fainted due to fatigue and lack of proper nutrition.

When we arrived at the cell he shared with Ingrid and his children the sight that greeted us was one right out of hell. Ingrid was unconscious in the floor. Her babies were crying, well all of them but one. Xavier the second lay on the floor not far from his mother. He was observably deceased. Keifer and I dropped the burly Headmaster onto the floor and rushed to aid the failing Ingrid.

Tears flowed in rivers as we discovered all the children were in various stages of illness. Xavier the younger had already succumbed to his, but Christiana and Lars weren't far behind. There remaining son, Henson, passed away only two hours after his brothers and sister. All these beautiful babies died in either mine or Keifer's lamenting arms. Death come to claim Xavier and Ingrid's brood so fast we barely had time to comprehend it.

The unfortunate children's parents were full of fever, hallucinations and barely clinging to life during all this. Me and Keifer attended them without takin a break, fearful that they would soon join their lost children. By the third morning, Keifer broke out in a fever of his own. That afternoon, the flu took me down as well.

The Haus doctor didn't have to guess the culprit behind the sudden illness of the Headmaster and his family. He sealed off the cells in the Dungeon, then fled to warn Amos. The deadly second wave of Spanish influenza had somehow invaded Das Kaiser Haus's foundation population. Within the week, almost every man and woman, submissive or non-collared was laid out on their backs suffering the ravages of the plague.

The upper floors weren't spared this horrific fate despite their quickly sealing off the door that lead to the Dungeon. The black collars that brought down the daily rations had been exposed to Xavier while he was contagious but had not shown symptoms yet.

Needless to say, these servants brought the flu to the first floors, unbeknownst to them. Over that five-day incubation period they'd been spreading it to everyone they encountered. Within one week of Heidi and Helga arrival, the entire Haus, all the way to the seventh floor, was sick, or dying of the flu.

I was far too sick and stuck below to have memory of the things I was told of this terrible tragedy. Those that lived above reported horrific conditions. It was inevitable that with so many incapable of attending to themselves, no one was around to remove the corpses.

Many that survived reported the halls were devoid of any life. Instead, they were lined with the dead and dying. The very air went putrid with the stink of their decay. Rats openly feasted on the copious amount of rotten flesh with free reign to run unchecked. The sounds of weeping, screams and prayers of desperation were deafening.

In the Dungeon, the story was pretty much the same. I'm still am not sure how the fuck any of us survived this illness from Hades itself. It's likely the months of short rations had let to most of us below suffering poor health.

For this second wave of the flu, the healthy, very young, and very old were the ones most likely to succumb. If your immune system wasn't too weak or too strong, your survival seemed to be more the case but not assured.

Obviously, I was among the lucky to claim life after the flu finished kicking my ass. Heidi, Helga, Keifer, Xavier, Kristian, Barham, Drexel, and both Schmidt brothers also recovered without serious damage. Max and Ingrid though weren't so lucky.

Max suffered significant lung damage from his battle with this sickness. He'd been a robust, strong fellow that could work for hours prior to getting the flu. After he recovered, slower than the rest of us I may add, he had a persistent cough. The rest of his life he had much difficulty maintaining a healthy weight and would fatigue very easily due to chronic breathing problems.

Ingrid, that poor woman, suffered the most of us all. She awoke from her fever, which induced nightmares to discover they were preferable to her new reality. I will never forget the moment she opened her eyes and asked to hold her babies, only to be told they'd been cremated in haste, along with all the others that died rapidly, in the mass funeral pyre.

Keifer and I did all we could, as did Kristian and Max, to console the broken hearted mother. However, what the fuck can you say to sooth the soul of the one that's lost her reason for being? Nothing is what.

If fate hadn't kicked that sweet lady's ass hard enough, within a few weeks of her recovery, it came back for seconds. Ingrid, weak from hunger, stress and the flu went into premature labor. She gave birth to a stillborn daughter before the Haus doctor could arrive to assist in the labor.

Finally, the horror of the flu epidemic within the Haus abated, and the final infected residents either recovered or died. The fall was nearly over, and the survivors among us were able to count and mourn our losses.

The once numerous Schmidt clan had been nearly wiped out. Only Xavier, Heidi, Helga, Bernt and Derbeck were left. The Krauss clan was hit even harder. Their relations that once had the potential to take on the huge number of rivals sharing the Dungeon with them boasted only three survivors and only one was a male.

All the Reinhardt lived on but above us the remaining Altergotts and Wagners suffered heavy casualties. Three of the Silk thrones were open and two of the Fur without a single relation left to fill the vacancies.

This was one hell of a disaster for both the powerful and the weak. It was recorded in the Haus history that of the three hundred residents that called Das Kaiser Haus home in September 1918, only two hundred and fifty still clung to life. The higher mortality rate seen among us was due to many factors. Lack of proper medical treatment, months of famine, and almost everyone getting sick at the same time, likely was the real killer more than that blasted flu itself.

As it was, I watched helplessly as Ingrid fell apart. The bubbly, loving woman I'd always looked up to withdrew deep into the darkness of her busted heart. Xavier also demonstrated significant changes to his once impeccable personality. The loss of his family literally overnight seemed to have released an inner rage. He began to be commonly seen using a far heavier a hand on his trainees than any deserved.

This coldness that came over Xavier could've been further fueled by the hateful reception he was getting at home. Everyone was aware that the once adoring couple had fallen out but few understood the reasons for it.

Keifer and I were perhaps the only ones around that were privy to Ingrid's reasons for the sudden hatred of her husband. She'd come to visit us not long after she lost the baby, full of fresh despair. In hushed whispers the grieving mother told us Bernt visited her and revealed a secret.

That shit stirring asshole was all too eager to inform Ingrid her babies were dead because her Mann recklessly snuck his sick little sisters through the back door. While this information was indeed correct, telling a mother that just lost all she had in the world, not wise.

Obviously, he intentionally picked that moment to put a wrench into Xavier's marriage. Bernt knew damned well of Ingrid's explicit demands that her husband observed the Haus lock down to the letter. He also realized learning that Xavier's betrayal had directly led to the death of her children would set that pretty woman ablaze with desire for revenge.

That's exactly what it did too. On the bright side, it renewed Ingrid's infamous inner strength. I think had Bernt not given her a fresh reason to fight on, she'd given up and gone home to be with her lost little ones.

Yet there was a darker perspective that grew from this discovery. With her love and trust in Xavier crushed beyond repair, Ingrid began having an affair. The man she chose to cuckold her husband with was the one she knew would piss him off the most. Ja, that rat bastard Bernt.

This terrible decision to sleep around with the cruel Bernt was perhaps one of Ingrid's biggest mistakes. Keifer and I realized her indiscretions with that brute long before she confessed them to us. I've often wished that one of us had stood up to either her or him before that revenge fucking got out of control like it did. But again, wishing is as helpful as sitting on your own nut sack.

As that horrible affair went on unchecked behind Xavier's back, his bed went cold. Ingrid wasn't going to rebuild his dynasty by denying him access to her fertile womb. While he assumed her refusal to sleep with him was due to grief, his brother worked often as possible to snag his brother's wife's treasures for himself.

And so it went that by the spring of 1919, Bernt managed to not only cockblock Xavier. He also damned up Ingrid's flow. She discovered herself with child. It was then she finally realized the dangerous position she'd managed to put herself into by slipping around on her Mann.

Fearful that Xavier would have her murdered when he found out what she'd been up to behind his back, she ended her game of freezing him out of her bed. Xavier, ever the fool, couldn't believe his good fortune. He honestly thought his wife had come back to her senses and all between them would return to the way it was.

He quickly and vigorously fucked his Frau and she pretended to be wanton for his sexual attentions. Then as fortune would have it, amazingly, Ingrid announced with a sly smile on her face to the stupid man she was once more expecting. Xavier was thrilled to his darkened heart. He celebrated for two full days, happier than I'd seen him in a very long time.

That clever woman didn't stupidly return her affections to Bernt. She spurned him with speed and refused to continue their secret affair. He was left ignorant of his success, believing like Xavier, his brother once again thwarted his attempts to gain what was never rightfully his to begin with.

Only me and Kiefer were aware of Ingrid's deception. We made a pact between us to never speak a word of his sister's moment of insanity. After all, she'd been through enough already. There wasn't any call for dragging up dirty truths, especially since an innocent unborn kid's life was at stake. Neither of us were sure Xavier would allow that baby to live if he'd known its honest paternity.

So, Xavier and Ingrid were once more the power couple they'd been in times past. Ingrid's belly grew larger as the summer approached. That was a miracle all in of itself considering by this point most of Germany that had survived the flu was slowly starving to death.

That pandemic had hit the young the hardest. Many submissives died because they were the target of that second wave. Amos, that still managed to hold on, ordered Xavier and his new Headmistress Ingrid, the women were hit as hard as the men so she took up that position, to seek out healthy replacements.

For a few weeks, the Headmaster, Headmistress team opened the back door and examined all the available children waiting in the yard. The ravages of war and sickness had left the country in dire straits. Orphans in numbers never seen in our lifetime wandered the lands, all of them looking for food, and shelter. Due to the scare supplies, even within the wealthy Haus, only a handful could be selected.

I couldn't believe my eyes the day Xavier and Ingrid opened the back door to do as Amos commanded. The crowd of desperate children had grown to an enormous size. All of them weeping and begging to be allowed inside. Make-shift tents fashioned out of rags littered the yard almost to the horizon. It was honestly horrific to view the near skeletal young people standing there in droves. This was a scene only the devil would appreciate.

With huge tears running down my face I leaned over to Keifer and said, "What is to become of the ones we cannot accept? Not even the church will have enough space and supplies to feed them all."

Keifer sighed and replied, "Honey, try to remember we didn't create this nightmare. Therefore we aren't responsible to fix it. They will realize soon that there is no help to be found here. Hopefully, they will move on. The ones still strong enough to travel that is."

I shook my head, "And what of the sick and weak? What happens to them?"

He flashed a woeful glance at me as he said, "They will do like the rest of us if something doesn't give soon. They will starve to death."

His cryptic words rang in my ears like church bells announcing a funeral. Xavier and Ingrid chose the requested number and put the lucky babies into the isolation cells. Amos ordered the new recruits be quarantined for a fortnight before allowed to begin their training.

Once the deed was finished, the back door was shut tightly. Xavier doubled barred it to defend against the hundreds of frightened, lost faces that haunted the Haus grounds. This horror wasn't even nearing its apex. I think all of us below were aware sooner or later if shit didn't improve something had to give.

And something did. Late that June, the Great War ended. Germany and all her allies were soundly defeated. While the country lamented her misfortunes, we in the Dungeon celebrated the end of the years of hardship. Boy, we couldn't have been more wrong.

The enemies of Germany didn't care that our Motherland had waved the flag of surrender. They continued to block all routes to the outside world. Their plan was to starve to death the population within her borders. As the fall began, the scarce food supply of the Haus hit a critical low. There was no longer enough left to eat for even half the residents to survive another month.

The dying Fur King was forced to make a decision no one should've had to. From his death bed, he drew up a decree that all submissives in the Haus were to be ejected immediately. The remaining residents were ordered to take up the slack and earn their keep or they could join them.

If that doesn't sound too bad, you'd be wrong to think it. Asking the rich to do their own laundry isn't the thing that made his decree so horrific. But exiling the servants to fend for themselves outside the Haus. Well, that assured they would die slow of starvation. Even if there was any food left anywhere to be found, there wasn't work for a kid that didn't know how to do anything but cook fancy dishes or suck a cock with skill.

I mean I understood why Amos did what he did. He literally was forced to choose who was to die first. If that blockade of our supplies wasn't ended soon, it really didn't matter. We were all going to starve anyway.

With heavy hearts among ear deafening screams of terror echoing through the Haus, all the submissive population was ejected into the awaiting arms of the cold world. I stood there in shocked silence as Xavier and Ingrid ushered out all the children that thought their prayers had been answered. It was not describable the fear and soul wrenching feeling of helplessness that overtook all of us during these dark days.

Watching through barred windows the collapse of our world was hellish enough to cause me foul nightmares for the rest of my days. The Gotts, however, weren't satisfied this was righteous punishment for the Dungeon Masters and Mistresses. They decided to pour on the hurt.

Three days later it became clear that the exiled submissives hadn't left the Haus grounds. Instead, they'd joined the growing forces of starving outside the back door. These desperate young people began to become the dangerous pack of hungry wolves. Many started to assault the outer walls, and others began to make wild attempts to break in through the windows.

Worse still, with so many crowded together in abject squalor and a third wave of the flu upon them, sickness began to rip through their camps. Amos knew the local authorities weren't going to lift a finger to help the residents being held hostage by the starving mob. He was forced to make the most horrific decision I believe any Fur or Silk monarch ever had to make.

The orders came down to us that we were to open the back door as if we were giving in to the loud demands of the crowd. Then, like a well-oiled machine, we were to falsely select the children by groups. Once we had them inside, Amos commanded we destroy them. This terrible action was to be repeated until every last one of them had been eliminated.

I felt like my soul left my flesh and floated above me as Xavier gathered us around with the news. Keifer nodded his approval, as did all the other Masters, when the Headmaster told us this was mercy we were granting the children.

I wanted with all my heart to believed there had to be a better solution but I couldn't deny the brutal facts of life. These youngsters were dying slow and painfully. There was nothing anyone among us could do to save them. Sending them to their grave quickly and with regret was better than allowing starvation to do its work.

So, we all drew straws. The two shortest pulled would be the ones to select the groups to be let in. The two mid-sized would drag the corpses to the back after the deeds were done. They would store them in the empty cells to await cremation in mass when the darkness came. The rest of the Masters would be expected to move with speed to breaking their necks or strangle the invited former submissives and orphans.

In the first day, Max and Drexel pulled the shortest straws. Me and Derbeck pulled corpse duty and all the rest, including Keifer, were tasked with the killings. I must tell you, this was not something I'd wish on my worst enemy. I have trouble retelling the terrible things I saw to this very day.

When the sun rose, Max and Drexel opened the back door. The awaiting mob was thrilled to see the Dungeon Masters coming out among them to select new recruits at last. The fellows had no problem gathering up about a dozen to invite into their lair. The excited children chattered happily as they were ushered into the pit.

Their voices fell to silence as they entered the cell to witness the awaiting Masters and Mistresses, ja, Ingrid, Helga and Heidi weren't excluded from Amos's commands. I sometimes still hear their screams of terror as the group of

Dungeon employees lit on them and made short work of their suffering.

Me and Derbeck worked without a word between us, but many tears. We moved with speed to drag off the broken little corpses. This brutality went on in the repeat for hours.

I lost count at fifty and decided it was best to never know how many babies I aided to murder. By the time the sun set, two things had happened. One, we'd destroyed every kid in that yard, and two, all of us had become numb to the act of killing the helpless.

When at last me and Keifer were permitted to return to our cell and get rest. I laid in his arms unable to cry a single tear. It felt like the world had gone mad, and we were hostages of the insanity.

Sleep didn't come to either of us but it wasn't the sights and sounds that kept our eyes open. It was the putrid smell of burning flesh that choked the air brought in through the ventilation. The flames of the pyre raged all night and into the next morning fueled by hundreds of what we thought were the last victims of the Great War.

Sadly, it only took two days for this very same situation to begin anew. A fresh mob of starving children was gathering at the back door. Amos demanded we cull the children with speed. Once again we drew straws. This time, I wasn't as lucky as the first.

Keifer and Heidi drew the shortest. Bernt and the remaining Kraus male drew corpse detail. I was forced to join with my brothers and sisters in ending the tribulations of dozens of desperate young people. A few times between breaking the neck of a sobbing little boy or girl, I'd steal a glance at the others in the cell.

Drexel, Barnham, Helga, Xavier and Ingrid (to my dismay) seemed to be enjoying their dark work. This realization bothered me far more than you can know. I wasn't too surprise to see this wasn't a hardship for the first four I mentioned. But to witness the one time kind hearted mother murdering with a glint of thrill in her expression nearly broke my spirit in two.

That night I managed to catch up with Ingrid before she returned to her cell and before Keifer returned to my side. I had to know the truth of what I thought I saw in her earlier that day. With fear of what she would say deep in my heart I approached cautiously.

I checked that no one was within earshot as I said to her, "Hard day, ja? I think I may have to increase my drinking habit to live with the crimes I've committed. I cannot imagine how tough it would be on my soul if I couldn't stay too drunk to demonstrate good judgement."

Ingrid looked at me and flashed a bitter smile as she responded, "My soul is at peace without the use of the alcohol shield. I'm sorry you suffer, brother Claus. I think you are looking at this situation all wrong if you honestly do feel remorse over it."

I was shocked to hear her say that. "How can you be so cold about this Ingrid? We are murdering children for Gott's sake. I would think you of all of us would demonstrate deep sympathy."

She shook her head as she replied, "I don't feel bad at all for them, Claus. Why should I? Do any of them deserve to survive any more than my own babies did? My children were as innocent, perhaps more so, than any I've sent to the grave today. As for your question about my lack of warmth. The answer is very simple, Claus. I view each one of them as competition. If I don't kill them, they will bust into the Haus and eat all the food we have left. Then me and my baby are going to starve. If you think on what I just said, you'd stop torturing yourself with feelings of misplaced sympathy. It's them or us brother. I choose us. See you tomorrow." She patted me on the shoulder and took off to join her husband in their cell.

This is the way it went for a few more months. Even when at last of the blockade of Germany's routes to obtain supplies finally ended, hyperinflation overtook the country. Many thousands died from starvation thanks to their inability to afford even the crumbs from the garbage cans. It seemed the woe and misery was never to end.

The year 1920 rolled in to find our people struggling to survive and a new government ruling the country. The Weimar Republic was rather ineffective at staving off the terrible punishments the world seemed to lay at the door of Germany. Though we weren't responsible for the outbreak of that war, most if not all the nations blamed us for it. Keeping the Motherland from ever rising again was the goal in mind of all countries that called themselves the Allies.

I cannot say there was nothing good about the Weimar Republic. One thing that happened under their rule was a universal progressive viewpoint. Under their governmental control women's status improved vastly. They were permitted to vote, hold land and no longer viewed as nothing more than property of their fathers or husbands.

There was also a more permissive attitude regarding the way a person expressed their love or with whom they choose to adore. Schwulers weren't completely accepted in the society as the whole but this was a period of time when less fuss was made about their existence.

All that aside, within the Haus, things started to change also. Amos was taking his final breaths as the early spring of 1920 began. His last wishes were witnessed by the remaining Princes of the Fur. The Silk King was among the many to succumb to the third flu wave late in 1919. His throne had remained open but no one was too upset about it. They were all too worried about where they would get their next meal.

In one of his last moves on Earth, Amos decided to give his old enemies the Schmidts a good kick in the hodensack. He ignored the tradition of raising the Head Dungeon Master to the throne and selected my husband Keifer in Xavier's rightful place.

This news both stunned and thrilled me and my Mann. We'd suffered terrible tragedies and been forced to behave like demons for a decade. All the while never daring to hope that one day it would pay off so soundly.

With excitement in our hearts we packed away our dungeon harnesses for the last time. Descending those stairs we'd cried our eyes out. As we climbed up them hand in hand, once again there was water bathing our cheeks. This time it was from tears of joy.

Amos wasn't a total idiot. He'd realized the wasn't enough Altergotts left alive to prevent Xavier's clan from taking power. The old goat brought the Headmaster and his nearly ready to pop wife up from the foundation as well. Amos named the Headmaster first prince of the Silk, knowing full well that insult wouldn't sit well with his nemesis.

To further deepen this discord among the united clans, he placed Kristian in the empty forth Silk throne and Max into the fifth. This left two hard to kill Wagners in the second and third placement. Amos realized Bernt and Derbeck's anger at being passed over for two Reinhardts that served far less time would set those men ablaze.

Last, he filled his empty Fur thrones with three eligible Elders of the powerful Wobben clan and raised that lazy Altergott to Fur King. Normally he couldn't do all that without Council's approval. But thanks to the huge number of fatalities that left most of the Princes' ten thrones, and Silk Throne, empty, no one held enough support to dispute his authority.

After that sly move to put a deadly wedge between the united Reinhardts and Schmidts, the bastard finally died. I was grateful to notice no one in the Haus mourned too much the day they screwed that sonofabitch into the Earth. No one ever forgave him for letting the flu in and kicking their beloved submissives out.

Well, Keifer and I weren't worried. Xavier was married to Ingrid, and even if we didn't completely trust him we could be assured of her loyalty to us. Xavier was smitten as ever with the still beautiful sister of my husband. He may have bitched about being misused by Amos, but we assumed he wouldn't dare to blame us for it.

That was our next biggest mistake, but once again, not even close to our worst.

We'd barely unpacked our meager possessions when a messenger arrived with a letter for Keifer in hand. It turned out Bladrick's life outside the Haus hadn't faired any better than most during those hard years. He informed his favorite cousin that he'd married that girl he'd been courting.

He went on to report their love had produced two beautiful children. Bladrick, as the proud pappa, had worked long hours in that factory job his wife promised her father would give him. That wasn't the career he enjoyed but his wife and babies made it worth the pains.

Then came the war and with it the flu. Bladrick caught a case of it from work in the fall of 1919 and before he knew he was sick, infected his little family. It was a tragedy to read that our old friend was the broken man. He'd survived his dance with the influenza only to end up burying his wife and children.

The reason he was writing Keifer was to request he seek favor with Amos to gain him permission to return. Bladrick no longer had reason or desire to continue in his colorless life as the widower factory worker.

Without his son to carry on his honorable name, he believed nothing he did honestly mattered anymore. A job in the horrible Dungeon was a better future for the broken hearted man than the one he was facing.

Kiefer went to Xavier, Kristian and Max to request their support in allowing Bladrick to re-enter the Haus. Kristian and Max readily agreed. Xavier stated he would do as Keifer asked if Bladrick accepted placement in the Dungeon as Headmaster.

This strange request didn't make sense at first. It was logical to assume Xavier would push to have either Derbeck or Bernt granted that coveted title. It was only after Ingrid visited with us and explained the situation we understood why Xavier desired this done.

He feared his brothers would someday become a threat to his bid to hold the Fur Throne. You see, it used to be tradition that only a Headmaster that served five years in that position could rise that high. Xavier was obviously attempting to block his power hungry brother Bernt and the overly popular Derbeck from meeting that criteria.

Keifer didn't like the idea of Xavier thinking so far ahead. Xavier was only twenty-seven at the time. My husband was aware that thanks to the war, many of the old traditions were being bent or broken. This led him to worry that his brother-in-law may have been stupidly planning to start a war with the newly risen Wobbens and left over Altergotts.

I was certain my Mann's fears were unfounded. Only a total idiot would dare to be gearing up to make a move on the Elders thrones before they were even thirty years old. Despite my statements of disbelief, Keifer insisted that Xavier was up to something. He insisted I keep my back to the wall and eyes open wide till he could figure out what.

So, in the Summer of 1920, Bladrick returned to Das Kaiser Haus for the last time. He spent an afternoon catching up on old times. He was forced to sit in the luxury apartment listening to the stories of our triumphs and tragedies. Later in his life, Bladrick confessed to me while Keifer blathered on, all he could do is think this could've been mine but I thought it a fools error to serve below.

Well, Bladrick learned his lesson. He went below to serve as Headmaster without a single word of quarrel about it. Not even after discovering that Keifer had the power to prevent him from serving below. That could only mean one thing. Bladrick was a man that was aspiring for future power in the Haus.

Not long after Bladrick came home to us, we received word that Ingrid had gone into labor. Keifer and I rushed to the Haus clinic. We arrived just as the doctor come out of the birthing room to announce both mother and son were healthy. He reported the baby was strong, well-formed and without visible disfigurement.

All three of us breathed sighs of relief. Xavier was already in the waiting area looking like a man about to have the stroke. The first Prince looked at his brother in law with a huge grin on his face. No doubt Xavier was thrilled to be once again the proud father.

I stood there watching the two men embrace wondering how Keifer could ever suspect this man of foul intentions toward us. It was at that moment the doctor approached Xavier and asked him if they'd chosen a name for their boy.

Xavier's smile melted to the frown as he replied, "Uhm, that's Ingrid's department. I just sire them and she pretty much does all the rest."

The doctor shook his head as he replied, "She said you'd say that. I'm asked by your wife to request this kid is given a name by his honorable father. Please honorable Voter I must have something to put onto the birth certificate other than male baby."

Xavier startled for a moment then after pursing his lips replied, "Ah, she grants me a great honor. Tell her I thank her for the mercy of it. Let's see, hmm, got it. I had the imaginary friend to play with as a boy. His name was Justus. I think if the Lady doesn't mind the name, I'd like to call him that."

Ingrid's voice called out, "That's a beautiful name darling. Justus it shall be." We all turned our stunned attention toward the pretty woman standing in the delivery room entry.

Ingrid smiled at Kiefer, and Xavier then stole a glance at me as she said, "He has his father's eyes. What do you think husband?" She looked at me then quickly winked with a diabolical expression.

Xavier was handed the baby while still appearing shocked his wife was out of bed as he replied, "It just like looking into a mirror, my beloved. Hello baby Justus. I'm your Daddy and this over here is your mother."

Well, at least Xavier had one of that kid's parents correct.

Chapter 7: Death of a Twin
Master Mad Maxx and submissive Meine Liebe

In truth it's impossible to understand the reasons behind the story of Master Mad Maxx without hearing all the details that went into his creation. On the surface it seems Claus is simply an old pervert trying to clear his conscious of all the rotten things he'd done in his life but if you listen very closely, you realize he is giving us the answer to every unbelievable brutal act we've been reading about for over twenty-one books. Now if only Maxximillian would be still maybe I can finish and move on before we are all as elderly as Claus was.

I fidgeted and snorted as I yelled out at Claus, "So Justus is Peter's brother. Why the fuck should I care? One brute Schmidt is bad as another. The whole lot of them not worth piss. For that matter, why are you filling my head with traumas of the past? Do I really need to add your Gott damned nightmares to my own? I've read plenty of history books. I know what happened to Germany and other countries during the Great War. It's terrible stuff no one disputes that. However, I do believe that my own suffering would be familiar to though poor children you knew back then. The way I see it, they luckier than me. None of them lived to face the damage done to dare flesh by the ravages of war and famine. They are at peace and I'm still fighting the losing battles. I beg of you to stop wasting my time with your personal tales of woe. I get it. Ingrid, Bladrick and you are products of your environment. Therefore I should just roll over and forgive all the horrible things you've done to me, yadda, yadda, and all that utter bullshit. Fine! If that's what you want to hear, then so be it. You are forgiven because you've opened my eyes at last. I'm the asshole for hating you. All this time you really are a saint and not a sinner. Happy now? If so, then get to the point, dammit. I sick of your head games."

Claus again came off his pillow with speed and grabbed me by Lucus's collar. "I am trying to do as you asked of me, boy. Did you really think all you've endured wasn't personal? Honestly? Surely you knew better. You are the most coveted soul that ever walked the halls of this fucking hell on earth. Everyone wants to be the one to force you to your knees to be called your Master. Why is that? Only one man can answer that question. Instead of being grateful, you insist on being a fucking rude brute about it. I'm not messing with you mind. Well boy, if you are ready to face what you been hiding from, then so am I."

I gasped and swallowed hard as Claus glared at me hard with his steel grey eyes. "I already know Jonas, Peter, Lucus, all them want to submit me so they can be called the Master of the Haus. That's not the question I asked of you. What I want to know is why…" He shook me by the collar with unexpected strength which caused me to go silent immediately in a stun.

He growled low as he said, "You think you got this all figured out do you? Ah, well you're dead wrong, little man. Each man seeking to possess you has reasons far deeper than what you think. If you don't hear the whole story, you cannot know their truthful motivation. Without that information, eventually one of them will get what he been battling for since me and Ingrid leveled you Priceless. That horror wasn't supposed to ever happen. There wasn't anything else we could do to save your life. We searched for you and your brother for two years. Praying against all hope you boys would be found alive. Me and Ingrid nearly died from the grief of losing our precious babies. When at last your mother agreed, we'd paid a big enough price to her for your return, we were overjoyed. But she returned only one of our twin boys. If that wasn't enough to send both me and Ingrid into deep mourning, the thing that Agnette brought to us wasn't our beloved Prince. Hell, it wasn't even human. It was nothing but a screaming, shutting, mindless beast completely broken by the horrors it had endured."

I shook my head slowly and tried to back away from the angered Elder. "I don't understand what you are saying Claus. Please stop the games. I withdraw the question. I beg your forgiveness for asking it. It's none of my business what you were doing with Ingrid down in the Dungeons. That's ancient history. So, it doesn't matter anymore, ja? I will never mention it again, I swear it. Can I have the candy you promised now?"

Claus's furious eyes began to water and a tear ran down his cheek as he said through clenched teeth, "Nein, I cannot face Ingrid, Keifer or your brother without being able to claim I tried one final time to fix what we broke. You listen hard Maximillian or Christian Axel. I want you to close your eyes and hear my voice. Don't you remember me? Your favorite Auntie Claus? Can you feel your grand mutter Ingrid holding you and your brother. Is that a nursery rhyme she is reciting? Does her hugging feels good, ja? Do you push your brother trying to get all her attention or do you cry and cling to her breast, heart broken by your siblings aggressions toward you?" I felt incapable of denying his commands as my lids shut against my will.

I saw an elderly woman. She was smiling at me. Her hair was white as snow, and her eyes blue as the sky. The Lady smelled of roses and her hugging made me feel safe. I could hear her sweet voice singing a pretty tune in my mother tongue: "Sing a song of sixpence. A pocket full of rye. Oh my goodness Maximillian. You are such a busy boy. Claus, sweetheart. I must beg of you not to give the little ones so much sugar. They are the handful as it is." Her laughter rises into the air like the sound of the songbirds.

I hear the man we know as our Aunt Claus, "Aw, Ingrid. Let the boys enjoy it while they can. Soon enough they will be old potbellied grouches like me. Oh what I wouldn't give to have the racing metabolism once more. Ha."

The woman we call grandmother giggles and we giggle because she does. "You still the sprig of a boy, Claus. I see you keeping up with Der Hund without breaking the sweat."

Aunt Claus nods his head. "The boys make a man feel young again Ingrid my dear. Come here to me my little lamb. Why the tears, honey? Did that brute Der Hund push you off granny's lap again? Well that's not nice, is it? Maximillian, what have we told you about picking on your big brother? Ah, how can a fellow be upset with you for long? Look at him Ingrid. He is the clever boy. He already knows I cannot deny him when he flits those big blue eyes of his. How can you stand it? The Princes are natural seducers, both of them. Das Kaiser Haus is gonna fall to her knees and worship at their feet I tell you."

Our grandmother nods and snuggles us close to her. Me and my brother wiggle hard trying to gain a tight grip, with grins on our faces. He looks at me, and I gaze at him. Our world is a place of love, safety, and joy. We are the Princes of Das Kaiser Haus. It's our destiny to save the Haus from the evil that grips it. We will unite the silver with the gold.

I open my eyes feeling frightened. "What's happening? What are you doing to me, Claus. Get out of my head. It's the candy. You drugged the candy. Let me go. I want to go home. Where is my mother? Help me. Someone, anyone…" Claus backhanded me with sped to end my calls of distress.

He stared hard into my eyes. "Be still. Look at me. You hear only my voice. You will answer me. You and your brother are sleeping in your soft bed. It's dark. The door opens and someone comes inside. It's not your grandmother. It's not your Auntie Claus. This person hits you and your brother hard. You're fading into unconsciousness. You see the face above you. Who is this you see?"

I look up into the face of woman. I know her. I cannot recall where I've seen her before. She hits us when we try to scream for grandmother. Darkness comes.

Suddenly I'm on the first floor of the Haus. I travel with speed down the hallway forced to follow. My heart begins to race. I see that Leo is leading us by the Elder's leash. All around me the collars are upset. I know why but my Master doesn't.

Stefan's corpse has been discovered by the Haus doctor. We see a woman's face. This is the monster the hit us. Max is sure of it. He pushes us from the wheel. He takes the knife we hid in our pocket. There is a flash of steel. Evelyn falls to the floor.

We are sure nobody saw us stab her in the back. She stares at us but cannot speak.

Her lips move to say without sound, "It's not possible, you were too small to remember…"

But Max, he did recall. Evelyn is the woman that took us away from our happy home with grandmother. She snuck us out of the Haus, but someone helped her by unlocking the Dungeon back door. Hemmel, he helped Evelyn hand us over to Gerard.

I snapped out of the trance. "Stop it, Claus. I know what you are doing. These memories are bullshit. You and Ingrid put them inside my brain. None of that happened. I didn't have a fucking twin brother. I'll kill you if you try to do that witchcraft shite to me again." I pushed the feeble Elder off me with a grunt.

Claus fell onto his back with a groan. "You need more chocolate. Let me call the black collar attendant. We are going to get to the bottom of this conspiracy if it's the last thing I do." He reached for the phone sitting on his nightstand.

I blocked his attempt by grabbing his wrist. "I don't want more of your Gott damned drugged candy, Claus. I think I've figured out what you and Ingrid were up to. You and her put false memories in my head so that I would kill all your enemies for you. That's the answer isn't it? She hated Xavier for killing her children with the flu. Same thing for Heidi and Helga. I'm guessing Hemmel pissed her off too and that horrible Drexel and Barnham. You said you didn't like them. That's a pretty shitty reason to kill someone but I can't deny both those bastards had it coming. Why didn't you and that bitch do your own dirty work? Why pick on me." I pushed his hand back at him angrily.

The Elder took a deep breath then calmly said, "Inside my dresser is a blue file folder. It's dusty and aged so you'll know it when you see it. Go get it for me will you love?"

I glared at him in disbelief. "You trying to distract me? Really? I asked you a question. Answer me dammit."

Claus smiled bitterly as he said in almost a whisper, "I'm trying to boy. You refuse to do this the easy way so, I'm forced to be cruel. Go get that folder and bring it to me. Tell you what. If you do this, I'll double the amount of candy I promised to give you."

I shook my head with vigor. "Nein, I told you I don't want more of your drugged sweets. Tell me the truth or I kill you." I leaned closer to him and poised my busted hands to make ready to wring his scrawny neck.

The Elder didn't even appear the least bid anxious as he calmly replied, "Ah, you dare to deny the mother Lamb the

256

treats I offer to her? Where is she boy? Wait, no need to answer that. I can hear her calling. She's in your pocket, ja? Listen. She's telling you to accept the candy and do as your King tells you to do. You know better than to disobey the mother Felicity. I'd hurry before you make her angry. We both know what happens when the mother loses her temper." He smiled at me with a glint of mischief in his expression.

I startled when he said that. "Huh? You can speak the language of the Lamb? How can that be? Nein, you're still fucking with my head. Claus, I don't wish to hurt you but I've no choice. You forcing me to do this." I rushed forward and ignoring the agony in my hands began to apply pressure to cut off his air supply.

Claus barely struggled against my hold as he rasped out, "I don't dare put words in the mother Lamb's mouth boy. Listen, Gott dammit. She is crying out for the candy. You must give it to her. Der Hund commands it." I let go of him with speed and pulled away as if he caught fire.

With my eyes wide in horror I whispered, "You know where Der Hund has gone? Please, tell me where he is. I beg of you, your Majesty. I cannot understand a thing Felicity says without him around to translate and that fucking Lamb raping Taube cannot be trusted. Help me Claus. I'm lost without him."

Claus nodded and coughed hard as he pointed at his dresser. "You go get that folder like I asked you, and with its help we will discover where he has gone together boy. Hurry, fetch it and I will call for the sweets the mother demands." I felt my heart racing as I rushed from his bed to mind him.

I pulled open the drawer and dug through it frantically. Behind me I heard the Elder speaking on the phone with someone. He told the person the Fur King wanted a batch of his Priceless candy bars and demanded they moved their asses.

I found the item he wanted rather quickly. With mild curiosity I held it up to look at it more closely. There wasn't any writing on the outside. Other than appearing quite old there wasn't anything usual about it. You could find one like it on every shelf in the Library at the Hall of Records. I shrugged my shoulders over this silly request he'd made and returned to his bedside the folder in tow.

Claus sat up in his bed and took it from me without expression. He reached out and patted my head. Then he commented that I was a good boy. It took all I had not to knock the hell out of him for treating me no better than a fucking pet dog.

If he realized my fury over that rude action, he showed no symptoms of it. I clinched my jaws while watching that bastard open that folder. He didn't say a word but his breathing began to go shallow. This sudden change in his demur surprised me.

I shot a stunned look at that file. His behaviors had perked my interest quite a bit. I decided to snatch it the second he wasn't paying it any mind. Whatever he was reading from it seemed to be disturbing to him. I sure as hell wanted to know any secrets that could upset this man like this one seemed to be.

A knocking at the door appeared to be my best chance to go for it. Claus sucked in his breath and trembled as he yelled out the visitor could enter. A male black collar come rushing into the room carrying three brightly colored candy bars. My mouth began to water and tummy rumbled upon seeing those yummy treats.

The Elder refused to break his attention from that coveted binder. "Give them to the Mortar King. Then get the fuck out. Lock the door behind you Deiter. You shall tell no one of anything you've witnessed or heard of this situation. If I discover you've disobeyed me, you will be feeding trees by the sunrise." The black collar bowed his head and quickly did as he was told in silence without hesitation.

I glared at him angrily as he tried to throw the candy bars at my head. "I don't want this poison. You get that shit out of my face asshole or what the Fur King threatens, I will do to you doubly." The poor Haus submissive shot a fearful glance at Claus unsure what to do with contradicting orders coming from two Kings.

Claus didn't look up from his reading as he calmly said, "Dieter, you will ignore the rude Mortar King. Drop the candy at his feet and do as I told you immediately. Don't force me to waste another breath. I thank you for the perfect service. Now get out." As you may have guessed that young man was more than relieved to let go of the sweets and run like hell.

I stared at the abandoned chocolate laying at my boots in the near trace as I growled, "You are the stubborn old goat, Claus. Why the fuck don't you stop stealing the precious air from the living and die already? I'm not feeling really fit these days but I bet I can manage enough energy to do at least one dance when you become the corpse."

The Elder sighed loudly and finally glanced up from his reading. "That was a nasty thing to say. You know you remind me of that brutal father of yours when you say shit like that. Is that what you honestly wish to become? A miniature version of the most hated man to ever live in the Haus?"

I scoffed as I responded, "You been so busy fucking me over to notice, but this man's not a miniature anything Claus. When I'm done with this motherfucking hell hole everyone will recall Xavier's reign as 'the good old days.'"

The Fur King tisked, "Well, that's a disappointment to hear you say it. Not really a surprise but no doubt the fact of it is breaking your grandmother's heart. She'd believed her greatest creations would rise from the ashes of the destruction we caused. and then liberate the trapped souls within these walls. Turns out, no matter what we've tried, there is no preventing history from repeating itself. At least the worst parts of it anyway." He blew out his breath with a frustrated sound.

I shrugged. "You'll be dead, so not sure why you care. Besides, if I'm the monster, you and everyone that lives here only have themselves to blame. I want to know what's so

260

important about that file you reading. Give it to me." I put out my hand to receive it.

Claus's expression went dark. "What will you give me for it? You know better. Nothing in the Haus is free of charge."

I groaned. "I'll give you the oral services."

He shook his head. "You are already obligated to do that, and we will get around to that soon enough. No deal.."

That pissed me off. "What the fuck do you want for it then? You know I'm the poor man."

Claus stole a glance at the candy bars. "Do as the mother lamb says. Eat that candy. Refuse my price and I rip up this folder. Then you'll never know of its contents."

With a growl I picked up the chocolate bars. "Fine. You are an asshole. Before I eat this, swear to me on your mother's grave they aren't drugged." I looked at the sweets nearly insane with desire to devour them like a starving hund.

Claus chuckled. "I'll do no such a thing. If you don't trust me then throw them away. I am happy to do the same to this blasted file the second you do. As it is I'd be thrilled to know it's gone forever. The fucking thing's been a stone around my neck for the last nine and half years. No doubt, I can die far more peacefully if you refuse this bargain. So, either eat that candy or stop bothering me with your questions that cause me torture that I likely more than deserve."

That caused me a bit of confusion and thrill. "You honestly are pained at having to speak with me? I thought you enjoyed forcing me to listen to your stupid old man stories."

He shook his head. "I suppose most elderly folks would find pleasure at re-living their days of glory. This worthless brute, however, isn't one of the lucky ones. My life had the potential to be one that'd give me pride to recall, but I think I had the reverse Midas touch. Instead of making gold I created shit. I drowned in it all my days, and even now I can barely breath from the stench of it. Are you going to eat the fucking sweets or are we done here? I'm growing tired and you still owe me a special service call, you know."

That statement made up my mind. I ripped open the wrappers and stuffed the candy into my eager mouth without any attempt at manners. Claus sat there watching me in silence. I thought it odd, but his expression appeared grief stricken or maybe pitiful.

At the time I didn't let it bother me. All I cared about was that chocolate and buying time not to have to service him. The more I ate, the more I desired chocolate. That cold sweating came over me almost the second that sugary sweetness kissed my tongue. Pleasure filled my senses to tingling and my breathing became labored. When the candy was gone, I licked each wrapper clean and considered eating them like I always do.

Claus cleared his throat and broke me from that weird trancing, "Okay, come back and sit with me boy. I will give you a moment to calm, then as promised I will share the contents of this folder with you." I dutifully returned to the spot next to him and attempted to gain a comfortable position never takin my curious eyes off the blue binder.

The Fur King leaned into my face and said, "Look into my eyes. What color are thy?"

I startled at the question. "I'm not sure Claus. Maybe grey or light blue? The same as the marble pillars in the Great Hall I think."

He chuckled. "You always say that. I want to speak with Christian Axel."

With a scoff I replied, "He's busy at the moment." I shot a look at the triple shard focusing on Christian.

Claus shook his head. "Then let me speak with Der Hund. Tell Felicity I need him to attend his Master. She can have him back shortly."

I groaned in dismay. "I told you Der Hund is missing, Claus. Christian has stupidly gotten himself into a mess by takin the wheel in triplicate. You speak with me, Maxximillian, or you shit out of luck." I giggled over the Elder's dilemma.

That caused him to gasp. "You are Maximillian, you say? Hmm, I usually speak with Christian Axel or Der Hund. Christian is in there with you but Der Hund is gone?"

I nodded. "Damn, you going deaf? Ja, that's what I just said daddy-o. Now what the fuck you want? Do you not see

I'm the busy man? I've got a Haus to run, you old buzzard. State your business then move on."

Claus drew in his breath and handed me the file. "Okay, Maximillian. This is the Coroner's report your grandmother Ingrid managed to obtain from Denmark the day they buried Christian Axel. If he is in the ground, then how can he be in the wheel room with you? If they buried you Maximillian under the false name. Then how can I be speaking with a dead boy? I want to speak with Der Hund so we can clear up this misunderstanding. I've been told he is in the green fields. Let's ask the lamb to lead us to him. She knows how to get there, ja?"

I snorted loudly. "Coroner's report? I don't know anyone by that name. Why should I care what he writes in that folder. I'm not dead but you're sure going to be, and soon. Is this man Herr Coroner the one I need to kill for burying some poor kid in a grave and saying that was me? He's in Denmark you say? Well I'm putting that motherfucker's name on Felicity's list immediately. When I escaping the Haus, I'm will hunt him down. Then before I murder him, I will make him tell everyone the truth."

Claus nodded. "Ah, ja. that's the wise thing to do, but how can he do that? No one knows what the truth is but you, my love. What he writes about you and your brother in this folder is only what he could know through observation of the end results of your horror. The details of it never have been determined because you cannot face the trauma of it and I never forced you to. Your grandmother and Uncle Bladrick believed your madness stems from the deep denial of what

264

happened in Gerard's barn. I refused to risk all that we'd recovered of the boy that survived. You're right. I'm dying Maximillian or Christian, whichever one you may be. Once I'm gone no one, there will be no one left to protect you from yourself, your nightmare memories, or the monsters in the Haus."

I sneered at him. "You call a lifetime of rape and torture protecting me? Wow! Get out of my face Claus. I'm sick to death of looking at you. You can take your so called protection and that Coroner fellow's words and shove them up your hairy ass."

The Fur King leaned in closer and bellowed out, "Maximillian, I command you to follow the lamb to the green fields. She know the way. Your brother is there. He needs your help. They cannot find him. You know where he is because…"

I gasped in terror, "I was in the green field with him."

Claus nodded and as he stifled a sob he said, "You and your brother are through the back door. The night is dark and cold. The big man called Gerard tells you to be silent or he will hit you. Two little boys, mirror image of the other, huddle together in the back of his truck. You are afraid. You cry for your grandmother but she isn't coming. Gerard drives for a long time. He stops only to take you to make water or slap the brothers for weeping too loudly. Where does he take you and your brother?"

I see the old barn. It's grey and withered against the cloudy sky. We think it's scary looking with many cobwebs and broken windows. We are frightened and cold. We cling to each other and this angers Gerard.

He stands like a giant over us,. "If you little brats insist on hugging like a couple schwuler cowards, then so be it. Less chain and space required that way. Hold still you bastards." He put the metal collars on our necks.

We weep helplessly as Gerard padlocks the short chain to the manacles. We cannot make a move without dragging each other along with us. The cruel man teethers us to the wall inside that scary barn with another chain of heavy links.

Gerard laughs as we hold each other trembling. "Ah, now isn't that adorable? Why don't you give each other kisses to go with the hugging? Ha! The Princes of Das Kaiser Haus, my ass. You boys be still, and keep those big mouths shut. If I hear so much as a fart from either of you, well the lambs will be feasting well this spring on the grass your flesh will feed." We watch him leave and close the door.

It's dark in the barn. The smell of rotten hay and decay filled the air. We are afraid of the big spiders that crawl around on the dirt floor. The chain prevents us from leaving the corner of the ancient horse stall. The animals that used to live in this place are all dead. No one knows where we are. We cry in each other's arms for a long time hoping this is a bad dream.

The days come and go. There is nowhere to go to make the yellow or brown waste. We are trapped sitting in the foulness. Gerard comes through the door sometimes with a bowl of mush and a jug of water.

We share this food but the hunger is terrible. We try to forget our troubles by playing games with each other or by singing the nursery rhymes grandmother taught us.

Most of the time, we spend all day weeping in each other's arms till we fall asleep from exhaustion.

The winter is coming. The cold makes our teeth chatter and toes numb. The clothing we wear have begun to rot away from the lack of vision. Gerard brings us a single blanket. We share it and struggle to stay warm. Maximillian says we are going to die. Christian believes this is true also. We think our grandmother doesn't love us anymore. Where is she? Why has she let this mean man lock us away in the cold darkness?"

The Fur King voice is trembling as he says, "Your grandmother is looking for her babies. Gerard has stolen the Princes from her. Tell me who do I speak with? Is this you my little lamb Christian? Or is this my tiny Goldene Hund Maximillian?"

"Ja. I am here Aunty Claus. I am Christian Axel. I am Maximillian."

Claus draws in a ragged breath. "One of you isn't here for long. Tell me boys, what did that mean man Gerard do when the spring came?"

"Maximillian learned to pick the locks. He freed Christian. We escaping the chains. The night was dark. Maximillian fell and hurt his legs. Christian helped him to keep running. Gerard and his woman were chasing us with their hounds. Our feet were too slow. They caught us. Gerard dragged us by the hair back to the scary barn. He was angry that we got away. He had a knife, Aunt Claus."

The Elder paused for a moment and then whispered, "What did he do with the knife?"

"Gerard cut up the little toy hund that nice lady gave to us. He tore out his stuffing because we forgot to hide him in the straw."

Claus frowned and leaned in close. "That's the lie I put into your memory to hide a painful truth. Think hard little one. Gerard did use that knife on something precious to you but it wasn't the toy puppy. It was your brother. Look again. I give you permission to remember and this time I don't block nor soften the blow."

"Gerard, he took that knife and stuck it deep in my brother's tummy. I tried to beg him to stop. Gerard didn't listen. He says my brother will feed the baby lambs in the Green Fields. No, don't do this. Leave us alone. Mother, help us."

"Oh my Gott, there is blood everywhere. He is screaming. Gerard puts him back in the chains with me. Oh nein, please don't cry, brother. I help you put the squishy things back inside your stomach. I hold the cut closed so they don't get out again. On nein, they keep falling out. Please, help us. Mother, where are you. He is hurt. Make him better. He says he is cold and cannot see. He cries and doesn't stop screaming. It has been two days and nights but he won't heat the food. He says it makes more pain."

"He thinks he is dying. Nein, don't die brother. Don't go to the green fields. Please wake up. Don't go to sleep. I'm afraid to be alone in the dark. Why doesn't he wake up?"

"There are flies and worms in his eyes. The are all over him. His flesh is falling off. Wake up brother. Help me put your skin back on your bones. He won't eat. He doesn't play or sing to me anymore. Mother help us. I cannot stop him from disappearing. What is happening?"

Claus puts his hand on my cheek. "Hush, it is alright, my little one. I'm here with you. Your brother is gone to be with the angels. He's not in pain anymore but you suffer still. Who is this boy I've given my heart to? Are you Maximillian or are you Christian Axel?"

"I am Maximillian. I am Christian Axel. Make him wake up, Aunt Claus. Don't you understand? He must put on his skin or he will catch the sickness from the cold nights. I put him under the blanket and share the food without arguing. I don't want to be alone in the dark. Can you hear him? He is singing to me."

The Elder nodded. "Those are the angels in Heaven he sings with, Christian."

"I am Maximillian. I am Christian. Nein, we are not the angels and there is no Heaven. That skeleton is not important. He is with me. His tummy fell out and the worms ate his flesh. I told him to come to live with me. My Haus is not falling apart. My brother is not dead, or in the Green Fields. He is in the chains next to me. We are here together forever."

269

Claus sucked in his breath then said, "Gerard didn't unchain you boys even after one died. For two years you suffered the horrors of that short tether to your beloved brother's rotting corpse. Alone, in that dark abandoned barn. Sitting in your own wastes, half starved, beaten regularly, and without hope. How did you survive the harsh German winters, Maximillian."

"I am Maximillian. I am Christian. The blanket. Gerard brings the blanket on the cold nights. We snuggle together against the cold. We play games with the baby lambs and the horses sometimes bite us. There are many animals in the barn to keep away the loneliness. We wish Gerard wouldn't have cut up the little Goldene Hund though. We loved that toy. It wasn't nice of him, ja?"

The old man shook his head. "Christian Axel, honey there were no animals in that barn. You couldn't have used your brother's warmth in the winter. The coroner's report stated the mummified remains they found chained to you were part of the corpse of your twin brother who was no older than six years ole. Sweetheart, you weren't rescued until after your eighth birthday. Your brother has been dead for over two years."

"I am Maximillian. I am Christian Axel. That's a lie. There are animals there. I can see and hear them. My brother isn't dead. He is here. You speak with him and we weren't rescued. We dies and came back to life. Gerard attacked us and he cut us up. See the scars? He thought he killed us. He took us to the Green Fields and buried us in the ground."

Claus nodded then gently stroked my cheek. "That's almost right Maximillian. Gerard didn't attack you, you attacked him, remember?"

"I am Maximillian. I am Christian Axel. Nein, he tried to touch us. He wanted to take our skeleton away. Nein, he wants to put it in the ground. That's not his. We won't let him do it. We see his straight razor. He's been shaving. He says he is going to take us home and he is to look nice for the membership ceremony. We hear him saying he is getting the money from our grandmother. He tells us we aren't to tell her about what he did to us. Nein, we will kill this man."

The Elder smiled. "You boys are the lions. You are making your Aunt Claus proud of you. Did you attack Gerard or did he attack you, Christian?"

"I am Maximillian. I am Christian Axel. Ja, we waited till he came for the skeleton. He has the key for the locks. Maximillian says to get that key. Christian will cause the distraction. Christian jumped on Gerard. Maximillian tried to grab the keys. Gerard used the straight razor to cut up our back. It hurts very bad but this must be done. We must escape to find our mother. Gerard is frightened. We bite him, kick him, scratch him and punch him. He is screaming. This makes us laugh. We hate Gerard for making the squishy things come out of our tummy. We must share the last because there is only one left. This is unacceptable."

Claus narrowed his eyes appearing suspicious. "Does Maximillian share Christian's flesh or does Christian share the skin of Maximillian?"

"I am Maximillian. I am Christian. There is only one of us."

He shook his head. "And what about Gerard? You boys attacked him, ja? He cut up your flesh. Did he knock you out and unlock the collar that held you to the skeleton?"

"Der Hund frightened Gerard. He pushed us off him but dropped his straight razor. Maximillian grabbed it and gave it to Christian. They wanted to die. It was agreed. It was the right thing to do. Too many of us have to share the boy. It's crowded. Gerard says he will take that skeleton to the Green Fields to feed the baby lambs. We want to go with him. Maximillian and Christian took turns cutting up the boy with the straight razor. Gerard demanded we stop this cutting. He was scared of all the blood coming out of the boy. We ignored him and cut faster. He hit us, and this caused the seizure."

Claus nodded. "Gerard thought he killed the remaining boy, ja?"

"We don't care what he thought Aunt Claus. We woke up in the ground. The skeleton was there with us. We couldn't breath and it was dark. This scared us. We tried to scream for help but the dirt filled out mouth. Christian and Maximillian worked the boy's hands to digging out of the grave Gerard put us into. We almost died before the boy got to the surface. We were tired but made the air hole. We took the rest for a nap before trying to crawl out of the hole. The skeleton, he didn't want to come out. We pulled and pulled but only his arm, shoulder and head was willing to join us in the revenge plot."

Da Elder sighed "Please sweetheart, you must stop attempting to shield your psyche from the pain of your trauma by telling yourself lies. Grief for your loss is necessary to heal the deep wounds within. The psychosis you suffering in the repeat is fueled by these delusions that your brother is still living, and you weren't chained up for two years all alone, with his putrefied corpse."

"You don't know shit, Aunt Claus. Shut up. Shut up. Move over dammit. There isn't enough room. Burn it down. Kill him. Call the lamb. Hurry. Sing a song of murder. A knife will make you die. Three and sixty black collars, baked in the pie. Where is the skeleton? We need the Haus doctor to put back on his flesh. Why did day take him from us? How can we fix him if we don't have it? You have no right to take him from us. He is ours. No one loves him. They never came to save us. Mother, where are you mother? Why do you abandon us in the cold darkness?

A loud popping noise followed by a stinging in my face awoke me from the nightmare I was having. I rubbed my red cheek and stared at Claus full of bewilderment. His expression was one of worry.

I groaned from the understanding he'd backhanded me yet again. "Why do you insist on hitting me, your Majesty? If you want the oral services, I won't give you quarrel. I must deny any penetration though. Doctor's orders. Call and ask him if you don't believe me." I glanced at the phone.

The Elder shook his head. "Now it is you that attempts to distract me. Nein, I may still desire such a delectable service call from my beautiful boy, but for the moment. I must insist you answer my question. Which one are you?"

I glared at him while still rubbing my smarting face. "Leave me alone. I'm not falling for your trickery. I remember what you just pulled. Shame on you Claus. That's pretty low to try to give me the hellish visions of dead people chained up to me for years in some abandoned barn. Gerard wasn't your fucking brother. He was my foul mother's husband. I didn't cut myself up nor did I get buried alive and dig myself out. Nor did I drag that corpse, still chained to me across an empty field either. You are a monster to even come up with a nightmare vision such as that. Gross, you've read too many horror novels."

Claus stared at me hard and pushed the blue folder in my hands at me. "You Gott damned right on that last statement. However, I only needed to read this once to never be able to sleep through the night peacefully again. Here you go boy. Open it up. The title of it might be of some interest to you."

I looked at page. There written in Danish in bold print it said:

Coroner's report for remains assumed to be of the child named Christian Axel Schmidt.

Cause of death: Shock and internal bleeding secondary to stab wound to abdomen. Homicide suspected. Age of decedent estimated to be five to six years ole.

Estimated time of death: Late fall or early winter 1963. Based on condition of remains recovered and eye witness accounts obtained from victim's twin brother: Maximillian Keifer Schmidt.

Condition of remains-mummified to skeletal. Partially recovered from shallow, unmarked grave. Partially recovered from shackles removed from the decedent's surviving identical twin.

Homicide investigation in death of Christian Axel Schmidt: Closed-due to death of suspect in Haus fire.

Suspect(s)/Decedent(s) name(s): Gerard M. Albrecht and Frau Ebba A. Albrecht.

Homicide investigation in death of alleged offenders Gerard and Ebba Albrecht: Closed. Alleged suspect apprehended and in custody. (see attached autopsy notes for above named suspect/decedent (s)). Both sets of remains are to be held in storage until all attempts to discover next of kin have been exhausted.

No further investigation into the above case is anticipated.

Additional comments: Special consideration granted for release of criminal evidence (decedent remains identified by relative's observation as: Christian Axel Schmidt) from evidence locker.

Case against suspect Maximillian Keifer Schmidt has been dropped due to diagnosed mental incompetence, with severe mental disease. (see attached psychiatric notes for further explanation).

A petition for guardianship and possession was filed by Miss Agnette Krauss. Her claim to full legal rights to take possession of both children has been upheld by court order. Miss Krauss has been provided undisputable evidence she is the biological mother of both the suspect and his decedent twin. She is, at this time, not considered a suspect in this suspected case of multiple kidnapping/child maltreatment/murder/arson.

Suspect Maximillian Keifer Schmidt has been ordered released by the West German authorities into the care of his guardian Miss Agnette Krauss. Decedent, Christian Axel Schmidt has been released for proper disposal into the care of his mother Miss Agnette Krauss.

Miss Krauss has received permission from the courts to return with her surviving son and decedent for burial in their country of origin, Denmark.

No further actions or notes in this case expected.

Filed 11/11/1965

-end-

Psychiatric Report. Patient: Maximillian Keifer Schmidt

Age: Eight years and six months.

Physician notes: Patient presents with numerous injuries. Physical exam of the patient records diagnosis of severe malnutrition, bacterial skin infection with wide spread pressure wounds due to poor hygiene and long term sedentary existence, wide spread deep lacerations both defensive and self-inflicted. Evidence of extreme neglect, physical trauma, psychological abuse - proven. Sexual misconduct enforced upon patient is suspected but unverified.

Maximillian was accepted into hospital care last week after being recovered during an investigation into a fire at a residence long abandoned by the owner. Two individuals believed to be the culprits of this child's deplorable physical and mental condition were found dead at the scene. He arrived heavily sedated from the surgeries to close his numerous lacerations and in strong restraints. Maximillian was permitted to recover from the calming drugs and once alert subjected to various psychological tests and observations to determine his mental functioning level.

After several days of intense investigation my findings/observations and recommendations are as follows:

Maximillian is functioning at the mental capacity of the child of less than three years. He is non-verbal and incapable of understanding communication prompts, even when presented in his reported native language. Most sounds the patient makes are guttural, animal noises but staff members have reported on some occasions they've heard him loudly call out the word, 'mother' in Danish. No other intelligible speech has been identified.

The patient is incontinent and demonstrates encopresis. Attempts to touch, speak with or offer any type of visual stimulation elicits extreme rage reactions with bouts of attempts at self-harm. The staff has been forced to maintain constant restraint devices and heavy sedation for patient to prevent significant injury to himself or others. Complete isolation from hospital population has been necessary to prevent rage outbursts from Maximillian. When stress of stimulation is removed, Maximillian calms quickly and demonstrates deep catatonic stupor.

Diagnosis: Schizophrenia, childhood onset with environmental factors present. Hebephrenic type.

Prognosis: Catastrophic. Improvement in mental functioning is not anticipated. Mental disease course is progressive and expected to worsen over time. Life expectancy is limited to less than thirty days without complete assistance in all daily functions.

Recommendations: Residential inpatient treatment for the course of patient's life span. Heavy restraint, with constant sedation and isolation from other residents and stressful stimulation is strongly advised.

Update: the patient has been released into the care of his biological mother, Miss Agnette Krauss. Maximillian's treatment staff and physician have informed Miss Krauss of the condition of his fragile mentality. A copy of this psychiatric record was given to Maximillian's caregiver. Miss Krauss has petitioned for and received permission to remove the patient and return him to the country of his origin. Physician orders this case to be closed. Further investigation and/or advising for patient treatment course is not required at this time.

-End-

11/21/1965

I stared at the words feeling sick to my stomach as I said, "This is a false document, Claus. You go too far with your attempts to gain my belief in your tall tales. I thought you were merely the pervert but you are something far worse."

Claus looked as if he was about to burst out into tears as he replied, "I won't deny I'm more deplorable than the simple pervert you accuse me of being. However, that isn't a forgery you're holding in your hands boy. This is the original copy that was filed with the German state where the crimes reportedly happened. That includes both the murder of your twin brother and the revenge you took out of the ones that did it. You see the mark at the bottom? That's the court seal. No amount of money can buy one of those from the unoccupied territories of our country."

I threw the file at him with force,. "Bullshit, Claus. Jonas managed to get adoption papers, a false birth certificate and even guardianship over me using the fake name of Maxximillian Weiss. I'm not so stupid to believe he can do such a criminal act but the great Fur King with all the money of Das Kaiser Haus is incapable of the similar rouse. The only thing I cannot for the life of me understand is why you going this far to try and convince me of such a crazy lie."

Claus caught the flying folder and frowned as he settled back into his pillow. "Okay Maximillian or Christian Axel. I think we need to takin a little break from this difficult subject for a bit. I can tell by your fury, we are very close to setting off one of those violent fits that the doctor was speaking about. I'm far too weak to handle your outburst if such a terrible thing were to happen. Honestly, I've always been anxious about pushing you too hard to face your terrible trauma. I don't care what Ingrid said. I believe it wouldn't takin much to cause that disturbed mind to snap in two for good. You have come too far and fought too hard for me to throw it all away. Though I confess, I'm more than a little eager to get this unsavory business put to rest at long last. So, tell you what. We both will be patient a bit longer, ja? I think for the time being I will go back to explaining what me and Ingrid were up to in the Dungeon with you. I know you said you no longer care about the answer. But like it or not, you will get it before I breathe my last. In fact, I swear to the Gotts, you are not leaving this room until the actions me and Ingrid did are explained fully. Now, you listen and for Gott's sake I pray you can do what we never could; learn from our mistakes. Ah, where did we leave off? Ah that's right, Justus had just been born and a well-kept secret along with him…"

I groaned but found myself unable to move a muscle or offer complaint to stop him from returning to that long winded story of his.

"So there me and Kiefer were. My husband took power as the Silk King and I was his adoring Queen. You see, even though we'd agreed I was the Dominant force among us after that mess with Vern you may recall. That understanding only held behind our closed bedroom doors. To all on the outside of our private life, Keifer was accepted as the top man of our union.

Xavier, Ingrid and their new baby Justus took to their position on the first Silk throne like they'd been born to it. Kristian and Max, as the fourth and fifth Princes, made our family clan's take-over of the Voter's floor almost complete. The remaining two Princes of the fading Wagner blood line were intelligent enough to keep their heads down and big mouths shut. They knew this was their single hope to surviving to see another sunrise.

The lazy Altergott that had managed to snag the title Fur King was more than a little irritated over this. He was pissed his late uncle hadn't managed to eradicate the resourceful Schmidt/Reinhardt factions. Keifer, Xavier, Kristian and Max all were aware the Elder monarch was bound to be seeking ways to do what Amos couldn't.

If this danger wasn't enough to keep me and Keifer sleeping with one eye open, there was plenty of other serious issues to do it. The long years of war, starvation, epidemic and hyperinflation had put Das Kaiser Haus into near shambles.

Many of the clients that historically had kept the Haus coffers filled with coin, lost their fortunes or lives during the repeated tragedies. Almost everything of any value within the walls had been stripped and sold off by the residents during the time of starvation and during months of hardships that fallowed. In short, the Haus was flat broke and no longer assured a steady flow of income to rebuild her lost treasures.

In response to this dearth of cash flow, instead of seeking out new sources of revenue outside Das Kaiser Haus's impoverished population. The Fur King stupidly decided to levy increased apartment rents and outrageous prices for meals in the Great Hall. As you may imagine, this set the residents into the mindset of near civil var.

Keifer and I had waited a little more than a decade to once again enjoy a decent meal and the most basic of comforts. The sight of our huge, but near empty Silk King apartment at first was a blessing we'd forgotten to dream about.

However, once the joy of our release to the world above abated a bit, both of us recalled the opulence that had been lost to us. As we traveled around the Haus, we did our best to overlook the evidence of utter devastation. We could hear the grumbles, murmurs and collective whispered complaints from all beneath us. Something had to be done, and fast, or it was pretty clear, Das Kaiser Haus was doomed to fall.

It was at this moment my clever husband came up with a brilliant plan. He was a native to your own motherland of Denmark and still continued to maintain ties to the country. In the city of Copenhagen, he'd been aware in his youth of a closed community not too unlike our own. Their rules and ways of management were different in many ways, but the services offered to the wealthy were pretty similar.

Keifer didn't have any associations directly with this Danish Haus. He wasn't even sure of its exact location nor if it'd managed to survive the var. He decided if it had, surely it couldn't be in any better condition than Das Kaiser Haus. It was rumored to be much smaller in size and of less fame among the coveted rich pockets across Europe.

The way Keifer saw it, suffering or thriving, either situation could work in our Haus's favor if he could form an alliance with their leaders. All he had to do is find some way to contact them. My husband didn't waste a moment to send out a call to all his living descendants residing in his homeland. Their collective mission: discover and make contact with the Danish Haus.

Weeks of anxiety passed while both me and Keifer waited to hear word of his attempt to beg for foreign aid. During this time, unrest among the resident's went from quite whispers in the shadows to overt curses hurled at all the Princes of the Silk and Fur.

Despite this overtly sinking situation, the Fur King continued to pressure the Haus peoples to empty dare pockets into his own, and those of his kinsmen. No where in the Haus was spared this continuing spiral into assured destruction.

Even Bladrick, Heidi and Helga and all the Dungeon dwellers milled about uselessly below. there wasn't enough coin to pay the training of new submissives to replace all those lost. The possibility of gaining entry by trading their services for the basic essentials of food and shelter wasn't possible anymore either. It wouldn't have mattered even if they had had a King's ransom to offer, the back door was devoid of willing volunteers for the first time in Das Kaiser Haus's recorded history.

The reasons for this strange lack of fresh servant applicants was soon discovered. The villages and towns in the lands for many miles around us no longer desired to send their orphans or unfortunate sons and daughters to serve what they viewed as wanton children killers.

They had learned the horrific truths of the fuel that fed those massive fires during the starvation times. Even though the war was to blame and many families all over Germany had to decide who was to live or die during that time of hardship. Das Kaiser Haus was more harshly held responsible for being forced to make the very same heart wrenching choices as most as them had.

For the rest of 1920, the Haus couldn't obtain even one third the number of new recruits it required for the Haus to run efficiently. Not many were willing to be subjected to wearing the honorable metal, unless promised far more than three square meals and a comfortable bed in a crumbling mansion.

Just when things appeared to be too far gone to salvage, Keifer received an excited message from one of his cousins. The news out of Denmark was hopeful. The Danish Haus continued to survive. More than that, according to Keifer's contact, this small Haus was thriving. The leader of the foreign community was more than eager to set up a meeting with Das Kaiser Haus's Silk King.

It was with a big smile and light heart my husband left for Denmark that early morning in the spring of 1921. I kissed him goodbye trying hard to hide my tears at having to sleep in our bed without him. I understood Keifer's actions were paramount to saving our failing world. That didn't make those long nights without him next to me any easier.

It goes without saying Keifer's trip to speak with the Danish Fur King Gregor Krauss was a huge success. He returned with not only enough borrowed funds to begin the reconstruction of Das Kaiser Haus to her former glory, but he also managed to strike a permanent alliance with him. The sister Haus in Denmark would become the saving grace on more than one occasion in years to come.

When Keifer come home victorious, with plenty of coin to go around. Well, you can imagine the suffering population embraced their Silk King with grateful arms. This would have been reward enough for a common man. My husband was anything but one of those creatures.

I was amazed at his wisdom when instead of keeping all this treasure for himself. He invested all of it. Both into reconstructing the damages within the Haus walls and to the surrounding lands.

This sudden demonstration of ability to afford the finer things in life began to soften the hearts of the angry outsiders. Not long after his return, Bladrick reported to his cousin the back door was becoming the popular destination for the destitute once more.

By the summer of 1921, the Haus had also managed to rebuild a lengthy list of client's with huge valets and exotic interests. I cannot tell you how proud I was of Keifer. My husband in less than one year single handedly managed to pull Das Kaiser Haus out of the muck of ruin.

As the residents celebrated the erasing of the evidence of war, death and poverty while worshipping their Silk King. others in the Haus weren't too happy to hear the people's grateful cheering. One of them was the Fur King himself.

That fucking lazy old Altergott was jealous as hell. It was the open secret the Elder was pissed off over the arrangement the Voter monarch had made with the Danish Haus. Not too many residents cared about the sour apple grumbling the Fur King was doing. They were all aware of his idle approach to problems solving. Even the youngest of the resident were aware that Keifer had merely done what the Fur King couldn't be bother to do."

I cleared my throat and shook my head. "You keep calling that fellow the Fur King the lazy Altergott. Was that his name or are you unable to lie fast enough to keep coming up with things to call all the people of your fantasy?"

Claus shot a glare of anger at me as he practically jelled, "Nein, I knew that idiot's name and I'm not making up a damned thing. I was attempting to spare you the pain of hearing it said is why I've neglected to mention it."

That made me chuckle. "You are a funny guy, Claus. You think it'd cause me agony to hear you speaking a false name you given to the characters in your tall tales. Is that supposed to gain my trust that you're not attempting to pull my legs? Well, you can let that hope go. I could care less what you decide to call the fellow. Better hurry up and come up with something real good cause I'm calling you out. Ha."

The Elder narrowed his eyes and without hesitation responded, "Kilian. The person Fur King Amos named to replace him with was the great grandfather of those boys you battled in the Palace and if I recall correctly, Heslach as well."

I sucked in my breath as if punched. "Seriously Claus? You dare to choose that name of all the horrible ones available to you? So be it. Your Fur King can be called Kilian Altergott the grandfather of the sonofabitches that I sent to hell. See if I give two shits. I still don't believe but half of what you telling me."

Claus shook his head. "I do believe you are aware the Hall of Records can verify or dispute whether I tell the truth of it. There is a book of the Haus history on the first shelf. When I'm done answering your questions, go ask the black collar attendant to allow you to see it. You will find within it a list all the men and women that held the Fur for the last two hundred years. Kilian Altergott held the Fur throne from 1920 until his death at age 80 in 1945."

I scoffed. "You probably call your black collar to rush down there and write it in. Whatever. You can keep wasting my time with your boring attempt to convince me you are really a good guy, and I had the twin brother. Oh and we were real Princes that were created to make Das Kaiser Haus into the heaven of your pretend dreams." Claus backhanded me with speed.

He stared at me hard as he said, "Silence. As I was saying before my ungrateful little brat nephew interrupted me yet again. So this jealousy that Kilian felt for Keifer didn't become the issue for several years. 1921 turned to 22, 23, and then 1924. All these years were quiet, peaceful and much needed times of healing. Das Kaiser Haus was thriving, and the people slowly recovered. Though the Haus and the people's flesh regained their fit tone, their heart were covered with scars that couldn't be forgotten.

Hoarding and constant panic attacks every time a rumor of famine, war, or sickness circulated kept even the easy going Keifer on his toes. We all tried to ignore the constant fear that seemed the ever present companion even when the skies seemed blue and sun shone brightly on our futures. It was in this atmosphere of perpetual underlying fear that Keifer was contacted for the first time by our sister Haus in Denmark.

The message indicated the young King Gregor was clearly seeking a return for the favor he's shown to Das Kaiser Haus during our past troubles. His request was quite simple. His young nephews were of age to seek membership within a Haus community. The problem was the Danish Haus wasn't as devastated by the decrease in population during the war and pandemic. Gregor reported he couldn't assure either young man even the basic provisions usually expected for fellows of their rank and heritage.

He respectfully begged the Silk King to allow the teenagers to enter as potential members of Das Kaiser Haus. Gregor reminded him such a thing shouldn't be of hardship. This was because according to the contract between them, Keifer was required to keep four apartments open on the third floor and offer them to any visiting member of the Danish Haus.

Though my husband was anxious about permitting two strapping young men of our rival Krauss clan such favor. He was aware refusal of Gregor's meager request could damage the hard won friendly relationship with this useful ally.

So, it came to pass that in the Summer of 1924, Hemmel and Heindrick Krauss crossed the borders and took up residence on the third floor. The arrival of two nothings from a foreign Haus culture shouldn't have raised an eyebrow, but it did far more than that. You see there were four eyes in the Haus that did far more than notice the pair of handsome boys that proudly carried themselves through the halls as the weather turned warmer. This sudden interest in turn reopened a deep wound in another. When the dust settled from this most unfortunate series of events it would leave one of the pretty males dead and the other one converted into one of the most notorious child killing Dungeon Masters the Haus has ever been cursed to call her own.

Chapter 8: A King Dies
Master Mad Maxx and submissive Meine Liebe

Heinrick and Hemmel Krauss. Ah, I remember the day the boys come through the door of Das Kaiser Haus. I confess, despite my honest loyalty to Keifer, it was hard to keep these eyes from stealing glances at those two. Dashing, good looking and full of the confidence all Krauss are notorious for. Mother nature had abundantly blessed them both with all they needed to be the natural born seducers.

As it was to turn out, I wasn't the only one feeling the lust whenever Heinrick or Hemmel was around. The brothers desired to become the full Haus members you know. Back in those days if you were from the outside there was only one way to be assured you got offered that honor. You had to serve at least five years in the Dungeon proving your worth.

Well Heinrick and Hemmel barely let the door hit them in the asses before they were making regular visits to the cells below. It was also common practice for newbies to be permitted to get a tour of the cells below. From there it was up to the sitting Fur King. Only that throne could approve anyone to serve as Dungeon Masters or Mistresses in training.

So, Bladrick fulfilled his duty by taking the handsome brothers under his wing. Every day for weeks you could expect to see Heinrick and Hemmel rushing through their breakfast at the Great Hall. They wolfed their meals and with gleams in their eyes, high tailed it down the stone steps with eager speed. These boys didn't appear too upset over the knowledge that in order to become a resident several years of their young life would be rather Spartan.

I supposed it didn't hurt that the only Krauss relatives of theirs to survive the flu epidemic were already serving below. They were almost assured an easy transition due to that alone. But there was an even more appealing reason for the boys rush to get to the dungeons each day.

Within only a week of their arrival, Bladrick reported to Keifer and Ingrid the Schmidt twins, Heidi and Helga, had managed to snag Heinrick and Hemmel's wanton gaze. His cousin added to no one's surprise, the girls seemed to be as smitten with the brothers as much as they were with them. He said things between the couples seemed to be progressing quickly. Our Headmaster suspected before the year was up, a union between the Krauss and Schmidt clan's was inevitable.

The brothers put in the request to serve below to King Kilian in record time. This probable marriage would finally put an end, at least for a bit, to the long-term rivalry between the powerful clans. A truce in the bloody battling was something both families seemed more than ready to enjoy. One would think this was wonderful news for the rising Schmidt/Reinhardt faction that controlled the Silk also.

Well, Keifer, Xavier, Kristian, Max and me were thrilled to have one less enemy to be wary of. Ingrid, however, didn't share in our relief. She hadn't forgiven

Heidi and Helga for bringing that plague that took all her children. I don't blame her for feeling that way either. Neither of the twins had bothered to offer a single word of apology to their brother Xavier. The also didn't seem too broken up that it was their fault so many souls had perished thanks to their dishonesty.

It was easy for Keifer, me and all the fellows to overlook the fact Heidi and Helga didn't earn the right to be happy. Though we had all suffered due to their actions none of us believed the girls should be punished for the rest of their lives.

We all felt sorry for Heinrick and Hemmel because those teenagers had no clue about the temperamental nature of the twins. I did notice none of us bothered to tell the boys. Truth is, all we were thinking about was maintaining our power as peacefully as possible.

All us Voters and Bladrick figured it was best to let the oversexed twins become Heinrick and Hemmel's problem. As for the insult to Ingrid's honor, that wasn't of any interest to her husband or anyone else for that matter. Even me and Keifer ignored her anger, much to our detriment. Well actually, I should say much to Heinrick and Hemmel's misfortune.

So, as I was saying, the boys asked old Kilian if he'd permit them to do their service in the Dungeon. Of course, the Fur King wasn't opposed to letting these young fellows head below where they wouldn't be an open threat to him or his kinsmen for at least five years anyway. It was settled pretty quickly. The sixteen year old Hemmel and his nineteen year old brother Heinrick started packing up their things with cupid's arrows in their heart.

Ingrid was hell bent to assure this convenient love affair was to end before it had the chance to begin. She learned that the boy's neighbors on the third floor had sought audience with Keifer to report a crime against them.

It happened to pass that one of the Wobben's young FemDoms had found herself in the motherly way. The girl claimed this happened against her will, and she wasn't aware of the identity of the father. In other words, the promiscuous teenager was attempting to cover up her illicit sexual conduct by saying she was raped.

All the residents were aware this Wobben's gal was sharing her stuff freely with one of the Baus boys. The Baus and Wobben's clans had been hateful enemies for as long as anyone could recall. She knew confessing this fellow was the daddy would result in her boyfriend finding himself pitched off the banister by an enraged kinsman.

To avoid pointing fingers at an innocent man she constructed they couldn't see the criminal's face' defense. This was a normal move made by unmarried FemDoms that got caught in the family way. It usually worked to protect the true offending fiancé from her family's reprisal and kept the young woman's reputation pure.

Without any evidence of a fellow to blame, Keifer was forced to dismiss the Wobben's complaints. The head men of the clan left the Council pissed but satisfied. This was because lodging the notice assured that if any proof come forward the family would receive swift justice.

Not long after the Wobben's voiced discontent, Ingrid managed to come across new information for the slighted girl. She told one of the sitting Elder Wobben's that the night their niece was dishonored she'd seen something disturbing. Ingrid said she was returning to the apartment after a night stroll. Her peaceful walk was interrupted by the sounds of a female screaming.

As her story went, she was unsure of the noise she heard. Before the honorable FemDom could go investigate the situation she saw two figure running down the hallway. This odd sight caught her attention. She swore on her life the owners of those dark shadows were none other than Hemmel and Heinrick.

She went on to say, at the time, she found their night jog strange but didn't realize the importance of it. Then rumors reached her ears of the Wobben's girl being misused around that same time. Ingrid openly wondered if the two incidents could be related. After putting that false bug into the Elder's ear she excused herself to attend to baby Justus.

Needless to say, the Elder hurried to meet with his third-floor kinsfolk. The girl was relentlessly questioned about the details of her alleged assault. It didn't take the Wobben's men long to coach the frightened young woman into recalling there had been two, not one, rapist. With a bit more prompting, the ignorant girl finally agreed it was Hemmel and Heinrick that attacked her.

They hauled the girl before Kilian and demanded he send the boys to the stake. The Fur King, while regretful for the girl's troubles, wasn't willing to anger the powerful Gregor. He wisely understood killing the Danish Fur King's nephews over a confession that obviously been coerced wasn't smart. He refused to order the death penalty.

The Wobben's refused to relent their demands the Dominants be punished. They demanded at the very least both fellows be exiled. Once again Kilian used discretion. He cautioned the Wobben's that such a grievous sentence demanded far more than coincidental evidence.

This family was then forced to leave Kilian's presence. He told them he wouldn't entertain any further discussion on the matter unless they could provide irrefutable proof that the Krauss boys were the criminals to blame. They left furious over his refusal to interrogate or even politely question Hemmel and Heinrick regarding their whereabouts that night.

Thanks to Kilian's oversight neither boy was aware someone had fingered them as possible rapists. They continued to obliviously walk about the halls and prepare for their move to the barracks below.

All the while, the Wobben's fury rose to the boiling point of near madness. By the time word got to me and Keifer of the Wobben's failed attempts, it was too late to try to derail the coming disaster.

I will never forget that morning in the Great Hall that Ingrid took a seat at our table. Keifer and I were quietly discussing repairs to the pool room as she sat down with a huge grin on her face. My lover asked her to share whatever it was that caused her such joy so that we might also smile.

Ingrid crossed her arms and with a snort said, "I already know you don't appreciate the subjects that thrill me this morning brother. As it is, it doesn't matter. In a few minutes, I finally will be able to call myself a mother that honorably protects her babies once more."

That caused Keifer to startle as he replied, "Come again sister? I don't understand. You are a wonderful mother to Justus. Everyone knows that. The boy barely can crawl without you hovering over him like the anxious bird."

Ingrid sneered at Keifer. "I'm not speaking of Justus, brother. I mean my other children. After this day, I can face them on the other side and tell them they have been avenged."

Before Keifer could ask her about the weird things she was saying, a FemDom come flying through the Great Hall doors and yelled, "The Wobben's are battling the Krauss boys." The entire room rushed from their breakfast tables eager to see the bloody show.

By the time Keifer and I, along with most of the dinners, rushed to the scene from the Great Hall a dark chapter in Haus history was already in progress. I spoke with a young Dominant later that day who was witness to the terrible situation from the beginning.

He said that Heinrick and Hemmel were making their daily rush down the steps for dare breakfast. When the boys reached the first floor their schedule was interrupted in the harshest of ways. At the foot of the stairs stood eight of the biggest Wobben males from that family. The Krauss brothers were completely taken by ambush, neither of them were aware these fellows were there to seeking undue justice.

Anyway as the story goes, Heinrick attempted to push through the Wobben's wall of flesh. He was immediately punched in the face and sent right to his pretty ass. Hemmel saw this nightmare unfolding and like any good brother would charge the brute that assaulted Heinrick. He also was knocked nearly unconscious with vigor.

The boy's youth was on their side. Both recovered and got back to their feet with speed. Only to be pelted with an unrelenting series of vicious blows by all eight of the angry Wobben men. It took mere minutes for the Krauss's handsome features to resemble the hamburger served in the Great Hall on Tuesdays. This insult should've sated the fury of the misguided Wobben's clan.

However, it would turn out this was the Wobben's sadistic idea of foreplay. We arrived just as the offending brutes were pushing Heinrick and Hemmel to their faces on the floor. No one bothered to try to stop these bastards from ripping down the brothers' breeches, right there in front of the gawking residents.

Then without the mercy of lube or even telling the near butchered young boys why this was being done. The eight Wobben's took turns holding the brothers hostage while their kinsmen soundly sodomized them publicly.

There was nothing Keifer or I could do to end this deplorable attack. Already Hemmel and Heinrick been sexually abused by at least two each of their assailants before we arrived. To add insult to their injuries, the entire crowd that'd gathered to watch the fighting, jeered and laughed while the brothers endured this open gang raping.

It was horrific to see, but I need not go into details about this. I'm aware you are personally familiar with this kind of crime that's exclusive to Das Kaiser Haus's culture. As I told you, this shaming of the male was and is a common weapon used in the family warfare of the Haus. To embarrass the Krauss boys in front of all the residents was and still is the highest form of disrespect, not to mention it destroys the reputation of the victims of it.

The worst of the damage was done before the threats Keifer was lodging at the Wobben men broke through their frenzy. They finally released the busted, bleeding, sobbing boys and hauled ass back to their apartments. The Haus doctor was called in to attend the many grievous wounds left by their cruel punishment.

Well, it took a week for the true extent of Ingrid's revenge to play to completion. At least in Heinrick's story that is. Heidi and Helga heard of their fiancés dishonor and immediately broke off their engagement. If the girls had honestly loved the Krauss brothers, as they claimed they did, something as petty as being raped shouldn't have mattered.

However, as suspected, the twins didn't care a fig for their boyfriends. This was crushing news, added to the traumatic incident and shame of knowing everyone was making fun of their pain. Heinrick knew neither of them dared to try to return home to Denmark. There was no explaining away the fact they were used as subservient mares in the repeat. Heinrick simply didn't believe he could live with his ego shattered to bits like it'd been.

So, it came to pass on the eighth day after their assault at the foot of the steps, Heinrick took a long drop with a short rope. His poor brother Hemmel, still reeling himself from his own injuries, found the dispirited Heinrick's corpse hanging like a cheap suit in their closet.

It goes without saying Hemmel fell into the dark, deep hole of depression. Most people in the Haus assumed he would be joining his brother soon enough. Suicide was, believe it or not, recognized by the Haus culture as the only way to reclaim honor after this type of disgrace.

Keifer, ever the good hearted soul, wasn't gonna sit back and do nothing. He wanted to try and save this unlucky youngster from more needless suffering. My Mann ordered Bladrick to take Hemmel down below, by force if necessary. He told the Headmaster to keep Hemmel too busy working to be considering the traumas of the past.

This seemed like a reasonable solution. Bladrick did as Keifer asked and at first, the reports from below appeared encouraging. Hemmel wasn't speaking about the incident and the young man was proving to be a fast learner in the skills of training new submissives.

Keifer was pleased to hear Bladrick expected Hemmel to become one of the great Dungeon Masters in a short time. The boy's prospects for a future of worth were looking up, or that's how it should've happened.

However, the residents of Das Kaiser Haus are a nasty lot. That you also aware of far too well, my beautiful boy. Even down in the bowels of the Haus, Hemmel was relentlessly hounded by his fellow Masters.

Every day, he was forced to endure the cat calls, whistles, taunts, jeers and crass jokes about sodomy. Bladrick did his best to quell the brutal treatment of his newest ward, but the second he turned his back, Hemmel was verbally harassed.

Then less than thirty days after that gang rape, members of the Wobben's family started turning up dead. Murder of a Dominant or FemDom no matter the reason was and still is a crime that carries a death sentence if caught doing it. There wasn't a soul in the Haus that didn't suspect Hemmel was the culprit of several Wobben's takin a dive off the banister. Supposing someone is a killer isn't proof they are though.

Keifer and Kilian informed Bladrick he was to keep a close eye on Hemmel. If anyone could find evidence of his innocence or guilt it surely would be their trusted Headmaster. Of course, without quarrel Keifer's favorite cousin agreed to never allow Hemmel out of his sight.

Interestingly, the Wobben's untimely deaths continued unabated. At first, it seemed the victims of the killer were simply crimes of opportunity. Some fell from the banister. Others slit their own throats.

None were spared. Males, females, young, middle aged, and old quickly made it to the list of the fallen. The only thing all the murders had in common, other than the surname of the victim, was each one found their eternal reward at night.

Bladrick was once again called to audience with Keifer and Kilian. He was questioned with harshness regarding his supervision of the one man in the Haus that had an axe to grind with the Wobbens.

The Headmaster reported he'd gone so far as to force Hemmel to share the cell with him. He again assured the Silk and Fur Kings the Krauss boy wasn't responsible for the serial killings, or if he was doing it the boy had to be gifted with magical talents.

Well, in less than six months the Wobben's had been slaughtered to such a high number that few members remained. The two sitting Elders, the girl that began this nightmare, and all eight of the rapists were the only ones still clinging to life.

I confess at first, I had faith in Bladrick's honesty regarding his close observations of Hemmel's every move. That all changed the second the two Elder Wobben princes come up deceased. You see, killing a number of lower Dominants that is something Hemmel could easily do. That is if no one was keeping tabs on him. Ending the lives of the highest upon high though, such a feat would require experience and a bid of assistance.

Without alerting Keifer to my anxieties, I slipped down into the Dungeons one late afternoon. I still had an affable relationship with a few of the lesser Masters that worked in the out of the way cells. I spoke with a couple of these men and learned of a disturbing rumor that ran rampant among them.

It was common knowledge that Bladrick had forced Hemmel to share a cell with him. He told Kilian and Keifer this was to assure no undue suspiciousness fell upon the already unlucky boy. This act appeared on the surface to be compassionate on Bladrick's part.

However, according to my old associates, there was a perception of dark motivation behind that move. Most fellows below believed Bladrick was takin advantage of the Krauss boy's unfortunate position. Some Masters even went so far as to claim the Headmaster was allowing Hemmel to gain his revenge. All the boy had to do was offer no resistance to his using him as the fuck toy.

I was aware of Bladrick and Hemmel's straight sexual preference. This was not a secret to the men that served under the Headmaster. But, Bladrick had been stuck in the Dungeons for almost five years. In that harsh environment without any company of females willing to attend his baser urges, seeking the favors of a notoriously good looking boy, well that wasn't as unusual as one may think.

Such arrangements happened down in the Dungeons all the time. Only, if my sources were correct, this situation was indeed different. Most believed Hemmel wasn't a willing partner in this mismatched relationship. The men told me they believed the boy was being blackmailed or even brutally coerced, you know, systematically raped, by the bigger, older Bladrick.

This idea was fueled by the fact Hemmel was often viewed sporting several bruises, cuts and other obvious defensive wounds without known causes. A few pointed out to me that the Krauss boy had arrived in the dumps. Since taking up the cell with Bladrick, most had observed his already crushed mood had taken a turn for the worse. They said the boy kept his eyes to his boots and no one had ever heard him speak a sound.

Instead of assuming my old friends knew the truth of it, I decided to investigate their charges myself. Without telling anyone I snuck down the Dungeon halls and hung out in the shadows. It was my intentions to wait till I could catch Hemmel alone. I was sure I could prove this was nothing but idle gossip the Haus residents are known for. I didn't dare to cause undo alarm by telling Keifer about the shit I heard without checking on the story, you know.

Well, I did manage to locate the young man in question. The second I found the boy, I realized getting a clandestine audience with Hemmel wasn't necessary. I passed by the pit and glanced inside. There before my horrified eyes I witnessed Bladrick forcibly holding the poor kid down while he sodomized him soundly.

Even from my safe vantage I could hear Hemmel sobbing as he whimpered, "Please Bladrick, I'm begging you. Stop hurting me. I give you anything else you want but no more I cannot handle this."

Then I heard Bladrick respond, "You shut up and take your medicine boy. Nothing in this Haus is free. I do for you, now you will do for me. Cry all you want my little bitch, but this is the way it will be for a long, long time sweetheart."

That was all I could stomach. I tore out of there like the four horsemen were chasing me. I swear to the Gotts, I didn't know what I was going to do, or if I should ever tell Keifer. I knew learning of his favored cousin's betrayal would break his heart.

After all, it was the Silk King's duty to punish anyone caught regularly abusing through blackmail another Dominant. Based upon Hemmel's pleas, Bladrick obviously was guilty. The sentence for such a crime was at that time castration.

However, the sentence for murdering of an Elder prince was burning at the stake. Though I didn't hear either man discussing the details of what Bladrick claimed Hemmel was paying with his flesh for. I knew in my soul the Headmaster was not only turning a blind eye to the boy's revenge behaviors, but he was also helping him seed the lawn with Wobben corpses.

For the next several days, I came close on at least four occasions to confessing all I knew of the Haus murders to Keifer. Each time I started to tell him, the words got stuck in my throat. I simply couldn't find the strength to do the right thing. I finally gave up trying by convincing myself seeing Bladrick and Hemmel punished wouldn't bring back their victims.

Then came the death of the eight offenders. A more gruesome series of killings, until a few of the ones attached to your name Maxx, had never been seen in the Haus. All the men were discovered over a period of two months. The murderer or murderers gouged out their eyes, cut out their tongues, disemboweled them, then castrated each one.

By this time, even my beloved Keifer began to suspect the offender was a huge fella. Hemmel's name was cleared since he was beautiful to behold but slight in build. A reward for any information leading to the culprit being identified was offered by Kilian, but as you guessed no useful tips come out of it.

I continued to keep my mouth shut. I assumed Hemmel's list was complete the second the last of the men that disgraced him and his brother fell. That was a gross underestimate of how angry that boy had become. He'd been saving his most hated enemy for last. The Wobben's girl whose false accusations resulted in the Krauss boy's misfortunes suffered the worst of all deaths handed to any of that clan.

She was found with her belly split vide open. Her unborn kid was torn from her womb, and strangled with is umbilical cord though it likely was already dead before that cruel attack on it. Her eyes were gouged out, and tongue cut out like the brutes that wrongly defended her honor.

However, the Haus doctor couldn't find that spongy member upon initial examination of her tortured remains. It wasn't until he looked a bit closer that the truthful brutality of her murder came to light. That missing item had to be dug out of her anus, where the killer had shoved it deep as possible while the girl still lived.

Her death effectively put the Wobben's clan into extinction within the walls of Das Kaiser Haus. Hemmel's revenge was harsh, cold and went well beyond the guilty parties. This obvious indication of the boy's deep rage still didn't loosen my lips about the things I knew of the crimes. I once again assumed this would be the last I ever heard of that ugly situation that destroyed two innocent boys and annihilated an entire family.

Of course, the true instigator of this sad situation, Ingrid, was as much the loser as Heinrick, Hemmel and all the Wobbens. Heidi and Helga escaped the carnage without so much as a scratch. Both girls continued to thrive and enjoy the fruits of their fading good looks. Neither thought a second nor caste a single glance at the poor jilted Hemmel, trapped reliving his trauma repeatedly only a few cells away.

For that unfortunate boy, things would continue like this for many years to come. Bladrick took Hemmel hostage when he was barely sixteen. The Headmaster didn't release him to enjoy the solitude of his own until he turned thirty-seven.

I believe the only reason he finally allowed him to leave was because Bladrick had become fearful. There wasn't a Master unaware of Hemmel's pent up rage over being misused as the powerful man's sex toy. Bladrick, always the cunning survivor, must have realized pushing that fellow any further wouldn't bode well for his continued good health.

With his reputation tarnished beyond repair and ego shattered to bits, Hemmel was without hope. He was viewed as worse than a leper by the females. None would touch him for any price. He'd probably never been with any girl prior to his being used as the unwilling catamite. This terrible ache to fulfill the sexual act with the gender of his interest, along with a desire to reclaim his stolen manhood, is to blame for his becoming the serial rapist.

You see the only females the man had any access to were the helpless silver trainees. After the second World War, virginity among rising pleasure submissives became mandatory. The punishment for any Dungeon Master found guilty of soiling a trainee was still exile or death, depending on the quality of the girl ruined by him.

These two factors resulted in Hemmel murdering scores of the silver collared girls. The gossip was that at first he would become mad with love for some pretty new girl. Then after wooing the innocent kid, Hemmel would takin advantage of her ignorance.

If she didn't willingly comply with his sexual advances he didn't shirk from enforcing her to. After the deed was done; he'd kill the girl. He couldn't risk the female pointing the finger at him as the Master that tarnished her silver. I mean, after all, the last time that'd happened to him, well, no need to repeat that tragic story, ja?

Over the years I have kicked myself a million times for not going to Keifer before Hemmel grew into the monster he became. I'm not sure anything could've been said or done for him to derail the nightmare created from this once happy, well adjusted, friendly teenager. But since I didn't say a word, I can never know what it might have been.

Hemmel's decent into hell was more far reaching than the end of the Wobbens or hundreds of unmarked silver graves. As you may or may not recall, he was involved in the plot that ended your brother's life and ruined yours. What I have failed to mention thus far is he is also likely one of the bastards that assured yours truly suffered a fate of loneliness and pain.

Before we get to that terrible story, first I wish to tell you of yet another boneheaded move of your grandmother. It was 1925, and the grisly murders of the Wobbens the year before put all in the Haus at ill ease. Xavier had begun to flaunt numerous affairs with several high ranking FemDoms in public. Many eyes were on the unhappy Frau of the First Silk Prince, and many of their tongues wagged behind her back.

Most expected she would attempt to sue for divorce. Such action to relieve a woman of a useless Mann was still difficult to do in those days, but it was possible. Even Keifer counseled his sister that allowing this open dishonor of her good name wasn't smart. This time, for a minute, it seemed that her brothers advice was sinking into her hard head.

Then to our shock, Ingrid withdrew her actions in seeking an end to her marriage with Xavier. The suddenness of her renewed interest in her husband rightly made me and Keifer suspicious of her motives. With only a little interrogation she privately confessed to us she'd once again found herself with kid. Like before, the father wasn't her Mann.

Ingrid didn't show a shred of remorse while she relayed that for over three months she'd been secretly sleeping with one of the Finks. This affair apparently had initially been the aging Frau's way of paying Xavier back for his cruelly disgracing her without care. That all changed as the two lovers discovered their feelings for the other were more than skin deep. Ingrid believed it was their honest affection that led to her womb opening up for business.

Whatever the reason for this misfortune, Ingrid was caught in a bind. A divorce wouldn't go in her favor if Xavier found out she carried another man's baby. Like the trooper she'd always been, she sucked in her pride and did what she had to. Xavier was again misled into thinking himself a worthy stud.

That would have been the end of this side story, except the Fink daddy was pissed over Ingrid's freezing him out. He began to actively stalk the pretty FemDom. His foolish behaviors were threatening to send rumors flying questioning her honor. No doubt, Xavier's wrath would have endangered both her and the life of her unborn kind.

She attempted to speak some sense into her disrupted lover. When all efforts failed, and he continued to take chances with her safety, Ingrid felt he had to be stopped at any cost. It wasn't too much of a surprise soon after that the poor fellow was found dead.

The Haus doctor told the Fur and Silk Kings someone had poisoned the man. He reported he believed the culprit was a spurred girlfriend. It was common knowledge tainted wine or food usually yielded the female suspect.

This theory never resulted in anyone being held accountable for the Fink's untimely demise. Ingrid had wisely kept their illicit behaviors as the tightly guarded secret. Only Keifer, me, the dead man and she were aware the two were more than loose friends. The case of his death was put on the back burner and to this day it remains unsolved.

Ingrid breathed a sigh of relief as her pregnancy progressed peacefully. Xavier continued to flaunt several new mistresses about the Haus, but it no longer bothered her. Your grandmother was never happier than when given the chance to play mother. She was simply born to the role.

Sadly, in the sixth month of gestation, something went wrong. Her baby boy was born prematurely and didn't manage a single breath. In the middle of this disaster the doctor cruelly told Ingrid she was no longer capable of producing viable offspring.

Her lamenting was deep as she laid the baby she believed to be her final chance at motherhood to rest. Xavier couldn't be bothered to come offer solace at the kid's graveside. Keifer and me were left to provide his grieving Frau the support that should've been his job.

So, that was the end of Ingrid's wild flings, at least for a few years. Xavier on the other hand continued to add names to his long list of conquests. Your grandmother responded to her hellish lot of a loveless marriage by clinging to her only living child, Justus.

The years marched on from 1925 to 1935 with almost nothing changing within the walls of Das Kaiser Haus. Ingrid and her baby boy Justus celebrated his fifteenth birthday, while his father made an ass of himself with two FemDoms half his age. Below, in the Dungeons, Bladrick continued to abuse the ticking time bomb Hemmel. Above us, on the Fur Throne Kilian grew weaker in physic due to the common ailments that come with advanced age.

Outside Das Kaiser Haus walls the government had changed rapidly. In January of 1933, a new Chancellor had risen by the name of A. Hitler. This charismatic man had enraptured the still wounded hearts of Germany's war torn peoples.

Many, even within the Haus, had great affection for this angry fellow. The word Nazi became part of the popular culture, as the country embraced the leader they were sure would make them a great nation once more.

Keifer and I, ever the liberal souls, avoided all subjects or contacts with this alarming regime. We kept our noses to the grindstone and eyes on the future of Das Kaiser Haus. It seemed best to let the rest of the world do as it pleased as long as it didn't affect the Haus.

Well, that was yet another mistake we made. This time, only one of us would live to regret it. The summer of 1935 found me and my beloved Mann staying busy with the many duties of the Silk throne. The two of us were too damned busy to notice, but with Kilian's power showing sign of waning, many began looking to the Silk throne with hungry eyes.

Our biggest threat to remain on the silver throne was the man sitting directly behind us, Xavier. I think from the start that bastard has been keeping a lid on his resentment over Keifer's rise. I also believe had Keifer not become the popular King he was, that shady fucker would've made a move to push him aside far sooner.

For whatever reasons, Xavier didn't attempt a single hit against his rival the Silk King for fifteen years. I must tell you, I'm grateful for every single one of those seasons I peacefully basked in the light of my lover's adorations. With that in mind I will take a deep breath and attempt to recant the horrible events of that bitter summer that I lost my beloved Keifer forever.

It took Ingrid, Bladrick and me many years after the dreadful assassination to put together the entire plot. Apparently, Xavier had been quietly tapping into the near bursting fury of Barnam, Drexel, Bernt, Derbeck and Hemmel. Every man but the last one, his reasons to be pissed we already discussed at length, hadn't escaped their Dungeon hell in all that time.

Needless to say, each was ready to see the rise to above the cells any way they could. It likely wasn't too difficult for their prince of the first Silk Throne to talk them into assuring he would be crowned the new King. All they had to do is help him remove the one already sitting in that seat of power.

This goes without saying, but the truthful ability for Xavier to herd these cats was a deadly promise. He would place the men that aided him onto a Silk prince throne, the second they successfully emptied them.

None of the remaining Wagners, Kristian, Max, me, nor my sweet Keifer were aware of the coming dangers. We honestly were too busy doing our jobs with honor, efficiency, and grace to notice the signs that spelled our doom. Even the usually paranoid Ingrid was deeply wrapped up in educating Justus to recognize her husband's sudden secretive behaviors as sinister.

June 15th, 1935 was a warm day with the clearest of blue skies. I managed to talk my overworked Mann into coming with me for a long stroll in the gardens. I can still see his handsome figure walking next to me, casting the most spectacular shadow across the green lawn.

Ah, what I wouldn't give for one more minute doing nothing more than takin in his scent and basking in the glory of his eyes, but I digress. I suppose old age brings out the best memories, along with the worst regrets, ja?

It was nearly dinner time when Keifer reminded me we'd been summoned to a private consultation meeting with Kilian. I really hated sitting there for hours listening to the old buzzard bemoan his fragile health, before finally getting to the point. My husband knew this fact all too well. He saw me roll my eyes and suck in my breath.

With a humored chuckle he said, "Baby, why don't you skip this boring meeting and go to the Great Hall. You know damned well Kilian will delay us until all the good tables are taken. Think of this as a win for both of us. You get to avoid having your ears assaulted and I finally can eat a meal with my best gal, taking in the finest view, ja?"

I shook my head. "Nein, you know the rules honey. Where you go, I follow. I realize there never has been any trouble but maybe that's because no one stupid enough to take on two big brutes," I said politely but without much vigor in my words.

Keifer halted our journey and with a glisten in his beautiful eyes replied, "I hate to tell you this lover, but there isn't a fucking soul in the Haus afraid of either of us Queens. Look, I insist you do as I am asking love. There isn't any reason for you to tag along to be bored out of your skull. Order me a large meal, and make sure to get an extra bottle of vine. I intend you take full advantage of my drunken state later tonight." He winked at me with a wicked smile coming across his gorgeous face.

I giggled like the silly schoolgirl over his promise of a passion filled night in his arms. "I'd never dare to misuse you without your consent baby."

He leaned in and kissed me with great vigor then replied, "I gave you my permission forever, remember Mrs. Reinhardt? I see you in a couple hours. Have that wine, supper and your lips warm as the weather." With that he let go of my hand and rushed off to meet with the aging Fur King.

I watched him shrink in the distance with a stupid grin on my face. It had been thirty-seven years since I first met this amazing soul. We'd celebrated twenty-nine years as lovers only a few weeks before that day. and still, the mere sight of Keifer could takin my breath away. I tell you Max finding a love like the one we enjoyed is a rare gift.

However, losing such a precious thing is perhaps as much a curse as it ever claimed the status as blessing. Something deep inside my gut went uneasy as I saw him disappear into the Haus back door. I shook off this foreboding feeling believing it was just me being the little pussy. I'd never liked being out of Keifer's sight. It was the open joke between us that I was like the tiny lap dog with a raging case of separation anxiety.

Well, you cannot fathom the number of times I've wished I could go back to that moment in time. If I could, I'd run up to that idiot I was and scream at him to behave the clingy baby all he liked. Honor does a man no good when he's alone with no one to share in the glory of it. Had I only, but I didn't, and sometimes there are no second chances nor room for mistakes.

I continued with my walk taking in the sights and sounds of mother nature scurrying about her daily routines. Eventually, I noticed the sun sinking low in the sky. I decided it was time to head to the Great Hall. I was hell bent to impress Keifer by wrangling up the best table possible.

With a light spring in my step I entered the Haus. My calm mood was abruptly shattered by the scene that met my eyes as they adjusted to the dimly lit hallway. The residents and submissive alike were rushing about wildly with looks of utter horror upon their faces. I immediately became alarmed by this chaotic situation.

I grabbed a young black collar male that was running past me. "Tell me boy, what the hell is going on? Why are you all behaving like the blitz is upon us?" I looked to the ceiling fearful that such a thing could be possible. It happened several times in the Great War after all.

The boy whimpered in my grip, "It's the Silk King."

My heart stopped in my chest when he said that. "What about him? Speak up or so help me I will beat you to a bloody pulp, Gott dammit."

He shook his head and looked at his boots. "He's been attacked and presumed dying or already dead. I heard they've taken his broken flesh to the clinic. Please honorable Voter, that's all I know."

I let him go feeling as if I was hovering above myself. Without hesitation and without breaking from that weird trance I took off like the shot for the Haus doctor's office. I prayed and pushed everyone out of my way as I barreled along. I hoped against all odds that collar was mistaken, but I knew, I knew, Gott forgive me Keifer, I did know.

When I arrived at the clinic door, I had to fight my way through the gathering crowd. Tears in the eyes of every gawker in that mob told me the boy's information was correct. This knowledge gave me the strength to move all obstacles out of the path between me and the man I loved.

The doctor saw me enter before I spotted him. He rushed over and pulled me to an empty room. I was nearly stupid with grief before he even said a word. His statement that afternoon haunts me to this very day.

He looked at me as he gave me that news. "Keifer is still alive Claus, but the damage, look I'm only the mortal man. What your Mann needs to survive is the sole property of the creator. He is in horrific pain, without any chance of recovery. We've been trying to give him mercy but he has refused all attempts to aid him out of his agony. Maybe you can speak with him and explain. Claus, there is no hope."

My eyes blurred with the stinging of tears as I stammered, "Are you absolutely sure doctor? I mean Keifer is strong. Maybe he could beat the odds?"

The doctor frowned deeply as he replied, "Claus, there is no way to gently tell you this, but the man or men that attacked him, they uhm, punctured his bowels full of holes.

There is no coming back from wounds like his. Even if we didn't do a thing, he's about to die slowly in the next forty-eight hours or less."

I could barely squeak out. "Man or men? Didn't Kiefer tell you the name of the sonofabitch that's done this to him?"

He grimaced then responded, "He, uhm, cannot report anything honorable Voter. They also removed his eyes, tongue, and broke his hands."

I let out a miserable wail upon hearing the gruesome details. "Oh my Gott. Nein, please let this be a nightmare. Wake me up, Keifer. Help him, I beg of you." I fell to my knees at the doctor's feet and took up his ankles unable to get a grip on my despair.

The kindly man gently pulled me back to my feet. "Claus, please don't debase yourself to the sorry likes of this worthless man. I swear on my honor I would trade anything for the ability to fix this or tell you it's all a bad dream. However, for this minute, you must remain strong for Keifer's sake. He needs to accept my offer of mercy. I can give him an overdose and he will no longer suffer. The King will fall into a deep sleep and pass away without any more unnecessary pain. Will you speak with him for me? I cannot stand by and watch him hurt like he is, and I know as his honest husband, neither can you."

I took several deep breaths and nodded. "Ja, okay I understand. Can I request the room be emptied while I speak with my lover about this? The things I wish to say are private. I don't desire an audience. I thank you for this and all the mercies you grant us in advance Herr doctor."

He flashed me a bitter smile. "Of course, Claus. I will keep the crowd at bay. Take all the time you need. I must warn you, brace yourself. The King, Keifer, the sight of him is disturbing. I would think he need not be focused on that, ja?" I nodded and did as he asked trying hard not to hyperventilate.

He led me to the back clinic room. The doctor wished me luck and informed me he'd be waiting for my word before coming in. I did my best to prepare for the worst and opened the door to go inside.

But nothing prepared me for the sight of my beloved laying there moaning in agony. Where his beautiful blue eyes one glistened were black empty holes. Blood stained the sheets, his face, his clothing and his fingers were bent at odd angles. I noticed right away his calls of distress were other worldly sounding. Without a tongue he couldn't do much more than make the guttural noises of an animal.

I gasped and swallowed hard. Then without a moment hesitation rushed to his bedside. I leaned down and gently kissed his forehead. His face turned with suddenness and he let out screams of terror. This traumatized behavior caused the rain to fall in torrents from my eyes.

I caressed his cheek as I choked out the words, "Hush, baby. It's me Claus. I'm here with you honey. You are safe now. I swear on my soul I kill anyone that tries to get between us ever again." His struggling calmed almost the second he heard my trembling voice.

I nearly fell into the weeping jag when he responded by lifting his mangled hand and laying it on my own. He groaned from the horrific pain in his flesh but managed to smile. I knew this was his way of trying to make me feel better. That was Keifer's way, you know. He could charm anyone even in the worst of circumstances.

Let me tell you something, Max. In all the hard decisions of my life, nothing has ever come even close to the one I was forced to make that night. Knowing the love of your life is dying, and you are sent to talk him into euthanasia, that's beyond brutal.

However, I could see that the doctor wasn't exaggerating. Keifer had no chance of recovery. He was suffering a fate that should only be reserved for the worst of scum. Even burning at the stake is more merciful than, oh shit, I apologize my beloved. I was so wrapped up in reliving this grief I forgot about your personal familiarity with this kind of torturous death."

I stared at Claus angrily, "There you go again trying to fuck with my head. I told you already. I'm not falling for your trickery. I never had a twin. I wasn't shackled to his corpse for years. Get on with your story will you? Shit, how much longer do I have to endure your nightmare tales? Seems to me you know me well enough to be aware nothing you said to this point surprises me. I'm more than a little experienced with the monsters that call Das Kaiser Haus home."

Claus frowned deeply and nodded. "That you are, my beauty. I suppose it's occurred to you that many of the things you've encountered, others before you suffered also. You surely don't believe that a coincidence do you?"

I shrugged. "Pushing the idea of a dead twin isn't working, so you try to gain my sympathy for the devil Hemmel? Ha. You will have to try harder than that Claus. Being forced to play the catamite isn't a valid excuse to go raping and killing hundreds of helpless children. Hemmel should've murdered Bladrick along with the Wobbens, then sated his blood lust with the bones of Heidi and Helga if he truly wanted justice."

The Elder grimaced. "Had he done that, Kilian or Keifer would have sent him to the hill for it. Surely you don't suggest that poor boy sacrifice his life when it was the only thing left of worth to him."

That made me laugh bitterly. "Sounds to me like he was the impoverished man if that's what he valued. The way I see it he had other options, but he decided to play the resentful little bitch. He agreed to that bargain he made with Bladrick to buy the right to get revenge. He took the prize but didn't want to pay for it. Then when he believed he was overcharged for the service. He took out his fury out on the innocent. He wasn't even high enough functioning to be called the bully. That motherfucker behaved like the pussy bottom until he finally became one heart and soul."

Claus chuckled. "Ah, you are so much like him, your Uncle Keifer. The way of cutting through all the crap is an art that I never could claim to possess. And what of him? You seem to have an opinion regarding Hemmel, Bernt and Justus. Do you believe the great Silk King Kiefer also a mere figment of an imagination I attempt to put into your mind?"

I shook my head and looked him directly in the eyes as I replied, "Nein, this man I think is not a fantasy. I can see your emotional pain as you speak of your love for him. That is real. I'm honestly sorry he didn't survive. If for no other reason then I doubt you'd have misused me had he lived to the ripe old age like you have."

The Elder laughed out loud. "Once again, a babe speaks more truth then I ever have. It's a sad fact that I'm drawn to you because you and Keifer are uncannily similar in looks, personality and strength. I've always been drawn like the moth to the Reinhardt flame. Not that anyone should blame me for it. You boys burn brighter than any fire on Earth. What is a girl to do?"

I groaned when he said that. "You can skip this part about the death of Keifer if you like Claus. There's no need for you to suffer over it. I don't require an example to understand the agony of losing someone you love. I have plenty of experience with it already." I soften my gaze and tone to demonstrate I meant what I said.

The Fur King smiled with his eyes turning into pools of water as he replied, "You offer me mercy, Maxx? That's not like you. If I didn't know any better, I'd think you don't completely hate me despite all the harm I've done to you over the years."

It was my turn to chuckle as I responded, "Ja, you've been wrong in the things you've done to me. However, I cannot lie. You may be the best ally and greatest friend I've ever known in my short life. I'm crazy Claus, not stupid. I cannot point out a single incident between us that you didn't do your best to make sure you paid for the service in equal return. If this stupid attempt to screw with my head is designed to gain my forgiveness, you can relent. The way I see it, you need none. I don't hate you, but I also cannot fib and say I love you either. Let's agree I'm indifferent and that's got to be enough."

Claus nodded. "Dat's fair and I do concur with your assessment of our relationship, dearest Maxx. That still doesn't release me from my promise to make you whole as possible before I go to face eternity. You must sit there a bit longer and endure the ramblings of an old man. I apologize for that, but your creation wasn't simple nor quick. Everything I tell you led up to that moment the cries of pretty twin baby boys called out to the awaiting world. I thank you for granting me a moment to recompose myself before reliving losing Keifer. But I'm ready to deal with it, one last time."

I shrugged and blew out my breath with frustration. "As you wish, your Majesty. I'm as always yours to do with as you please."

Claus laughed with tears streaming down his haggard face. "Don't I fucking wish that were the reality. Anyway, all fantasy aside, where was I. Oh my Gott, that's right. Keifer lays dying in the Haus clinic and this worthless man couldn't do shit to stop it from happening.

I spent the next thirty minutes cuddling, petting and weeping onto my beloved husband. He couldn't speak a word but he mouthed 'I love you' in the repeat. We did our best to hold on tightly to each other during his last few moments we had together in this life. I would repeat the many things I said to him, but I prefer to keep that between me and the man that earned hearing them.

As the seconds ticked away, his pain was growing observably more unbearable. I confess, I happily would have sat there fawning and sobbing until he succumbed from his injuries. It was honestly what I desired to do more than anything, but it wasn't right to behave selfishly. Keifer had been good to me all our lives. He'd earned a peaceful end, no matter what my regret at having to let him go.

After he'd suffered a particularly bad spasm I leaned into his ear and whispered, "When you and me met, you were there to help me when I fell. This time, baby, I'm the one that offers you aid. The doctor has the concoction that can make the pain go away. I swear I won't leave your side as you start the last great journey. You'll die in my arms just as you promised me long ago. Before you decide to leave, allow me to make one to you. I will never love another as I have loved you. If I live to be a hundred, sweetheart, it will still be only your name that falls from my lips with my final breath. You have my permission to let go if that's what you need to hear. I must demand you save a seat at the finest table for me. I will be along soon, you can bet on it." With those words I nearly lost all composure.

Keifer gently rubbed the wet from my cheeks grimacing from the pain. I watched his lips make out the words, 'I will wait for you baby. I will miss you. Pray for me. I will give Mother Felicity your love.'

I nodded and did all I could to breath as the grief crushed the air from my lungs. "Do you want me to send for Ingrid before the doctor ends your torment baby?"

He shook his head nein then mouthed, "I want her to remember me as I was, not like this."

With that he motioned me to called for his mercy. I stood up and walked to the door. It was as if the walls closed in on me, and time stood still. I wanted to run back to my broken lover. To never allow that syringe to take him from me, but I mustered the strength to think of Keifer's comfort instead of my own.

The doctor true to his word was standing ready outside in the hall. I didn't have to say a word. He knew from the look on my face Keifer was ready to meet his maker. Without a moment hesitation he rushed into the room and closed the door behind us.

He whispered to me, "You may take a moment to prepare yourself and his majesty. When he is ready for mercy, nod your head and I will do the rest."

I didn't respond but rushed back to Keifer's side. With much care I took a seat next to him and cradled his head. I leaned down and put my forehead to his. He lifted his head and begged for my lips to meet his own. I engaged him in a deep kiss that had to be beyond agony for him. To his credit he didn't even whimper. Then he mouthed, 'I love you Claus. Goodbye for now. We will be together again my beautiful Queen.'

I broke down but motioned to tell the doctor that Keifer was prepared. I didn't remove my forehead, open my leaking eyelids, nor stop clutching his head as the needle went in. I felt my lover jerk slightly at the stick, then almost immediately his tense flesh went limp. His ragged breathing suddenly went quiet and came to a halt.

And then with a final moan caused by his last breath, my beloved Keifer suffered no more. I won't lie. I wailed uncontrollably the second I realized he'd left his mortal coil. The doctor ended up having to call for help to pull me off my husband's lifeless corpse. I'm sure it was a pathetic scene to behold but I won't apologize for my behavior. I was lost without him, and honestly didn't believe I could survive now that he was gone.

I wasn't the only one going bonkers over the death of Keifer. Ingrid arrived about thirty minutes after the doctor sent her brother on his way. She'd been in the village shopping with Justus when the tragedy took place. Her greeting upon her return home was to receive the horrific news of the King's murder.

You could hear her screams of grief for minutes before anyone could see her. I rushed and caught the wailing woman before she could push her way into the room that held his defiled flesh. He didn't wish for her to see him like that. Even if I risked her hating me for all her life, I was hell bent to grant him this final dignity.

Luckily Max and Kristian arrived on the heels of their despondent cousin. With these poor fellow overcome by their own bouts of intense grief, they managed to hold it together enough to help restrain her. Bladrick arrived not long after his other bereaved kinsmen.

I must tell you that was the wettest summer in Germany's history. The five of us practically flooded the Haus and fields of the nation with our tears. I didn't notice it at the time, because of my hellish pain, but oddly neither Drexel nor Barnam made a single appearance in the clinic. Not during the first hours of Keifer's death nor later on as preparations for the royal funeral began.

As the Haus coroner attended his dark work, I finally realized their absence. I asked Bladrick about his cruelly demanding his half-brothers keep their distance. He informed me he'd given both Reinhardts a pass to come above to show their respects. Apparently, the fellows didn't feel moved enough to bother with even faking they cared.

This insulted Ingrid more than it did me. All I knew for many weeks was that I was truly alone in the world. A widow at only forty-five years old, and I didn't kid myself. I knew that status wasn't ever going to change. My happiness was buried deep in the earth along with my beloved Keifer. There it rots to this day, held tightly in the boney grips of a long dead corpse.

We all held each other crying until at last, we were sapped of our mourning fluids. My river never seemed to go dry. To their credit they didn't leave my side for the next several days.

I imagine they assumed I was prepared to do something stupid. Well, to be honest, they were right. I sure did consider following Keifer as I'd always done. Shit, he was all I'd ever known. I truly was lost without him.

Ingrid and Bladrick were broken hearted, but they managed to handle their grief more constructively than I did. Ingrid and Bladrick thought beyond saying goodbye to their beloved family member. They wanted nothing more than to gain revenge on the person or persons that took that beautiful soul from us. After careful inspection of the facts in the attack, the pair slowly began to develop a theory of who was to ultimately to blame.

It really came down to simple deduction and observation of behavior upon receiving news of the King's demise. Drexel, and Barnam were natural suspects from the start over their lack of demonstrating common decency.

Despite my deep grieving I told Ingrid I wanted to add Hemmel to their list of suspects. This was based upon the way the crime was committed. Without revealing my source of information I told her I thought cutting the tongue and gouging out eyes was too similar to the Wobben murders to ignore. She agreed and the disgruntled Dungeon Master went to the top of that list.

Next we all had to consider Xavier and his brothers could be behind the plot. Keifer wasn't even in the ground before that pushy bastard showed up at the apartment door demanding I pack up and get the fuck out of his haus. I was merely the Silk Queen and had no rights to the throne proper.

However, his cruelly demanding I leave a home that I'd shared with my beloved for many years before being formally named King was more than rude. It seemed a bit more than suspicious. Ingrid admitted she couldn't account for Xavier whereabouts during the time of Keifer's mortal assault.

Bladrick added more pieces to the puzzle by stating he'd been unable to locate Bernt or Derbeck hours prior to the murder. He also couldn't account for the movements of Hemmel, Drexel or Barnam. All these men had plenty of motive to desire Keifer be eliminated. It felt to me like in the end we would never be able to give my beloved the justice he deserved. Not unless we intended to kill every fucking fellow on Ingrid's list. That was what Bladrick thought we should do. He rightly believed it was best to send them all to the grave and let Gott sort out the guilty from the innocent.

Well, Ingrid wasn't keen to wait around till Xavier was either cleared of murdering her brother or his guilt discovered. She wanted to flee from this Haus of horrors. It was no small thing to understand she'd found only misery and suffering since the moments her tiny feet crossed the threshold. Ingrid lamented everyone she'd love except me and Bladrick were taken from her.

I couldn't argue as she had a point. Her marriage was sour and her bed empty of the lover's embrace. Justus had taken to spending all his time following in his father's footsteps, leaving his lonely mother to fend for herself. It seemed the poor woman was cursed. But then again, if she was, I could claim such a terrible fate doubled.

With the rise of Xavier to taking the dishonorably emptied Fur Throne, I assumed I would be tossed back to the main floors or quite possibly out the door. To my complete stun, and everyone else's, Xavier's first action as King was to move all princes of the Silk up one seat. He then named me to the opened fifth Silk throne.

I took the offer out of fear of what would become of me if I refused Xavier. Ingrid met with me after the announcement. She bitterly informed me the only reason her husband showed me kindness was because it was in his favor. Xavier didn't view me as a threat to his authority. I was universally seen as the nelly bottom remember.

She honestly believed Xavier feared the rise of his brothers. He had no honest loyalty to Barnum or Drexel. It made strategic sense to move a non-rival to the weakest position in the Silk. Ingrid wisely counseled me to keep my mouth shut, agree with all her Mann wanted and never question his authority if I desired to remain overlooked as a serious threat.

The idea that Xavier could've been the one that killed my beloved, caused me to accept her advice. It is far easier to get close enough to kill your prey if they don't see you coming, ja? Ingrid wasn't willing to play that game any longer. With tears in her eyes she told me, she was leaving the act of revenge for her brother up to the man he loved the most.

As for that lost man's sister, she was preparing to make an escape from the sinking cesspool called Das Kaiser Haus. Her intended destination both surprised me and at the same time didn't. She informed me that Kristian and Max had made arrangement with the Fur King Gregor.

Her loyal kinsmen must have paid the Danish Haus a fortune to aid slipping the dispirited FemDom from under Xavier's cold claws. Well, whatever Gregor charged the fellows to take Ingrid in, it was minor compared to what they ultimately paid for their part in this conspiracy.

Looking back on the weeks following Keifer's funeral I can clearly see that Ingrid's move to leaving Xavier must've been one he hoped she make. He wasn't too broken up to discover his wife gone. In fact, I witnessed him in grand spirts. To this day I'm unsure if his giddiness was due to the moments of freedom he could enjoy while he worked to retrieve his wayward woman or if it was due to his thrill over having secured evidence he needed to smite a few more of his rivals. Well two of them to be exact. His golden eyes were full of diabolical delight as he ordered the arrest of the Silk princes Kristian and Max for the crime of kidnapping his Silk Queen. The sentence for their slights against him was to be a trip to the Hill for death by fire.

And so it came to pass that in the summer of 1935, madness caused by many tears of grief for her lost brother managed to set a fire that consumed the last two beautiful hearts left in our grim world. Their fires burned so brightly it seemed to blind the Haus resident to the darkness that was fast approaching us all from the horizon of our bleak futures under the bloody reign of Xavier the Child Killer and that angry little man that had promised to make Germany great again.

And so we are about to enter WWII and discover the origins of many of the names we've all come to know over the many chapters of Christian's story. I know this story Claus is telling seems never ending but it will end very soon.

To be continued in book two entitled "Xavier Saves the Haus" in The Most Brutal Man in Europe Series

About the Author: Alexandria May Ausman

Alexandria May Ausman in her 16th year was diagnosed with Schizophrenia. She was quickly abandoned by her foster parents. While still only a teen, she was forced to battle this devastating illness alone.

Alexandria has struggled with lack of a support system, numerous psychotic episodes, exploitation, homelessness, and an uncaring mental health system.

Alexandria raised two healthy children. After obtaining her bachelor's degree in psychology she worked as a child abuse investigator and became a diagnostic psychologist while acquiring her Master's in psychology. Alexandria never forgot the experience of 'slipping through the cracks.' Her life's goal is to help people suffering abuse and/or mental illness have access to necessary services. By accident, she became a model of 'gothic attire' and the World Goth Queen.

She began writing a fictionalized account of her life experiences after a catastrophic return of psychotic symptoms. Today, Alexandria is retired, and homebound due to crippling symptoms of Schizophrenia. She currently lives in Tallahassee, Florida, with her loving husband and a loyal support dog.